This is a work of fiction. Names, characters, businesses, places, schools, events and incidents are either the products of the author's imagination or have been used in a fictitious manner. Any resemblance to actual persons, living or dead, or actual events is purely coincidental. All conversations, actions, and descriptions of any government figures are imagined and purely fictitious.

12 PILLS

AN AGENT WHELAN MURDER MYSTERY

KIRK BURRIS

Look for other titles by Kirk Burris:
MURDER AT PARKMOOR
Breaking Sandcastles
Soul Survivor

You can find purchase links on his website:
www.KirkBurris.com

Follow Kirk on Twitter: @BurrisKirk
Follow on Facebook: @KirkBurrisAuthor
Follow on Instagram: @KirkBurrisAuthor

ACKNOWLEDGMENT

During this challenging time in 2020, with so many affected by the Corona Virus, Covid-19, my heart goes out to the family and friends of those who have suffered.
Please be aware that this book was written more than a year ago, and so the omission of any mention of Corona Virus is not out of indifference, but rather that it simply didn't exist when this novel was penned.

Please enjoy this for the escapist reading it is meant to be. We get enough reality on our television sets every day.

Thank you,
Kirk Burris

To all my friends and family,
thank you for your support.

Dedicated to my Mom and Dad, with love.

Chapter 1

"Go!" Pierson yelled through the near darkness of the woods.

Special Agent Thomas Whelan couldn't see Agent Pierson yet, but he readied his sidearm and pointed in the direction he believed it came. Two shots rang in the air fifty yards in front of him, the second one flashing through the trees. His hands were shaking after forty-six hours with little sleep and less food, but he managed to balance his trusted Glock on the hood of his SUV.

Twenty seconds ticked off his watch. No more sounds came from the forest in front of him.

I should have gone in with him. Why did I listen to him?

Whelan wasn't sure whether to call out to his partner or not. As he was about to chance a whisper, Pierson came bursting through the tree-line, thirty feet south.

He was gasping and clutching his left shoulder, blood spilling from between his fingers. His face was wild in the setting sun, and he pleaded to his younger backup. "I said, go! Save yourself!"

Before his fellow field agent could make his case, Whelan hopped into the driver's seat and did a 180 in the mud. "Get in back!" he said, pulling alongside his partner.

As Special Agent Pierson grabbed the rear door handle, three more shots rifled through the air.

Whelan saw the face of Eddie Morrison, the man they spent the past three months tracking down. He stood inside the first line of foliage bordering the forest. Eddie was grinning behind the hilt of his pistol as he lowered the barrel. More gunfire whistled through the air deeper in the woods, at least five rounds hitting the side of the SUV.

Whelan opened his door, ducking low to the steering wheel. Pierson lay face up on the ground, riddled with holes, his eyes distant.

Mud sailed as Whelan gassed the pedal and flew back down the road. He watched the sunset in his rearview mirror, casting long rays through the parting rain clouds. One lit up Agent Jay Pierson for the last time, providing a highway for his soul to travel.

"Godspeed Pierson." Agent Whelan's prayer was sound-tracked with more gunfire as he sped toward darkness.

Breaking the news to Pierson's wife was going to be difficult. They had been married for six years and still carried on like newlyweds. But when his thoughts shifted to their son, little Jack, stuffing his cheeks with Cheerios while watching the perils of his favorite superheroes, Thomas released his first and only tear.

"I will end you, Eddie Morrison." Agent Whelan spoke aloud to himself often when alone at the wheel. "Whatever it takes, I will end you."

"Whatever it takes" was two and a half years of hell undercover. It cost him his time, his health, his wife, and his son.

After the first year, his wife filed for divorce. This wasn't what she signed up for. He knew and understood that. Reason dictated he let her go. He was selfish a bit at first, but he conceded and signed the papers by the end of year two.

His health was shot. Down fifteen pounds, and not in a good way, he looked gaunt and abused. Some in the office suspected he was using narcotics to fit in and obtain information. If he went beyond what was considered "acceptable" risk, his superiors turned their heads.

His wife filed for full custody. He conceded that too, as long as he could maintain visiting rights.

Connor was eleven now and understood life better than Thomas did at that age. Thomas believed that his son knew, deep inside, and despite missing him, his dad was doing the right thing. When he was able to show up, the day was packed with fun activities and presents. He felt it eased Connor's pain somewhat.

Thomas' ex-wife always called him a "poor excuse of a cliché," stereotyping him into some category of a divorced father she felt was sadly textbook. He could only hope Connor was mature enough to understand his limitations as a dad so he could best perform his job. "Someone has to catch the bad guys, son," he would tell him.

Thirty-one months after Special Agent Thomas Whelan watched his partner get gunned to the ground, he sat in a D.C. courtroom testifying against Eddie Morrison. The judge's docket had opened up to clear Morrison through the system, from arrest to trial, in record time—payback to someone in the federal building.

Eddie was convicted on multiple charges of murder, drug trafficking, illegal firearms trading, and smuggling of at least a dozen outlawed substances. He had also been charged with human trafficking, but none of the girls would squeal, so the charges didn't stick. The rest was enough. Eddie Morrison received three life sentences plus forty years. Eight of his goonies received the same or worse.

Whelan broke the news to Pierson's widow on a Sunday afternoon in the rain. They stood in the driveway and held each other for some time. Whelan declined the invitation to come in for coffee and say hello to Jack. He'd delivered the message. It was time to deliver himself back to the world of the living.

Six weeks later, while fishing two hundred yards off the north side of Grand Cayman, Thomas Whelan's life would take a new direction.

3

He casually reached for the ringing phone, resting his beer between his legs, his other hand on his fishing rod.

"Whelan," he answered.

"Special Agent Thomas Whelan? Of the FBI?"

"Who's calling?"

"This is Supervisory Special Agent Miranda Jones. I have a case we could use your help on."

Thomas was still in vacation mode, recovering his sanity. He didn't feel like returning to work yet. "How did you get this number?" It was a local phone he borrowed from his friend Gerrard on the island. No one had the number except his mother and his wife; for emergencies. *Ex-wife*, he corrected in his head.

"Oh, it didn't take Gerrard long to break," she said.

"Yeah, well, you can tell Gerrard he owes me a case of beer, the bastard."

"Why don't you come on in," Jones wooed from the other end, "it looks like you could use another beer *now*."

Thomas bolted upright and looked toward the beach. He was too far out to see the faces at the Tiki-Taco, his favorite hangout south of Rum Point. He gave his outboard a tug. "Fine, but you're buying dinner too. I haven't caught a damned thing out here today."

❀ ❀ ❀

Miranda Jones met Thomas Whelan at the shoreline. He tied off the dilapidated Panga to a monstrous trunk of beached driftwood and stood ankle-deep. "I see how you broke Gerrard. He always was a sucker for beautiful, exotic things."

Thomas nodded toward Gerrard, sitting on a stool at the Tiki-Taco bar, nursing a beer. Gerrard acknowledged him, holding up his bottle in toast and wearing a cheesy smile. This elicited a high-pitched but infectious laugh from Thomas.

He shook it off and looked squarely at Agent Miranda Jones, taking in her appearance. He'd done well in his profiling classes at Quantico, and his Masters in Psychology didn't hurt. His doctorate path toward pharmacology was interrupted when an FBI Assistant Director recruited him. He read Agent Jones and knew she was sincere in her need of his help.

Miranda Jones' skin tone was a deep, dark bronze. Her hair was jet-black, with some natural, loose curl, and her light copper eyes glowed warmly in the Caribbean sun. She could pass as a native islander. Her linen blouse attempted to conceal a sizable chest and a loose skirt pulled tight at the hips before flowing down to the sand. When the wind caught it, Thomas could see muscular thighs and calves. She was extremely fit, head to toe, and just as dazzling.

He hadn't felt any real attraction to a woman for over a year, despite having to commit a few unseemly acts in the past few months. One look at Miranda Jones had him smitten.

"I'm normally sharper with genealogy, but damned if I can place where you hail from," he said.

"That's because I'm a mutt," she explained. "I must have ten different nationalities in my gene pool. They mixed around for a hundred and fifty years, and out popped me."

Thomas tilted his head slightly. "It was worth the wait."

Doing a little curtsy, Agent Jones smiled wide and mustered a southern accent, "Why, thank you, Agent Whelan. Care to escort a belle to the cotillion?"

Thomas held out his arm, and she took it. They strolled the thirty feet up to the giant bamboo hut with table seating and barely had a chance to sit before Gerrard arrived carrying a bucket of light-beer bottles packed on ice, each with a lime wedge poking out of the top. He placed them in the middle of the table next to Jones' binoculars and scurried back to the bar without uttering a word.

"Uh-huh," Agent Whelan snapped at Gerrard's back, "you know you were a bad dog! Shame!" He snickered and picked up a menu, pretending to look while he pondered on why Agent Jones might be here. He already knew he would have the Mahi Tacos. He always had the Mahi Tacos, with mango-pepper sauce and a side of plantain chips. The fish was undoubtedly on the grill the moment they saw him tying up his boat.

When he put the menu down, he was caught off guard by Jones' stare. It was unapologetic as she did some profiling of her own. She liked Thomas' reddish-brown hair and hazel eyes. They matched his freckles. Those with Irish roots weren't usually her type, but he possessed an undefinable appeal. He was thirty-three, a little young for someone already so accomplished in his career, but he wasn't setting any records either. Tallish; a tad on the thin side—she knew he was in rough shape from the past two years and supposed he was already putting some weight back on with his vacation time. He'd certainly regained some color in his face.

Most importantly, she'd caught his curiosity. He was hooked. And when she hooked a fish, she always reeled it in.

Without saying another word, Gerrard again showed up with two baskets, each with three Mahi Tacos and a monstrous heaping of freshly fried plantain chips doused in sea salt.

Thomas wolfed down his first taco without taking a breath. Halfway through his second, he paused and took a sip of beer. "Okay. What've you got?"

Agent Jones reached into her bag and retrieved an extensive dossier. Three murder victims were tossed under Whelan's nose. The photos showed two men and a woman, unremarkable and appearing unrelated. There were no indicative marks on any of them. They all looked healthy. Outside of their deceased status, of course.

Whelan looked up. Jones was watching him.

"Poisoned?" he asked.

She nodded.

"Herbal?"

"Mostly. Aconite."

"Wolfsbane? Classic." Whelan looked at the photos. "Mostly?"

"That's the interesting part." Agent Jones looked around quickly to make sure no one was eavesdropping. "One of them had succinylcholine traces. The others probably had it, but you know it can be hard to detect. Agent Whelan, there were at least two other substances that came up as unidentifiable."

He squinted and cocked one eyebrow.

"Someone out there," she continued, "is creating new compounds. Our lab guys are stumped."

"Well, your lab guys have PhDs. I didn't get that far. They recruited me before I could finish. Why do you think I'll know more than your team?"

"I don't. But your experience there will be an asset. And at least you speak the language."

"I'm still not sure why you want me on this at all?" Whelan was confused.

Agent Jones tapped the forehead on two of the victims. "Because these two... you went to elementary school with."

❀ ❀ ❀

Chapter 2

"Come on, Tommy, throw the ball!"

Tommy was trying to read the arranged signals from the catcher behind the plate. None of the finger combinations were making sense. One of them forgot what they meant, and Tommy couldn't be sure who. He threw the pitch.

Jackson Kenny swung and knocked it far into left field. The runner on third came home, and the game was over. Tommy lost the game for his team. *Or maybe that damned catcher.* Either way, he would take the blame for over a decade. The incessant ridicule would prevent him from competing in any sports for the rest of his school years. However, it allowed him time for his studies, and he excelled in every class he took, especially the sciences.

The week following the game, Jackson came up to Tommy and admitted he suspected Fat-Bobby didn't know what he was doing behind home plate, and no doubt muddled the signals. Jackson's gesture was appreciated since none of his teammates bothered. It would be the start of a friendship, but peer pressure would wind up separating them as the years went by, and the last time Tommy spent any time with him was at the end of eighth grade.

"Drink?" asked the flight attendant.

Thomas Whelan woke from his light sleep in the back of the plane. "What?"

The attendant interrupted his dream. "Would you like something to drink?"

"Coffee, if it's fresh. Do you have real dairy cream?"

"Sorry, the powdered stuff. Still want it?"

"Yeah," Whelan conceded with a frown.

As the attendant poured his cup, she noticed the photos in Thomas' lap. Her face altered its usually-permanent grin, and she scampered up the aisle.

Thomas looked at his lap. Jackson Kenny's still body and vacant eyes were staring back at him.

Who wanted you dead, Jackson? Who did you piss off?

Before Eddie Morrison, Whelan's dreams were normal, filled with visuals of his family. Once colorful and vibrant images were now replaced with muted, distorted shapes, like looking through a screened door. It was just as well he was awake.

The flight back to Washington, D.C. gave Agents Whelan and Jones time to go over the case again. There were three people killed. So far.

JACKSON KENNY

PAUL DUKE

TRACY STAMFORD

The two boys went to school with Thomas. "I had Jackson in my third and fourth-grade classes, and I think Paul was in my second or third, and fifth or sixth? I'm not sure. I knew them both. I was pretty close to Jackson for a few years, but Paul and I weren't really friends. Of course we knew each other. Everyone knew each other." They grew up in Independence, Missouri.

"And you're sure you didn't know Tracy Stamford?" asked Agent Jones.

"To my recollection, I've never heard of her." He glanced again at the file, but he already had it memorized. He knew her address, the distance between his house and hers, what school she went to, all of it. "She grew up in Lee's Summit. When you're ten years old, eight miles apart might as well be eight hundred."

Jones let out a sigh. "I'm at an impasse in the case. I've been working on it non-stop for three weeks."

"I still don't understand how you connected the cases in the first place and knew to run such elaborate tests," said Whelan. "You're holding back on me. You ready to fill me in on the rest?"

"I didn't want you distracted by the obvious until you had a chance to dig through your memories and formulate any connections."

"The obvious?"

Agent Jones handed him a new file folder. This one had "CLASSIFIED" stamped on the front.

"SAC Kendrick said I'm not supposed to show you this unless you agree to transfer to the Kansas City field office. I know you have a son in D.C., and if you're not able to be farther away yet, I'll understand."

"I'm lucky to see him once a month now as it is. I can take a flight."

Jones clarified, "This would be a *permanent* transfer, with a new partner assignment."

"I don't want a new partner yet." Whelan glanced at his lap.

"Hey, I get it. But the bureau...they gave you tremendous latitude while you put together your case against Morrison. You put that to bed. Now, it's time."

Whelan stared at her. *Put that to bed? I should have put him in the ground. I could have.*

"They'll put some babysitter with me," he continued. "They know I'm frazzled right now and nursing my way back to normal after two years of hell. I don't need someone watching over me every second. I need to get back to work and focus on a new case."

The second he vocalized it, he knew it was true. "A fresh start in K.C. might be the right move. But I don't need some damned babysitter."

"No, you don't. I've already evaluated you. You passed."

"That's why they sent you? To evaluate me? Great." His sarcasm was laced with the acceptance of truth.

Jones turned in her seat to face him directly. "I've evaluated all of my previous partners—from the Navy to the K.C.P.D. to the FBI—everywhere I was given the requisite authority."

"*You?*" Agent Whelan's voice cracked. He'd looked her up and knew she already had a partner.

"Agent Whitfield and I aren't working out. He has rather antiquated views and a chauvinistic attitude that should have never made it out of the '60s. They granted me permission to bring you over. What do you say?"

Thomas looked her in the eye. She smiled. Her teeth were perfectly straight and white. Some orthodontist took excellent care of her.

He was tempted to say yes because he was captivated by her. But if he agreed, he wouldn't be able to pursue his attraction. That was a hard-fast rule and in place for a reason. His emotions played across his face like a transparency on an overhead projector.

Again, Agent Jones laughed. "Easy there. You're strangely cute and all, but I'm involved."

Well, of course she would be. What was he thinking?

"Show me what else you have on the killer and let me process this whole moving and new partner thing for a few minutes, would you?"

"Break the rules? Why Agent Whelan, you scoundrel. Putting me in such a compromising position."

11

His mind went to a darker place with her comment. *Am I nothing but damaged goods?*

He kept trying to avert his eyes from her lips. "You have that Georgia accent down pat."

"I've been around. Wait 'til you hear my Jersey Shore."

She plopped the classified folder onto his lap.

New photos she'd withheld were shocking. It had been quite some time since a serial killer left such a distinct calling card, let alone announced there were more to come.

Stuck in the mouth of each corpse was an orange, plastic pill bottle with a white cap. The kind you'd find at most any pharmacy in the country. Written in Sharpie on the top of the caps were the words "1 of 12", "2 of 12," and "3 of 12." One for each bottle. One for each victim. One a week.

Agent Thomas Whelan's skin tingled. Hairs rose on his arms and the back of his neck. It was the "thrill of the hunt." Those without this calling in their nature could never relate, but it drew Whelan fervidly. It was part of why the FBI recruited him. His graduate file was flagged when the professor of his criminal justice course tipped off his friend at the bureau. Whelan took the class on a whim as an elective. There were no expectations he'd excel and devour the course material.

Miranda Jones' expression was bitter-sweet. "I know that titillating sensation. But after twenty days of coming up empty-handed, I'm not turned on by it any longer."

She studied her air vent a moment before adjusting it. "I am glad, though, to have fresh eyes take a look. And the fact that you knew two of them…." She turned in her seat and locked her eyes on his. "It leaves me optimistic for the first time since being handed this case."

"And Whitfield's going to walk away from this?" Thomas couldn't believe it. "No way!"

"He won't have a choice," she answered. "I'm running this one. I get to pick my team, and he's getting in my way."

A low whistle escaped Whelan's lips. "You're ballsy."

Three of twelve. There were going to be nine more if they couldn't catch the killer. And soon. Week four was almost here.

"You really should have led with this," said Thomas. "I'm in."

Chapter 3

Sonja Cuevas was wrapping up her bartending shift at her Ocean Drive restaurant on South Beach in Miami, Florida. It was a little before midnight. The clubs were getting into their grooves nearby, and while usually, she went home and straight to bed, tonight was a special occasion. It was her best-friend Janine's twenty-eighth birthday.

Sonja's mother babysat her daughter for the night so she could go out with her girlfriends for drinks and dancing.

While Sonja loved her daughter, a night off from her once in a while reminded her she was still young and pretty. Usually, there was no problem finding a guy willing to shake it on the dance floor in hopes of getting her into bed.

The final drink she poured before clocking out left her a hugely generous tip. She rang the bar's bell in appreciation and headed up the street toward frivolity. It was a muggy night in the middle of June, with slight breeze coming off the ocean to cool her down. Hordes of people were scurrying about in various levels of dress, depending on their destination.

By 1:15 a.m., Sonja was in the middle of the dance floor with three sour-apple martinis in her. She'd caught the looks of several men, one of whom she was grinding against for the better part of an hour to deafening beats with scant rhythm. Her "Huge Tipper" from earlier sat in the corner of the club, staring and smiling, unnoticed.

Around 2:30, Sonja's friends collected her from the middle of a group of men and made excuses to go home. She was five martinis in now and was hesitant to leave so much fun.

"After one more dance," she said, pulling one of the guys to the floor.

Her friends trickled out, save the birthday girl, who stayed behind with Sonja. They lived in the same apartment building four blocks over and always walked home together when going out.

Last call was given at the club, and a final round of shots was ordered to end the celebration, a Hail Mary attempt by one of the guys to get into someone's pants before throwing in the towel. Sonja didn't notice that the person delivering the tray full of Sex On the Beach was Huge Tipper. She tossed hers back and continued flirtations in progress until the lights came up.

The group meandered across the street to wake up in the fresh air and maybe even dip their toes in the Atlantic. Toe-dipping became skinny dipping. After splashing around for a bit and cooling down, Sonja's grinding partner offered his own version of sex on the beach, and they got busy in a hammock on the nearby palm trees in Lummus Park.

Janine was content to visit with the other two remaining men on a park bench, testing which one was the better kisser.

Huge Tipper lingered in the darker shadows, hidden from the streetlights, silently observing both spectacles. They were over in minutes. The guys grabbed a taxi, and the girls walked home.

Sunday morning, at 7:20 a.m., Señora Cuevas stepped out from her daughter's door to see if perhaps a newspaper was delivered that she could read with her Cuban coffee and guava pastries. Her screams were heard from every apartment in the building when she discovered her daughter Sonja lying face up in the courtyard in front of her. A pill bottle jutted out from her mouth. She couldn't make out the writing on the cap without her glasses but would soon find out it read, "4 of 12".

❀ ❀ ❀

Between the flight home to Washington D.C., then to Kansas City, and now down to Miami, Special Agent Whelan spent more time in the air the previous thirty-six hours than on the ground. He rode with Agent Jones, first to the morgue to see the body, then over to the precinct where the local police were putting together their case.

Captain Vicente Mansilla was none too happy when they walked through the door. He'd returned from the hospital where the victim's mother was resting after suffering heart palpitations following the discovery of her daughter in the courtyard.

"You have news for me?" he asked. His nerves were shot. "Because if you don't, go the hell home and let me work my case."

Agent Jones managed a moment of compassion. She'd been there. "Can we find a private room?"

"Why bother. Everyone in ear-shot's going to get filled in by me anyway. Save me from repeating it."

Jones spoke up a bit. "This case is federal jurisdiction. You're all to hand over everything you've got so far. I'll expect files on this desk in five minutes, and we'll begin questioning now." She looked the captain in the eyes. "Starting with you."

"What makes you think this is federal?" he asked.

Agent Jones looked at the seven other men and women in the bullpen. She sighed. "Fine, I'll do it here," she mumbled.

She pulled out the photos, pre-bottle removal, of the first three that were murdered. While a low whistle was released somewhere behind her, all the captain could do was walk to his office and slam the door shut behind him, mumbling expletives the whole way.

When Agents Whelan and Jones opened his door twenty seconds later, Captain Mansilla was pouring himself a bourbon. He glanced at them, swallowed his jigger, and re-filled. He gestured with his eyes toward a shelf with more glasses on them. Jones grabbed two and filled them finger-full. Whelan took one, and they sat down opposite Mansilla.

For three minutes, no one said a word, then Mansilla opened up. "The mother's about to have a heart attack. They're keeping her overnight for observation. And this little angel," he threw a picture of an eight-year-old girl toward Whelan's glass, "is Lorena. She'll be sleeping on some stranger's couch tonight while trying to grasp that her mother won't be coming home. Ever."

He took a breath, and a sip, before continuing. "The last memory she'll ever have of her mother is this." Another picture flew across the desk of Sonja Cuevas, "4 of 12" in her mouth. "And I was foolish enough to promise both daughter and grandmother that *I* would find the son of a bitch who committed that sick crap."

Captain Mansilla looked both federal agents in the eyes. His own moistened a bit. "Let me be the one to tell them when it's time."

Agent Jones instinctively reached out and placed her hand over his. "Of course, Vicente." She pronounced his name with a perfect Miami-Dade accent. And then she continued in flawless Spanish. "Whatever it takes, we'll keep you in the loop, and if it's at all possible, we'll even let you be there when we catch him, so you can tell those ladies you saw the evil bastard fall."

Whelan's eyes opened wide. His Spanish was nowhere near the level of Agent Jones', but he caught enough of what she said. There was little possibility the killer would be apprehended in Miami or that after they had all they needed from these men, they'd ever see any of them again.

And she'd already assigned a gender to the killer.

How convenient, Whelan thought. *She's taken the potential perpetrators list down to forty-eight percent of what it was two minutes ago.*

Jones had sold it. Captain Mansilla opened the door and declared, "Everyone, give these two your full cooperation. I want nothing held back. This psycho's been halfway across the country. Let's do our best to ensure his capture."

Everyone started hustling for the first time since the feds' arrival. It was clear who ran the show.

Whelan whispered to Jones, "So what makes you think the killer is a man?"

"You know ninety percent of serial killers are men. The odds are in my favor. And this *feels* like a man to me. I can't imagine a woman doing this."

"Sounds like a vengeful woman to me. And silencing them with a bottle in their mouth? Women have a greater fascination with mouths than most men do."

"I concede; it could be a man or woman at this point. I also recognize that poison is a more preferred weapon choice by women. But I would disagree with you about that "mouth" thing. You've been staring at mine since we met." Jones licked her lips, opened her eyes wide with a smile, and headed toward an agent's office down the hall, leaving Whelan alone to ponder in Mansilla's doorway.

Two hours later, the agents finished reading through the available files: testimonies, interview summaries, lists of matches from the database of fingerprints, and initial conclusions. The case was fresh, but an entire team of Miami's finest had moved quickly. DNA testing sent to the lab resulted in no known hits. The victim recently engaged in sexual activity, but she had shown a history of promiscuity, according to witnesses in her building, and no evidence of rape was indicated.

Of course, Miami-Dade's best were stumped on where the first three bodies were located, as nothing had been released on the wires. The feds delivered the first confirmation of what they already suspected.

The chief witness—so far missing—was the birthday girl, Janine Cook, Sonja Cuevas' friend from the club with whom she was last seen. According to the officers posted, there was no sign of her at her apartment complex all day. She worked at a different restaurant, two streets up from Sonja's on Ocean Drive. She was supposed to show up for a 6:00 p.m. shift, but the manager told them she was a "no-show" when they called at 6:30.

"I've booked us a hotel three blocks up from there," said Agent Jones. "Let's check in and have some dinner?"

By 8:00 Sunday night, Whelan and Jones were sitting at a sidewalk table at Janine's restaurant, sipping on beers and watching the ocean turn orange from the setting sun.

The beach was golden. Even more golden bodies were still walking up and down it, or playing volleyball, or taking a swim before dark. The temperature was tolerable from the ceiling fan attached to the awning above them.

"Well, isn't this beautiful? I can see why it's so popular," said Jones.

"Too crowded for my taste. Too commercial. I'll take my eleven-dollar Mahi tacos in Cayman over their thirty-dollar fried cod sandwich any day," replied Whelan, putting his menu down in disgust.

"So get a burger. Someone tipped me off. They're supposed to be exceptional here."

"For twenty-eight dollars, they'd better be. I wonder what taxpayers would say if they knew they're about to buy me a twenty-eight-dollar burger."

"They'd say, 'Thank you for working to catch a killer on the loose and keeping our cities safe, despite it costing you any quality relationship time to grow or care about a family of your own. Why don't you have the prime-rib? It's our treat for all you do'."

"Prime-rib?" asked Whelan.

Jones nodded. "Yes, with creamy horseradish and mashed yuca in garlic oil."

Whelan laughed. "Sold me. Make it two. You know, you sure sold Captain Mansilla. That was impressive."

"Thanks. I've developed a technique or two over the years."

"Where'd you learn Spanish?" he asked.

"My mother spoke Spanish and Portuguese, so those are my first languages. I picked up English in the school system and took French and Italian in high school. It would seem I had a knack. I'm working on mastering Hindi now. I can speak it, but the accents aren't where I want them."

"Fascinating. I took Spanish in high school, and it stuck well enough. I speak German—from my dad's mother—and I took Russian and Czech in college. I guess combined, we'll be pretty well covered."

"Yes, I read your file. As long as we don't have to question any Chinese on this investigation, we'll be good to go."

"So," Whelan began, locking eye contact with his new partner, "tell me about this person you're *involved* with."

Miranda Jones let a soft chuckle escape.

It was charming and excited Thomas somewhat.

"Well—" she started.

She was interrupted by the manager approaching. A young woman was in tow. "Agents, this is Janine Cook. She showed up at the back door."

Chapter 4

"I've been hiding out at a friend's all day," finished Janine, ending her story of last night's events. "I was afraid to come to work, but I didn't want to lose my job, so I came by to explain to our manager what was going on, and now, here I am."

Janine lowered her voice to a whisper. "I knew it had to be one of those guys we hung with at the club. One of them followed us home! They knew where we lived! I had to get out of there."

Jones put her fork down for a moment and looked sweetly at the frightened woman. "And this morning? You heard the screams from Señora Cuevas, and...?"

"By the time I got to the courtyard, at least ten people were there. Some were crying; some were in shock. At least three had their phones out, taking video. Sick people, you know? And poor Mrs. Cuevas. All she could do was sit on her knees, howling over Sonja's body. I shielded Lorena from it as best I could. She ran up when she saw me. I babysit her sometimes. I took her to her bedroom and told her to put her music on until her grandma came to get her. Then I bailed."

Agent Whelan was curious about that. "Why? Why not stick around and give your story to the police?"

"I watch cop shows! The killer always returns to the scene of the crime! We were pretty lit. For all I know, one of those people in the courtyard could have been the killer, and I wouldn't have remembered his face. He could have been ready to pounce on me next!"

Agent Jones patted the top of Janine's hand in comfort. She was tremendous at playing with empathy to get what she wanted.

Or is she sincere? Whelan couldn't be sure. Either way, it worked for her.

A police car double-parked at the curb in front of them, and an officer came to retrieve Janine.

"If we need anything further, we'll be in touch," said Agent Jones. "This woman is going to make sure you get home, and we'll have someone posted at your door for protection."

Janine Cook thanked them and was whisked away toward safety.

"Well," said Agent Whelan, "at least that saves us a witness hunt. You think the mother will be up for talking with us? The locals didn't know the right questions for her."

"Yes," agreed Agent Jones, "I think she'd better be ready tomorrow. Our killer's already down to six days before he strikes again."

She caught Whelan's raised eyebrow and snapped, "Oh, don't look at me that way! What am I going to do, say 'he/she' for the next few weeks?" She was getting frustrated.

"You're conditioning your mind to rule out potential suspects before you can fully process them."

"I—," Jones cut herself off. "You're right. I'll try not to use those pronouns. At least not until we find some evidence with a Y-chromosome attached."

"Well, if this takes a few more weeks, we aren't going to save *any* of them. We need answers," said Whelan. He stood up and emptied the last few drops of his beer onto his tongue. "We need answers now. What time do you think visiting hours are over?"

❀ ❀ ❀

They knocked on Victoria Cuevas' hospital room door a little after 11:00 p.m. Agent Jones stuck her head in. Señora Cuevas was sitting up in bed, alone. Her eyes pointed toward a muted television, but their focus was elsewhere. Jones made it to the bedside before Victoria realized she was there.

Her head pivoted, and she re-positioned her pupils on Agent Jones' face. "I wondered when you'd be here."

Whelan came further into the room. "You did? Did someone tell you that FBI agents were looking into this now? Who's been here?"

"No one. I've had a few hours of silence to think, agent...?"

"Whelan. And this is Agent Jones."

"Agents Whelan and Jones. I doubted the killer was local. There's been nothing on TV. Every night, they report the daily murders. My Sonja didn't get an ounce of air-time on the ten o'clock. You guys are keeping it secret, so you don't frighten the public. I get it. Some "sick-o" is out there randomly killing pretty girls. I'll bet he's going city to city so he can't be caught."

"I don't think it's random at all, Mrs. Cuevas," said Whelan. "Somehow, they're connected."

"Victoria," Jones jumped in, "we've read your report to the police. We have some other questions to ask you."

Señora Cuevas sighed. "I doubt I'll be able to tell you anything I didn't already tell the police."

"When did you live in the Kansas City area?" asked Agent Whelan.

Turning to sit on the edge of the bed, Señora Cuevas turned off the television with a click of the remote. "I stand corrected. The local cops didn't ask me that. Is the killer from K.C.? Have you caught him?"

Agent Jones stepped back to let Whelan move in front of the woman.

"No, Mrs. Cuevas, I'm sorry, we haven't. But if you can tell me about your time there, it might get us a step closer. The first three were from the K.C. area."

"I'll be damned. So not random..." She paused before rushing to share her thoughts. "We were there a couple of years—'97 to '99. Sonja was five when we moved there. I met a man who was kind to me, gave me work at the stockyards. A desk job, filing, paying invoices. I had a distant cousin living in Raytown, so we stayed with her for a few months, then moved into our own apartment in Independence. We were happy for a while. But then there were some cutbacks, and I lost the job. I waitressed for a few months so Sonja could stay in school there. A better opportunity brought us home to Miami. I hated to do that to her. She made a lot of friends in a short time and was so happy."

Victoria started to tear up. She let them fall unwiped as she continued, "Sony—that was her nickname back then—she attended Kindergarten and first grades there. She made passing scores and loved to participate in school activities. Her English was a bit rough then, but those two years saw her come a long way. She was an angel."

Whelan interrupted. "I'm sure she was Mrs. Cuevas, but what I need to know are any names you can remember. Friends? Teachers? Social activities? After school lessons—maybe music? I need to know everyone that might have been in her life back then."

"That was over twenty years ago," she was overwhelmed.

"Yes," chimed in Agent Jones. "Take your time. I'm recording this on my phone. Close your eyes a moment, and think about when you first moved there. You lived with your cousin? Was there more family? Who did you work for? Did they ever meet Sonja? Who else was in her life? Let the names you remember start flowing as you go through those two years."

An hour later, Agents Jones and Whelan were walking out with over forty names to investigate.

Victoria Cuevas yelled out to them before the door closed. "Agent Whelan!"

He stuck his head back in, "Yes?"

"Tell me you'll catch him. Before there's a number five?"

"That's the plan." He let the door click behind him.

His brain went to work on the way to the parking lot, puzzling until it went from questions to theories. *That's the plan. Plans. Not random. The killer's making plans. Planning. Planning on killing number five. Who's number five? Planning. Planner. The killer's a planner. Planner. Teacher's planner.*

Whelan knew it must be a teacher connection. Perhaps a teacher who transferred from his school to Lee's Summit, and then Raytown? *A substitute!*

"We need to look into all the substitute teachers who were traveling around the K.C. area from '97 to '99."

Jones agreed. "Yes, excellent. I looked into teachers in Independence already. Figured that had to be it until Tracy Stamford. I got off that train when she showed up. I knew I brought you in for something besides those pretty eyes."

Whelan's "pretty eyes" opened wide for a moment before realizing she was kidding with him. She had his number already.

Perhaps it was too soon to get back on the horse after Eddie Morrison after all? He sighed and sank into the passenger seat.

Staring out toward passing trees, Thomas Whelan counted the number of royal palms he saw on the way back to their hotel. They lined the swale between the lamp posts.

The last time he was in Miami, he used his "pretty eyes" to plead entrance into a known sex-trafficking den in Hialeah. His former partner—Agent Pierson—had leads for the place, holed up in a run-down shopping center. It took him over a year to get the introductions needed. He was undercover and represented himself as a buyer for a chain of massage parlors in Chicago.

The stench of the lair was a mix of dirty sex and pot smoke with a sickly-sweet bourbon and cocaine chaser. He was forced to "taste" the merchandise. The merchandise was forced to taste him. It would spiral out of hand for sixty-four hours while waiting for forged green cards.

Agent Whelan uncurled his arms and turned his head back to Agent Miranda Jones. His eyes were red and moist. He wiped at his nose, attempting to erase the odor still lingering there five months later.

Miranda Jones took pity. "I'm not sure where you were, but welcome back. Look, I'm sorry, Thomas. It's been a long day. Your mind's working fine. It just needs some time to get back in the groove."

"I guess. Speaking of time, at least this trip wasn't wasted."

"Not at all. Now we have a time frame. Whatever the inciting incident was, it happened between '97 and '99. Sonja Cuevas narrowed down our search to a two-year window."

"God rest her soul."

It was not an off-handed platitude. Jones shot him a glance and felt a deeper connection to her new partner.

The following morning, she made some calls and got her researchers working on substitute teacher names. By the time they landed at Kansas City International, they were caught up on sleep with fresh places to start.

They went door-knocking the rest of the day.

Whelan laid his head on his pillow at the hotel around midnight with no new developments from their efforts.

Before his alarm could ring at 6:00 a.m., Agent Jones' call startled him awake. He looked at the clock. 5:50. Close enough. "Whelan," he answered.

"Turn on the national news!"

"What channel?"

"Doesn't matter! Find a damned news channel!"

Thomas fumbled with the remote a moment, landing on a national news network. Reporters were breaking the story. He channel-surfed a moment until he caught one at the beginning of the tale.

The morning anchor looked young and ambitious. "An anonymous YouTube account appeared overnight with raw footage of a murder victim in Miami, Florida. Neither the address nor the deceased's name has been revealed. We have reason to believe there may be a serial killer on the loose in Florida. That's right, folks, I said it. A *serial killer* is on the loose in Florida. The video footage and the account were taken down from YouTube, but copies were recorded before it was discovered and removed. We have obtained a copy of the footage, which we are about to show you. Please be advised what you are about to see is gruesome and disturbing. You might want to ask younger viewers to leave the room."

The reporter paused for dramatic effect, then a phone camera's vertical video started playing on the screen before Thomas. It was a video clip from Sonja Cuevas' courtyard. Señora Cuevas' wailing lament could be heard the whole time over other voices shouting and screaming. The backs of onlookers filled the screen a moment as the videographer worked his way through, and then suddenly, poor Sonja's body was there on national television. The camera zoomed in closer and closer until Sonja's face filled the screen. Stuffed in her mouth and protruding out about an inch was an orange pill bottle. The handwritten "4 of 12" on the cap was distinctly legible in the frame. Sonja's eyes were open, and a look of fear was captured in them before she passed. Captured forever, and now literally, for the world to see.

The news anchor appeared on-screen again. "Twelve victims, ladies and gentlemen. There will be twelve victims before it's over, and we've just witnessed number four. Who will be next? Who's being targeted? Is *your* family safe? We have calls in to Miami-Dade police and the FBI. We expect to be hearing from them momentarily with some answers."

The journalist was seeking to sensationalize this moment. "Someone out there has targeted twelve people to kill with what is presumably a custom pharmaceutical. How well do you know *your* pharmacist? Do you trust the pills *you're* taking? Could the pills you're taking be custom-made by a psychotic killer? Is *your* name on the list? Twelve pills for twelve victims, ladies and gentlemen. Twelve pills. Hug your children close tonight, folks. The 12 Pills Killer is on the loose!"

And there it was. One of a detective's worst nightmares during an investigation of this sort was realized right before his eyes. They named the killer. Within twenty minutes, all the other networks fell in line. He or she had an official media name now: The 12 Pills Killer.

Miranda's voice could be heard on the other end as Thomas came back to reality.

"I hear you," he mumbled into the speaker.

"Well! What do you think?"

He sighed. "Shit."

Chapter 5

Agents Jones and Whelan met up around 7:00 a.m. for a quick breakfast and headed into the Kansas City field office. In the parking lot, Jones caught sight of her former partner getting out of his car.

She mumbled to Whelan, "There's Whitfield. I don't want a confrontation this morning. Let's hang back a minute."

Whelan turned to get a suitable look at the man he'd replaced as Jones' partner. Whitfield's face looked somehow familiar to him.

Whitfield caught Whelan's stare and "bee-lined" straight for them.

Jones shot her partner a look. "Subtle."

"Agent Jones," Whitfield commented flatly with a nod, then held out his hand to her new partner. "Agent Whelan? Mark Whitfield."

Whelan shook his hand. "Agent Whitfield." He cocked his head and blinked. "Mark Whitfield... You look familiar. Didn't you go to Truman? Class of... 2001?"

Mark's face was blank for a moment. Then, "Tommy? Oh my God, you're Davie's little brother! How've you been?"

"Good. Well, better, now. I'm good. Gosh, I haven't seen you in ages. Not since you and David shot bottle rockets off the back of the boat on Lake Jacomo. Hell of a way to fish, man! Wasn't enough left to eat!"

"We weren't exactly interested in eating them," Whitfield snorted. "Man, that was about... 2002? What were you? A sophomore?"

"Yeah, graduated early at the end of '03, then went straight to UMKC, did the three-year thing there too, then Princeton for Grad School. Talk about a blast from the past. You look well, man."

"Yes," said Jones, interrupting the high school reunion. "You look well, Mark. You been golfing? That's quite a tan you've gotten this week."

Mark looked at his old partner. "Miranda, I took the week off and played a few rounds. I had time coming. Are you going to give me shit for enjoying myself after you had me reassigned? I don't know which A.D. you fucked to get so high on the totem pole, but you've got a lot of nerve, woman. Half that building's in on this manhunt, and you managed to get me assigned to a 'suspicious' vehicular manslaughter near Dodge City involving Congressman Delaney? The guy was drunk. But now I have to go check in, then spend over *five* hours driving across Kansas! The Garden City resident agents could easily handle that without my oversight."

Agent Whitfield turned back to Whelan. "Tommy, it was great to see you. Say hi to your brother for me. I haven't thought about Davie in years. I can't believe I didn't figure out who you were when I heard the name. Small world. And you're back in K.C.?"

"Looks that way." Whelan looked at Jones. He'd been thrown for a loop and was finding it a challenge to work his way back to the respectable, grown adult she'd split a bagel with thirty minutes ago.

"Well, welcome home. I'd say, 'let's catch up some time,' but the circumstances aren't quite in favor of a reunion." Agent Whitfield headed toward the building. He yelled upward without turning his head around, "Watch your back with that one, Tommy! She's got an agenda. Ask around!"

Neither Whelan nor Jones spoke for close to a minute. Whelan couldn't stand it. "So...you took that a lot better than I would have."

"What would be the point? He's an ass. A forever member of the 'old-boys club.' And you! For a minute, you had me scared I'd misjudged you."

"No. You're safe. He was friends with my older brother, David. They were stereotypical teens. Guys being guys. I was the weird one that didn't fit in. I can see what you mean about Whitfield being chauvinistic. It would seem he never outgrew that. Shame."

Whelan grinned at her. "And you have an *agenda*?"

"Oh, yes. My evil plot to catch criminals and work my way up respectfully within an organization and a career path I love and have given my life to. But because I'm a woman, he thinks I must have some 'agenda' and be a man-hater. God, I can't believe I didn't insist on re-assignment sooner!"

"Man-hater?"

"Yes. He liked to infer I was some sort of power-hungry lesbian slicing and sleeping my way to the top. What a dick!" She was getting herself riled up.

Whelan's interest was piqued, but instead of following up with the multiple questions that raced through his head, he took the high road.

"Okay... sorry I asked. Put it out of your head. We've got work to do."

Agent Jones calmed herself and headed toward the front doors. "Thank you, Thomas. I want to reconfirm a theory with the addition of Cuevas to the list."

"Oh?" asked Whelan.

"I think he's killing them in the order of their birthdays on a twelve-month calendar. Sonja was born in April, and Stamford and Duke were in March and February. I'm pretty sure Kenny's was January."

"It was," said Whelan, remembering his old friend from elementary school. "I went to a few of his parties. They were always right after new year's."

"Then I'd say there's a favorable chance target number five was born in May. Any childhood parties you remember in May?"

Agent Whelan jogged a step to catch up to Jones as she headed inside. "I'll have to give it some thought," he said.

❀ ❀ ❀

Agent Jones looked at the list.

JACKSON KENNY

    b. January 3, 1987 - Independence Elementary

PAUL DUKE

    b. February 18, 1987 - Independence Elementary

TRACY STAMFORD

    b. March 12, 1987 - Lee's Summit Elementary

SONJA CUEVAS

    b. April 6, 1992 - Raytown Elementary

"What do you think? Anything coming to you yet?" she asked her partner.

"No. I knew the boys, not the girls. I wonder if that means anything?"

"Possibly. If he's targeting *you*."

"Well," said Whelan, "if he is, I have a few weeks. I was born in December."

Jones sighed. "I'm at a loss. I've been focusing on those born in 1987 as a key factor. Sonja Cuevas threw me for a loop. She's five years younger than the rest. Was she in the wrong place twenty years ago? Or was it more than that? I'm starting all over here."

"I doubt 12 Pills went all the way to Miami for someone who was simply 'in the wrong place,'" said Whelan.

"12 Pills?" asked Jones.

Whelan shrugged. "It's out there…."

"Well, maybe *12 Pills* was tidying up witnesses?" Agent Jones plopped into her desk chair. "We have agents working on all the kids that went to elementary school in the area between '97 and '99, who were born in May, June and July. Anyone who remembers one of the vics more than passingly will be put on a list so we can follow up. If we haven't caught—the killer—I'm not calling him 12 Pills from now on. So far, it's only four! If we haven't caught the killer by number seven..." she paused and looked to the ceiling, eyes wide.

"We'll get them," Whelan stepped in and put his hand on her shoulder.

She nodded. "I think we're back on interviews today. Here's your group." She handed Whelan a sheet of paper with names and addresses. "Substitute Teachers" was centered at the top.

"*My* group?" he asked.

"We're splitting up today. We're short on people. Kendrick's got forty agents in there now, working their leads for this, twenty-two of which are back in the field working their own lists today—in pairs. I've given you and me the most likely suspects. You're used to working alone. You really need me babysitting your interviews?"

"Of course not. But protocol… Did SAC Kendrick sign off on this?"

"What he doesn't know won't kill us. Oh, and that reminds me. Stop by his office," Jones continued. "He wants to give you the official 'welcome to the team' speech. He's giving me a lot of latitude on this case, but I think he wants to make sure you know who's really in charge here."

"Okay."

Special Agent in Charge Alan Kendrick was in his early sixties, Whelan guessed. He was lean, except for a small protrusion above his belt; too many beers with whiskey chasers over the years. Whelan thought perhaps he caught the smell of whiskey now on the Special Agent in Charge's breath. Maybe it was the cinnamon breath mint. The past two years left Whelan needing more breath mints than usual when reporting in person to his superiors.

They went through "official motions" for five minutes. Kendrick conveyed his confidence in Agent Miranda Jones to run their investigation. Assistant Special Agent in Charge Henry "Hank" Monroe was on emergency medical leave, and this was an excellent opportunity for Jones' career. He'd set her up in Hank's office to work when not out in the bullpen.

Kendrick shook Whelan's hand and walked him to the door. "Agent Whelan, your track record and experience are invaluable here. Agent Jones is Supervisory Agent on this, but you're her partner now. Watch her back. I've known her for over eight years. She's tough. But no one's invincible. There's a side to her that...well, watch her back like a partner should."

"Of course. Sir, if there's something you'd like to share with me, I can keep a confidence."

"I'm sure you can." Kendrick stared at his newest agent a moment. "There's been an occasion or two where she's reacted before thinking the situation through. Sometimes, her passion and her energy get ahead of her. She's always feeling the need to prove herself."

"Well, if Mark Whitfield is an indication of the majority of agents she's had to deal with here, I can see why."

36

"Yes, I'm working on that." His eyebrows shot up, and his head rattled. "Look, forget I mentioned it. You're in skilled hands."

"Yes, sir."

"And while I'll be getting my updates from her, my door's always open; to you and anyone else that needs me," Kendrick threw in.

"Thank you, sir."

Whelan wondered if there was a deeper meaning to Kendrick's comments. It was like a father watching out for his child. Eight years was a long time in this business to foster a relationship with someone under your command. Whelan dismissed it. His focus now was on catching the 12 Pills Killer.

By the time dinner rolled around, Whelan had finished interviewing six more potentials and was no closer to a real suspect. Substitute Teacher Number Seven agreed to meet him for a beer at one of his old college watering holes on The Plaza, Slap-Happy's Bar and Grill. The locals called it "Slappy's."

He was tall and thin, with greasy hair and loose pants, which would have dropped if his belt were not cinched tight around his navel.

Agent Whelan shook his hand upon arrival. "George Beckford? Special Agent Thomas Whelan. Thank you for meeting me."

"Thanks for offering the beer. It's been a long day, and I could use a drink."

"My pleasure. Long day?"

"Yes. I teach fourth-graders now. Full time. Down on Prospect. Some days can be challenging."

Whelan took a sip of his beer. Still served in a frosty mug the way he remembered it. "How so?"

"Oh, you know, the usual bullcrap." Beckford's voice went high-pitched in an attempt to sound like a woman, "You gave my boy an 'F' because he's black! You don't like Tiffany because she's black! You put LeBron in detention because he black!" The more he spoke, the more his diction took on an urban vernacular.

He took a breath, "All I tell them is, lady, look around. *Everyone* here is black. Not everyone is in detention or making 'Fs'! They all think I'm a racist despite clear evidence to the contrary. I can't help it if my skin's white. I'm trying to educate their fucking children. You know I had three threats to my life last year? By fourth-graders! One even brought a knife in his bag. Metal detectors caught it right away."

"The district won't transfer you?"

"Nope. I've submitted five requests in two years. Can't afford to quit."

"So, tell me about subbing out in the burbs back in the mid-'90s."

Beckford lit up. "Oh, those were the good ole days!" He slammed down the rest of his beer and motioned the bartender for another. "Times were simpler then. Money was flowing into the district. There were fewer restrictions for a substitute, and we were in high demand. If you were willing to travel anywhere within a half-hour of the 435 loop, you could work every day. Students were kinder out in the burbs. And smarter. Not these *delinquents*, like now."

"So you were happier, then? No issues. Not with the board, or any particular student issues you can recall?"

"No. The students loved me. Especially the girls. I think I reminded them of their dads, but I was more down-to-earth and relatable—younger."

"You were how old, in '97?" asked Agent Whelan.

"Ummm...I guess I would have been twenty-eight, twenty-nine. Is that important?"

"I'm not sure. So, you don't recall any trouble with any students between, say, '97 and '99?" He watched closely for any facial reactions on Mr. Beckford.

There were none. "Nope. Happy times. I'd give anything to go back to those days." He started cackling. "Well, wouldn't we all. Take away twenty years? I think everybody would like that."

"Maybe," said Whelan, standing up and throwing a twenty on the bar. "Except I'd be thirteen, and I don't feel like repeating Jr. High."

George Beckford continued blathering. "No, I guess no one wants that! Thanks for the beer."

He stayed behind for a third while Whelan took to the street.

Agent Whelan believed Beckford was a little creepy and a racist. *But not my guy.*

As he got in his car, George Beckford stood watching him through the front window. His face was relaxed except his lips, which were still conflicted with a twisted pucker. He raised his brow and returned to his seat at the bar. Happy Hour was kicking into full gear.

Chapter 6

Three days later, Jones and Whelan were comparing progress at the office. Agent Jones had built an old-fashioned investigation wall on a rolling corkboard. The victims' photos were posted with names written in sharpie across the bottom. Post-its littered the side with potential suspects and random ideas.

"Anything to add?" she asked Agent Whelan.

"Not really. I'm drawing blanks. Interesting board, though. You like it old-school? I prefer 'i2 Analyze'. Data's always with me that way. I keep it updated in the cloud so I can add notes from my phone when and wherever I need to."

"I get that as a field agent. I keep my phone updated in real-time as reports come in. But I find if I come in each day and I'm slapped in the face with *this*, it motivates me to keep going. And there's something about seeing it larger than a phone or computer monitor. It's more real, somehow."

"Hey, if it works."

Jones sighed as she ripped off three post-its. "*Nothing's* working for me right now. That's the problem."

"We'll catch a break soon. The killer *will* slip up. My subpoena for the airlines' flight records from Kansas City International to Miami and back was granted. We should be able to start comparing the names of everyone who was in Miami from Kansas City last week. We can cross-match them with the list of teachers. I've already put two agents on it. I hope that's okay? As your new partner, they're kind of looking at me as being in a supervisory role, even though that's not official."

"That's perfect. I didn't bring you onboard to sit on your ass and wait for instruction. I'll get Kendrick to issue a memo that your 'lead' on this one with me. I can't do it alone any longer. Whitfield sat on his ass and twiddled his thumbs in resentment. I'm glad to have real help."

"Of course. We should have the flight records within the hour."

"With my luck, the bastard drove down." She rubbed her eyes. Not much sleep was coming to her lately.

"Where are we at with those substitutes?" she continued. "You finish them all?"

"In person, except for the ones who aren't local anymore. My gut tells me our killer is still living in the area."

"How many aren't *local* anymore?"

"About four. Well, I profiled out a few. I have four left. I've spoken with all but one. She's not returning any of my calls." He handed her a sheet he'd printed out from his software.

Agent Jones studied it for a second, then jerked her head up. "This Judy Ward's number starts with 305. That's Miami. Book us a flight. Your killer might be a woman yet."

Whelan nodded. "I've wanted to get back down there anyway. According to Janine Cook, there were at least three people taking video. We need to see the footage from the other two. One of them might have caught the person who released our crime scene to the world via YouTube. Maybe we can get more answers. If we can find the other footage, there may be additional people in the crowd identified that we can track down and talk to."

"Mansilla said no one in the building admitted to recording it."

"I know. Someone's lying."

❀ ❀ ❀

Felix Perez sat in his boxers, frantically shaking his PlayStation controller. He liked any game slated with an 'M' rating and which allowed him to shoot people. When the knocking on his door wouldn't stop, he paused his gameplay and opened up his condo in South Beach.

"Felix, I'm Special Agent Thomas Whelan with the FBI," said Whelan, holding his ID up to the young man's face. He was alone, split up from his partner once again to save time, acutely aware that tomorrow was likely going to present another body. Agent Jones had gone in search of Judy Ward.

After going it alone for over two years tracking down evidence on Eddie Morrison, it didn't bother *him*, separating for interviews. However, he was concerned that Agent Jones was so comfortable breaking policy and reflected on Kendrick's comments. He brushed it off, knowing full well they were on a rapidly ticking clock.

"I already spoke with the police," Felix moaned. "I ain't got nothin'." He would have shut the door were it not for Whelan's blocking foot. "Go 'way, man! I don't know nothin'."

"*Nothing?*" asked Whelan, moving his body into the doorway. "One of your neighbor's swears you were taking video of the dead girl. How well did you know Sonja Cuevas?"

Agent Whelan surveilled the room, noting a bong and some papers on the coffee table. The unmistakable smell of pot was permeating the air. "You got a prescription for that?" he asked, nodding toward the table. "Some debilitating medical condition you're suffering from? You'd better enlighten me fast, or I'm going to have to bring you downtown, Felix."

The twenty-year-old had been smoking it pretty heavily. "You can't bust me, man. Ain't nothin' here, and you need a warranty or something, man. You can't come in here, man."

"I'm not *in* here. I'm out *here*," said Whelan. "Why don't you *invite* me in to discuss Sonja, and I'll forget all about calling for a 'warranty' to sack your place for more drugs?"

Felix gave in and walked back toward his sofa. "Fine." He picked up the game controller and resumed his play.

Whelan moved into the living room and glanced at the TV. Mr. Perez was blundering through the challenge, shooting the crooks—and the civilians—along the way and failing to remember to reload as often as he should.

"You like games?" Whelan asked.

"Yeah. I like this one. Got it yesterday. Already on level four."

"If I can beat you to level five, will you turn it off and talk to me?"

Felix whooped, "Sure old man. Whatever you want." Because some Fed showed up with a badge didn't mean he could shoot his way through *this*. He handed Whelan the extra controller. He doubted Whelan had played a video game since Pac-Man. When you're twenty, thirty-three looks like fifty.

What young Mr. Perez failed to realize was Whelan had a son who also enjoyed video games. And the last time he'd played this one with Connor, they'd made it to level eighteen. And in under a day. Ten minutes later, Felix was sitting open-mouthed as Agent Whelan jumped off the boat, sprinted down the pier, stole a car, raced to downtown, and opened the door to the bank. He grabbed the flag on this level, advancing his character to level five while Felix was still sitting behind barrels on the dock.

"No way, man! You cheated or somethin'! You didn't tell me you'd played this, man. That's not fair."

"Sure it is. You never asked me. You made assumptions. Now, if *I* made assumptions about *you,* Felix, I don't think they'd be very favorable." He turned the TV off and faced the young man directly. "Do you want me to start making assumptions? I need to know what you know about Sonja Cuevas, and I need a copy of the video on your phone. I need this *now*. Then you can go back to your life. That was the deal. Man."

Felix opened his mouth with a retort. He sighed instead, then closed his mouth and handed Whelan his phone. "I didn't know her. I moved here two months ago. I'd seen her come and go and stuff, but I didn't know her really—just 'hi' and stuff. Pretty lady. Shame man. That freak scared the shit out of us. There's still a cop car outside on the street every night, watching us, man—creepy stuff. You haven't caught him yet? You think he's still here in Miami, man? I bet he's in Tijuana. That's where I'd be. Living it up and shit."

Once his tough wall collapsed, he was an onslaught of not-so-helpful verbal diarrhea.

Whelan blue-toothed the file to his phone and returned Felix's. "See there? That wasn't so hard." He smiled with as much insincerity as he could muster and stood to leave.

The young man checked his phone and jumped up. The video was gone. "Hey man! You said you were gonna *copy* it! Not erase it! I need that back, man. I was savin' that for TMZ or some shit. They pay big bucks for that crazy shit. You can't take it. That's stealing!"

Whelan didn't have any more time to waste. "I don't need this showing up on YouTube, Facebook, TMZ or anywhere else. Man. You get me? You want to complain, come on downtown. I'm heading there now. And by the time we get there, that 'warranty' I called in when I first arrived should be on my desk. You can save us the delivery. And when they escort you back here, they'll want to double-check your closets, your bathroom and kitchen, your computer. Oh, and all your games? Well, I'm afraid they'll wind up needing checked out too." Whelan glared at the kid. "Well. Come on! I don't have all day. Let's go!"

Felix plopped back down on his sofa. "Nah man. It's cool. But if I see that on TMZ, you owe me half, man! Deal?"

"Deal." Whelan returned to his car. As he turned over the ignition, he began to chuckle.

Judy Ward's home was quite different than the tiny condos that Felix and Janine rented in Sonja's building. She married into money. Her winter home was a mansion in Sunrise Harbor, south of Coconut Grove, directly on Biscayne Bay. There were six bedrooms and over ten thousand feet under air.

"May I help you?" asked the servant who opened the door.

"I'm Supervisory Special Agent Miranda Jones, with the FBI. I need to speak with Judy Ward." She flashed her credentials.

"Mrs. Ward isn't home right now." Her Haitian eyes grew wide with fright, and she tried to close the door.

This time it was Jones' turn to foot-block a door. "I'm sorry, but it's urgent. Do you know when she'll return? I'm happy to wait."

"Mrs. Ward won't be home today. Please, I must get back to work."

This wasn't Miranda's first illegal immigrant. "Oh. I'm sorry to keep you. I'd hate for you to miss any work. If you'll show me your green card so I can confirm you're actually *allowed* to work, then I'll be on my way. Oh, and I didn't catch your *name*?"

The woman ran deeper into the home, screaming, "Mr. Ferretti! Mr. Ferretti! There's a woman here to see you." She disappeared behind a wall.

Agent Jones helped herself into the foyer. It opened wide, so the first thing you saw was the living room with floor-to-ceiling windows. The view of Biscayne Bay and the ocean off in the distance to the right was breathtaking. Sailboats decorated the water; parasailers the sky. Splashes of red, yellow and green crisscrossed horizontally in front of her. Foxtail Palms lined the sides of an infinity pool, which cast a complementary shade of blue to the teals of the bay in front of it. It would be easy to lose yourself in a home like this. Every day would feel like a vacation. She took a deep breath and expelled it slowly.

"Can I help you?" It was a man's voice.

Agent Jones spun around, expecting to find an old and decrepit body one breath away from being able to cash in a life insurance policy. But the man was attractive, with salt and pepper hair, in his early sixties and unduly fit. *Ahh, money.* She noted his Italian-made suit and dress shoes. *Those are not off-the-rack.*

"I'm Supervisory Special Agent Miranda Jones with the FBI," she repeated herself. "I need to speak with your...wife? Judy Ward?"

"Judy's on holiday. She went to L.A. with some friends for some late spring shopping. A 'girl's week.' What's this about?"

"I need to ask her some questions about her time in Kansas City back in the '90s. How long have the two of you been married?"

"Coming up on ten years."

"And she didn't take your name? Mr. Uberto Ferretti, is it?"

"No. She didn't." His Italian accent was faint but present. He'd been in the States for quite a while. He was becoming guarded.

"You know, I've been traveling all day, and I'm parched. Could I trouble you for a glass of water?"

Mr. Ferretti looked for a moment like he'd decline. He opened his mouth, "Adelaide!"

No one showed.

"Adi?" He looked around, then turned and disappeared behind the same wall as the maid.

Agent Jones immediately went into reconnaissance mode. She walked the room, inspecting every photograph. Rich people loved displaying professional portraits of themselves. She could find nothing taken before the past few years—no early images of Judy Ward. The pictures hung showed her as blonde, aging well, mid-fifties now. Not as fit as her husband, but not heavy. They made a handsome couple.

Other items on display in the room were static. Nothing intimate. It looked more like a showroom of impersonal art. *Or 'show-off' room.*

"Your water?" Ferretti appeared and handed her a glass full of cold filtered water from the fridge. It was a gorgeous crystal, not ten for ten dollars like those in Miranda's cupboard back home.

"Thank you!" She took a sip. "Oh, that's refreshing. You have the most beautiful view. How long have you lived here?"

"I bought this in 2000. But I'm sure you knew that already. Ms. Jones, what do you think my wife can help you with from her time in Kansas City?"

"She was a substitute teacher back in the mid-90s. Does she ever talk about that time in her life?"

"Seldom."

"Ever mention what she taught?"

"I can't remember. Why are you here, Ms. Jones?"

Miranda was trying to size the man up. His eyes were heated. He was shut down at this point. Perhaps a lifetime of learning to do that was quite natural for someone with his status in the business world.

"I'm investigating a murder."

Interest showed on Mr. Ferretti's face for the first time. "The 12 Pills Killer?"

"What makes you ask that?"

"It's on the nightly news here. We can't escape it. Perhaps where you're from—Kansas City, is it? —they don't show it every hour. But it's like no other crime has happened in Miami for the past five days. One of the others was in Kansas City?"

"Yes."

"And you think Judy's involved somehow? Hah!" he burst. "That's funny."

"Why?"

"Judy is the sweetest woman you'd ever meet. It's part of why I married her. She has the biggest heart and no room for nonsense. She could never be involved with someone psychotic."

Hmm. Maybe she dated *the killer.* "Well, people change over time, Mr. Ferretti. Perhaps she was a different woman twenty years ago."

"Not according to her mother. She comes every year for three months in the winter. 'Always been an angel that one'—says it all the time. Loves her dearly."

Yes, and my mama loves me, but it doesn't mean she really knows *me.* "Can I get her cell phone number?"

"No."

"How about Judy's?"

"No. Leave your card, Ms. Jones. I'll have her call you when she gets back on Tuesday."

"Tuesday! Lucky girl. Sure would hate to pay those credit card bills!"

"Good day, Ms. Jones." He was quite stern.

48

"Good day Mr. Ward. I mean, Ferretti! Sorry. Wasn't thinking for a moment."

Uberto Ferretti knew she was trying to bait him. He'd sat across more than one negotiation table in his career. She was trying to shake him, an obvious ploy. He nodded toward the front door.

Miranda turned the door handle, but before leaving, wheeled back around to Ferretti, still in the middle of the living room. "Chemistry! I just remembered she taught chemistry *and* biology. You think she retained enough after her early retirement to make custom pharmaceuticals?"

Ferretti managed to keep his mouth closed, but his jawline dropped on his face.

Agent Jones smiled wide. "I'll be back on Tuesday."

Chapter 7

Saturday morning came, June 20, and in a quaint Tudor in the Westwood area of Kansas City, 12 Pills, a once-inhibited sort, was whistling a tune from the radio as bacon and eggs fried away in cast iron. Arranging the breakfast tray brought pleasure. Accompanying toast and half a grapefruit completed the meal. *Vitamin C is better when it's natural.* A tall glass of low-fat milk over ice was in the corner.

An unfinished but tidy basement held a large oak table, a hand-me-down loaded with memories. The cleared end was set with a placemat and the meal eaten in silence, save for the sound of the Kansas City Star's thin pages rustling as they turned between long fingers. 12 Pills looked up over the corner of one page and noticed that a Bunsen burner was turned up a bit high at the far end of the table. The flame was adjusted to the appropriate height. Several other beakers were held up to the light bulb and examined for cleanliness. Two were wiped free of dust on the white lab coat worn by the pseudo-scientist.

Mustn't have any dirt. This isn't a poor farm.

A mesmerizing process took place for the next two hours, as tubes were filled with carefully measured chemicals from unmarked bags. They were weighed to the milligram on shiny scales, and liquids were poured and cooked.

A fresh piece of root, severed from a flowering stalk out of a small pot, was placed beside two others, harvested from the backyard. They were all cleaned, peeled like carrots, then measured and diced. The pieces were wrapped in cheesecloth, then placed in a heavy press. With each turn of the handle, a few more drops of liquid fell into a waiting beaker. 12 Pills added their "nectar" to the concoction in progress.

Leaves from a different plant were chopped fine, then placed in boiling water for twenty minutes. A few milliliters were added to the batch. Halfway through the cook, flower petals were squeezed and pressed—for color. *Don't be afraid of color. God created all the colors. Revel in them.* This particular petal also insured additional toxicity. In the end, a medium-blue residue powdered the bottom of a flask.

Delicately scraped and weighed, 12 Pills placed it into the stainless hopper on the pill press. Ebay started listing them at under three hundred dollars, but this was top-of-the-line and allowed for various pill shapes and sizes. Soon, four blue tablets a little larger than a regular aspirin sat in the repository.

Peeling off rubber gloves, 12 Pills popped the final corner of toast with raspberry jam onto a waiting tongue, a reward for a completed task. *And we don't waste any food in this house.*

The lab was cleaned, sanitized, and put back to order. It wouldn't be needed for another week. Dust covers were returned to protective positions, not that there was any dust to be collected.

Tweezers removed the pills from the catch-cup on the press and then dropped them into a tiny, plastic zipper-locking bag, about two inches square. A pocket on the lab coat would house them for now. 12 Pills cleared the breakfast tray and wiped the table clean of the single spilled crumb.

A yank on the light cord threw the room into relative darkness, save a little table standing beside the stairwell. It was lit up by light spilling down from the opened door at the top.

Time for someone to get their medicine.

51

Stored neatly in a row were eight orange pill bottles, their caps marked with Sharpie. The first one was grabbed on the way up. "5 of 12."

❧ ❧ ❧

Tony Balzano grew up privileged in a large estate home in Sunset Hill, about a half-mile south of Kansas City's Country Club Plaza. His family came from money, generations of Italian connections in the trade industry, and other revenue streams best left unmentioned within a mile of any courthouse or police precinct. They cleaned up across the area in the early '80s when the post-modern "Memphis Milano" scene took over a niche in interior design, and everyone who wasn't a fan of Laura Ashley florals thought black lacquer was making a comeback in bedroom furniture and entertainment units. Tony himself was conceived beneath such a headboard in 1985.

He fell in line and joined the lucrative family business, now owning and operating Balzano's Fine Italian Furniture and Imports, "with three locations to serve you" around the greater Kansas City metro area. Massive warehouses were revamped, and when you step inside one, it's like going to a theme park.

Each visitor, greeted by a "tour guide" dressed like a gondolier, is offered an Italian Ice in five flavors, though the Honey & Sambuca is considered the house favorite.

The retail floor sections off into five furniture styles, each representing a different area of Italy. Matching displays, murals, faux buildings, landscaping and lighting all add to the attraction. Bridges cross over small canals with flowing water to move from theme to theme, and hidden speakers pipe music to match the style of furniture and convey a mood.

Tony Balzano caught a lot of attention in high school for his charm and superior looks, but his hair was now disappearing, and his old wrestler weight of 154 more than doubled. He sat in the office of one of his showrooms, going through the day's sales as they populated into his accounting software. Leisurely sucking on his Honey & Sambuca as he did most nights at this time, he said goodnight to the last employee as they punched out.

It was a little before 10:00 p.m. Tony settled out P&L statements while comparing them against an old paperback journal with other figures written in ballpoint. Occasionally, a family deal still needed to be laundered through the business, so numbers were adjusted before the bookkeeper came in on Sundays to prepare files for the accountant meetings on Mondays. By the time a final pair of eyes were on it before being filed with the IRS, no one could say for sure that a bedroom suite didn't sell for $4700 instead of $2800, or a piece of art didn't sell for $15,800 instead of $6250.

Without warning, a sharp pain hit Tony's stomach, and he stood up to see if it could be relieved. Spasms hit a little lower in his intestinal tract. He was about to go and find some seltzer as a fresh agony grappled his heart. He fell, clenching his chest with one hand, his stomach with the other. While on his knees, a stranger appeared in the doorway and looked on without remorse. Tony's eyes widened as the stranger approached.

His visitor was eating an Italian Ice and watching the "Death of Tony Balzano" show.

Tony believed he was experiencing a heart attack. He was unsure why he had stomach pain. "Help!" he gasped.

The stranger smirked.

Tony rolled onto his back to stretch his legs out and allow his guts to stretch with them, hoping that would end the burning working its way down. At one point, he was sure vomiting was inevitable, but his nausea passed. His heart pain also ceased as abruptly as it started. All pain soon eased. Smiling with the abatement of agony for a moment toward the ceiling, Tony realized he was losing motor control over his limbs. His hand tingled, and he couldn't lift his arm. *What's happening to me?* Paralysis was setting in.

A rubber-gloved hand appeared in his peripheral vision. It set an Italian Ice on the edge of his desk, next to his. He managed to turn his neck so he could see the top of the snowball and knew from its color, it was Honey & Sambuca. He looked at his cup beside it. For the first time, he noticed his ice wasn't quite the proper color. Not the normal soft yellow. It had a slight bluish-green tint to it. Subtle but different.

The visitor's face appeared, glaring into Tony's.

Who are you? Balzano wanted to speak out, but his voice wasn't cooperating. *My heart! Is it beating? Please beat! Dear God...*

His eyes could still see, but the light was dimming. His face began to show the fear his mind was processing. It fought the darkness as the lack of fresh blood to his brain overcame him. The last thing it would ever process was the bottom of a little orange pill bottle pushing toward his face.

By the time it entered the mouth, Tony Balzano was dead.

Tony's eyelids were forced open, so he might properly greet those who would discover him. They captured forever the fear he felt in those final seconds.

The visitor polished off their own Ice, and threw the cup in the office trash, along with Tony's. The thirteen-gallon liner was collected, and the desk lamp shut off. Making the way by nightlights, the 12 Pills Killer went out the back door of the building and walked three blocks to a car without being seen. "5 of 12" was in the bag; another week would mark the halfway point.

12 Pills stared into the rearview mirror a minute. Discontented eyes stared back as the engine turned over. There was no rush. The car pulled out slowly and made its way home.

Gertrude "Gertie" Balzano was Tony's aunt by way of marriage but participated in the family business for over a half-century. She liked to work the floor some weekends to alleviate boredom and chat up the locals. She missed being social, and since her husband died three years prior, her little eighty-two-year-old body found a lot of free time on its hands.

Tony failed to show for service that morning, so she went straight to the store from church, beating the regular employees who started drifting in before the doors opened at 11:00 a.m. She marched herself to Tony's office, planning to give him a proper lecture about how important a sermon he missed. She saw him on the floor and turned on the lights.

"Ahh, Tony..." She was disappointed. "Who did you fuck over now?" A German native, she took to the family ways as if she were Sicilian born. She wasn't surprised. Looking around, she wondered for a moment how she was going to hide the body. He was too heavy to drag.

"Oh my. You fat little fuck. Ah, well, serves you right."

She looked at the pill bottle. "5 of 12." *Oh, Heavens!*

This was not "family" business. *Thank God.*

She dialed 911.

Sitting in Tony's desk chair after the call, she opened the bottom drawer and eyed a bottle of Sambuca. It was half full. She started to take a swig. Then it dawned on her it might be poisoned. "Oh, mio!" She set it down hard on the desk. Reaching into her purse, she pulled out her own tiny flask and took a swig of whiskey. Her eyes darted back and forth between Tony's face and the clock on the wall. It was nearing 10:30, and she knew the sales staff would be showing up soon.

Thankfully, her great-nephew, who managed the store on the weekends, walked in first.

"Uncle Tony!" He ran to his side.

"Don't touch him!" snapped Gertie. "Go wait outside for the police and keep any sales staff from entering the building for now. I don't think we're going to be open for business today."

Chapter 8

Agents Whelan and Jones poured over the security video footage while a forensics unit swept the office of Tony Balzano.

"There!" Jones pointed to the monitor. "He's walking up to the back door! What's he...? He's covered head to toe."

The surprisingly clear footage showed a figure in a dark raincoat with a hood, hands covered with gloves, shoes wrapped in— "Is that duct tape?"

"Clever," said Whelan. "No shoe prints. Can't get a proper shoe size. They measured maybe size eleven or twelve in the dust. I'm guessing it's more like nine or ten. No way to be sure."

"So he came up from nowhere and cut the back door camera around 8:00. No one detected him, and from there, what? The back door was locked with an emergency exit bar. He went in the *front* door? And of course, there's no camera in the front, just the back and here in the office. Cheapskates."

"They must have figured they didn't need any more. It's not easy to shoplift sofas and ottomans," said Whelan.

"What about that $12,000 figurine I passed on the way in? That could slip into a large coat pocket easily enough."

"True. I would guess video footage doesn't corroborate their yearly write-offs for theft, so why bother?"

"So, he could have been one of two-hundred or more customers they had in the hour before closing. Then he hid out anywhere in this maze of a showroom until everyone else went home."

"I'll bet our killer knew this building from previously scoping it out. This was well planned. 12 Pills knew there were only two cameras and exactly where they were."

Miranda looked back to the frozen image on the screen, captured right before the cord was cut. "They couldn't have placed the damned camera higher up? He didn't even need to reach up to snip it. From this angle, I can't tell how tall he is, anywhere from five-six to six-three. Those hedge cutters have at least a two-foot reach."

She sighed. "Unless forensics finds more evidence, we're no closer from this."

"Yes we are. We know he, or *she*, is five-foot-six to six-foot-three and wears at least a size nine shoe. That rules out a lot of people." His tone was facetious.

"Maybe," agreed Miranda. "Unless *she's* wearing lifts and wrapped up her size sevens in *two* rolls of tape." Another sigh.

Whelan laughed, his patronizing finished for the evening. "Go home. It was a long flight from Miami. Rest up in your own bed. I'll wrap up here. We've got four agents interviewing the employees. I don't think 12 Pills is going to have stood out as a raving psychopath, but you never know."

"Put four more on following up with every customer who made a purchase in the last two hours the store was open."

"Already on it. And I've got two going through every bit of footage to see if anyone looks like they're scoping out the place, paying special attention to the cameras. Unfortunately, their DVR only records up to 30 days. If this was as well planned as I think it was, the reconnaissance could have been months ago."

Agent Jones pursed her lips as she patted her partner on the shoulder and slipped out.

Whelan switched the camera view back to the office and replayed the footage for the fourth time. It showed Balzano coming in around 9:40, sucking on a cup of Italian Ice. He nursed on the little cup while pouring over a record book and his laptop, then the camera went dead, and the footage stopped recording.

"Joe!" yelled Whelan.

Lead Forensics Agent Joseph Cusack appeared from out in the hallway.

"Get Gertrude Balzano back in here," snapped Whelan.

Gertie arrived in short order. She was tired from the long day of incessant interrogations. "Yes?"

"Where's Tony's laptop?"

"I sent it to the accountant already. Didn't occur to me you'd need it. We still got a business to run."

"I'm touched by your commitment. We need that back ASAP. I need to see if there's anything on there that might make someone want to murder your nephew. I need that record book he was logging entries from too."

"Sure, I'll have his laptop for you first thing in the morning."

Gertrude walked over to a bookshelf behind Tony's desk. She grabbed a record journal off the top. "Here's the latest book for anything not in the computer system. The furniture always gets input directly into the software as it arrives, but Tony did things the old way for the imported art pieces."

"Why not inventory *them* into the computer's software?" asked Whelan.

"Because his system worked and that little logbook is a lot lighter to carry around than a computer when he goes on purchasing runs to Italy," Gertie lied.

"Write down your accountant's contact information. I need to send a car to retrieve that laptop. Now, not in the morning."

She obliged. "Anything else?"

"No. You can go. And again, my condolences."

Gertie raised her eyebrows and gave a curt nod before leaving.

Agent Whelan stood and surveilled Tony's desk. *What are we missing?*

And then he caught it. On the edge of the desk, there were two water ring stains on the glass. They were faint and easy to miss if the light didn't catch them the right way. Whelan double-checked to make sure there was only one cup in the video. He looked at the empty trash can.

The killer had an Ice and then took both of them with him! No trash liner. They were bagged and removed. The killer was eating an Italian Ice. What flavor? Does it matter? Might matter. What flavor does a killer like? Flavor...might hide the taste of poison. They put it in his fucking Ice. Could the whole bottle still be out there? Could they be that careless? Maybe they slipped up!

A few years back, Agent Whelan adopted the plural pronoun 'they' when gender-neutralizing even individual suspects. He would have to work on instilling this in his partner. It bothered him that she was so confident the killer was a man. Because the statistical odds favored it, didn't make it fact. There was room for error, and he'd seen a couple of psychopaths in his rookie year that bucked the trend. Eight years seemed like a lifetime ago after chasing Eddie Morrison for so long.

"Joe!" Whelan yelled out again.

"Right here." He was outside the door and popped his head in.

"Sorry. Pull every bottle of syrup."

"Already ahead of you. But I can tell you none of them are going to have your poison."

"Why's that?"

"Cause the bottle with the flavor he liked to suck on every night is missing."

"Oh. Thanks. Night."

Agent Cusack left to gather his crew and head out.

Whelan looked back to the two water rings. *You will slip up. I will catch you when you do.*

He wasn't sure he'd sold himself on his pep talk, but he left for the evening feeling like something was about to shake loose on this case.

Chapter 9

"We're flying back to Miami tonight," Agent Jones spoke over the phone to her partner the following morning. "Pick me up at Stronghold's Gym, would you? I'll text you the address. I've got to get in a proper workout before I turn to jelly."

Jelly was hardly the thing Whelan saw when he looked at her. He arrived ten minutes early and decided to saunter in instead of waiting in the lot as requested.

Stronghold's was the latest gym to open up in the Westport area of Kansas City and within a quick mile jog of Miranda's home. Filled with a mix of Millennials and Gen-Xers, they were each trying to outdo the other's generation with harder, longer workouts and the proper amount of parading around to be noticed when you broke a sweat. There was a smoothie station in the front and a vegan cafe on the left wall, far from the type of gym Whelan envisioned she attended.

He spotted her lifting free weights in the back, staring into a mirror.

"I took you for more of a 'dirty old boxing gym downtown' sort of girl," he beamed at her duplicate in the mirror. "With smelly floor mats and a little ninja teaching karate in the back."

She returned his smile. Her face was damp from her routine, but she let it run down her cheeks instead of patting it dry. "There's actually a boxing ring *in* the back, and I think they *do* teach karate three nights a week—you have to check out the schedule up front."

"Boxing ring! You mean it gets even bigger than this?" Thomas looked around. It looked like the place could have been a large grocery store at one point.

Miranda grinned. "Hey, it's a mile from my house, and I happen to have a free membership courtesy of one of the personal trainers. So..." she stopped for a moment and turned to look at him directly, "...why would I drive through rush hour traffic and pay for parking to work out on smelly old mats?" She was a blaze of fiery joy.

"I'm sold. Where do I sign up? And how do I get the family discount?"

She continued to jubilate while a few of the other early morning "before work" crowd milled around her admiring her workout's payoff.

One of them approached, scrutinizing Whelan, but went straight for Miranda. He was towering, with beautiful ebony skin stretched over a frame of solid muscle. He weighed close to 240, and all of it in his chest, arms and quads. His head was bald and a bit shiny still from his own workout. He wore a tank top, drenched in sweat. It clung to his six-pack and failed to hold in his massive pecs and their nipples. There was a small Stronghold's Gym logo in the center. His face was model-caliber, and Whelan guessed he was around thirty.

Miranda placed her arms around his neck, and he curled his back to reach down and kiss her.

"Derrick, this is Thomas Whelan," she said, stepping aside. "Whelan, this is my friend, Derrick Domino."

Derrick stuck out his hand and smiled warmly. "Wonderful to meet you finally. I've heard so much about you! Miranda thinks you're going to solve this latest murder investigation. That's awesome!"

"Nice to meet you too." Whelan took his hand back apprehensively. "I've heard absolutely nothing about *you*."

Derrick was boisterous. "That's Miranda!" He bent down and gave her another kiss. He stroked her hair, placed his monstrous hands on either side of her face, and gently planted a third kiss, holding it for a few seconds longer than was socially acceptable in a public place.

Whelan looked around the room, trying not to be present. Onlookers smirked, some of them jealous, but most took it in stride. They'd seen this display more than once.

Derrick exhausted his lip-lock. "I'll wait to hear from you when you're back in town."

He looked at Whelan. "Nice to meet you, Thomas. Take care of my girl." With that, he was gone, headed to the machines to meet a new client.

Thomas watched him leave. He turned back to Miranda, speechless for a moment, while she wiped her body down with a hand towel. "So...not...a lesbian?"

"Uh-uh."

"He's crazy about you. How long have you been together?"

"A couple of years. But we aren't 'officially together.' He'd like to be, but I'm not ready to commit to anything but my job right now. He knows and understands. We're both so busy. Maybe one day." She looked over at him, where he was spotting a young man on a bench press.

"I'll be in the car."

"I *did* ask you to wait outside." She looked at a large clock on the wall. "Give me five minutes to run through the shower and change. I'll be ready to go at exactly 8:00. When I *said* I'd be ready."

By the time Agent Jones joined him in the parking lot, Whelan had already looked up Derrick Domino. That was his given name. It marketed itself. He was an ex-Navy Seal, college-educated, and doing personal training for the past four years. He was thirty-two— six years Miranda's junior. Whelan was a year older than Derrick, but it felt like a dozen at the moment.

He studied his face in the mirror. He had more lines across his forehead and in his crow's feet than most men his age. *Reflections in the rear-view mirror may appear deeper than they are.*

As Miranda opened the car door, he was looking at his bicep, flexing it as best he could. There was scant tone in the tiny muscle. He needed to start bulking up after his two-year ordeal chasing down Eddie Morrison.

She noted the bio on Derrick still sitting on the screen.

Whelan sighed. "So, all that...and he's a *personal trainer*?"

"He's got an eight-month waiting list, an online video channel, three 'healthy living' books on the market and brings in over $140,000 a year."

Whelan processed her statement for a moment. He sighed again and started the car.

❀ ❀ ❀

Miranda didn't know where to take the conversation on the way to the office. "You found a place yet?"

Thomas shot her a squint. "And I've had time for that *when*?"

"I don't know, online, at night maybe, in your hotel room. You want to move back to Independence?"

"No. More central. Perhaps around the Plaza."

"You called your mother yet? She know you're in town?"

"Keep drilling me like this, and I won't feel the need to make time with my own mother."

Miranda laughed. "I'm sorry. I… I care."

"Thank you. Now drink the rest of your protein shake in silence like a good girl."

"Yes, sir!" Miranda took a large sip and quieted herself into bemused reticence.

At the office, Agent Whelan was handed a tablet by one of his associates. "Here's the list of everyone who's flown from K.C. to Miami and back in the past three weeks. We've taken out all children and ruled out everyone we know for sure could not have been in K.C. during the '90s."

Whelan scanned down the list, sorted alphabetically. He went straight to the start of the letter W. He mumbled aloud when he hit upon "Walsh. Walsh, then Warsaw. No Ward." He jumped to the "Fs" and looked for Ferretti. Nothing.

"Where are the private airlines? These are all the major carriers."

The agent took the tablet for a moment and brought up another screen. It was a lot shorter list. Judy Ward's name jumped out.

Whelan drew a line with his finger over to the flight data. "Agent Jones, we need to cancel our flight to Miami. Judy Ward's not flying home from L.A. tomorrow. She's right here in K.C.!"

❀ ❀ ❀

By the time Agents Jones and Whelan knocked on the front door of Judy Ward's mother's home in Westwood, a residential neighborhood southwest of The Plaza, a protracted review of Judy's flight records revealed frequent visits to Kansas City.

Evelyn Ward was in her mid-seventies. She held a strong resemblance to Judy, with more wrinkles and a gnarled nose.

"One or two sugars in your tea, dear?" she asked Agent Jones.

"A drop of cream, please, no sugar."

"Agent Whelan?"

"Two sugars, please." Whelan was doing his best to remain calm after Mrs. Ward insisted she put on tea before she'd sit and answer questions.

He passed the time by giving himself a tour of Evelyn's home. "I like this floor plan. Would it be impolite if I asked what the market value of homes in this neighborhood go for?"

Evelyn paused a moment. "I think Francine up the road got around four-fifty for hers last year."

Whelan looked at Agent Jones. "I need a raise."

She chuckled, as did Mrs. Ward, who was the intended target.

Agent Jones began, "Evelyn, why does Judy come to Kansas City every few weeks? Is she that homesick? Are there problems in her marriage?"

Evelyn took a sip and exercised prudence before she spoke. "Problems in her marriage? Yes. But that's on her. She's a big girl now." A burst of laughter escaped her before she spirited through. "She comes to see *me*. I'm dying. Cancer. Breasts—well, it was my breasts. They're gone now. Also, my lungs and liver. I imagine it's everywhere now, but I quit going to the doctor three months ago. I've got another two to four weeks, I'd say, then I'll be up in Heaven with my Laurence."

"I'm so sorry, Evelyn! I didn't know," replied Miranda. "We wouldn't bother you now if this wasn't imperative."

"Well then, go on, dear."

"Problems with her marriage?"

67

"Yes." Mrs. Ward set her teacup on the ottoman tray. "Uberto Ferretti. Biggest ass I ever met."

"I've met him," agreed Agent Jones.

"Well, I think he's abusive. I'm not sure. Judy stays mum about it. Last October, he accused her of coming to see me so often because he believed she was having an affair. I mean, *Judy*! Of all people! Well, they got in quite the fight, and she threatened to leave him if he didn't come to his senses. Then, about five months ago, he came here around ten o'clock one night, drunk as a skunk, and kicked in the door when I wouldn't let him in. Judy was asleep in bed. I think he expected to find her in there with another man. She was exhausted from taking me around to all my doctors for two days straight and glad to have a whole night's sleep away from that brute. I usually go down to Miami to get away from the snow, but this year, I didn't have it in me. Well, the following morning, he realized how foolish he'd been. He apologized to us both and bought me a new door, lots of flowers. He was all mushy with Judy, and she seemed to buy into it. I don't know what she sees there."

Mrs. Ward paused a moment to make sure she made eye contact with both her visitors. "Money doesn't buy happiness, kids. Can't buy health or happiness. You have to work on both of those yourself."

Agent Jones was growing fond of this kind, wise soul in front of her. She hated to keep up her interrogation but knew she had no choice. So far, this was all "buttering up."

"Evelyn, Judy was a substitute teacher in the mid-'90s. Biology and Chemistry. Did you notice any... *strange* behavior during those years? Was she dating anyone at the time?"

"Oh, you could call it *strange behavior,* I suppose. I did, for years. But we all came around to a new way of thinking after a time.

She was dating this one fellow. Ken, I think was his name. They were together in the '90s, but you'd have to ask her what years exactly. They were pretty hot for each other; then it ended abruptly. I think Ken wanted children. When he learned Judy couldn't have any…" she shook her head. "Part of why she bonded with Ferretti. *He* didn't want children. *Ever.*"

Whelan observed the mantle full of old photos during his home tour. He pointed to one on the end now. "That camping trip… is that Judy's brother? They look like they could be twins."

Evelyn sighed. "That's James. That was taken in '91, I think. Last photo I have of him."

Jones felt sorry for this poor woman who lost a husband, and a son apparently, and would soon lose her own life. No wonder Judy was coming home so often. "Evelyn, when will Judy be in? It's urgent we speak with her. We're investigating a crime which we believe she might be able to shed some light on."

"Judy? Did she witness something? What was it? Was Ferretti involved? I'll kill that bastard."

The "kind soul" grew a little rough around the edges.

Agent Jones asked, "Why do you think Ferretti's involved?"

"He's a psychopath, that one. Mean. Loves threatening people. Vicious. He'd sell his dead mother for a dime if it could turn a profit. If there's a crime, I'd look to him. I never did get the full scoop on where he got his millions from—embezzlement, fraud—a white-collar felony I'd wager, and with lots of wire transfers."

"I'm sorry, but we need to discuss this with your daughter. Will she be back in soon?"

"She's not due 'til tomorrow, I'm afraid. Her plane's supposed to land around lunch."

Agents Jones and Whelan exchanged puzzled looks.

Jones spoke up, "Evelyn, according to the flight logs, Judy's in town *now*. Since *Friday*."

❀ ❀ ❀

Chapter 10

The surveillance team showed up to keep an eye out for Judy's arrival at her mother's home. Agents Whelan and Jones headed back to the office.

Whelan filled two coffee cups before opening his laptop on his desk.

"I'm starting to get the feeling our killer isn't a former teacher, substitute or otherwise. I think they knew these people as a peer," he said to his partner.

"Really? I still feel it's the most feasible candidate. A five-year gap between Cuevas and the others doesn't make sense—*eight* between her and Balzano. What twelve or thirteen-year-old hangs out with a five to seven-year-old? Did you?"

"Not by choice. David's four years older than me, and he didn't want to hang with me when we were kids. But, many of us had siblings, older or younger, who we were forced to invite to certain gatherings. Birthdays, camping outings, boy scout groups, church functions... I'm betting Cuevas was simply in the wrong place. A friend perhaps, of one of their little sisters who tagged along?"

"Hell, we're guessing. We shouldn't still be guessing. If we don't start putting more together soon, there's going to be another innocent person killed."

"Innocent? Why innocent? Maybe they all did something to the murderer. Traumatized them in some way."

"*Twelve* people?" Agent Jones' head jerked. "I'd buy four or five, not twelve. This wasn't somebody bullied. Not in that way, at least. Our killer snapped. After twenty years. What would make *you* snap after twenty years?"

Thomas slurped his java. "A stolen love. A murdered love."

"There'd have to be someone you loved involved, for *most* people. Now, a true sociopath could snap over that, or anything else—with the right provocation built up. What was that list you started spitting out a minute ago? Birthdays, camping, boy scouts, church groups...what else?" She started writing it out on a notepad.

"Are you kidding? You're going down an endless street. Sports teams, drama productions, debate squad, cheerleading, social media friends, *all* the regular social groups, choir, band, extra-curricular groups, the YMCA, Boys and Girls clubs, holidays, vacations... the mall... Santa Claus..." Whelan stopped, his prospects spent.

Jones looked up with a new fire in her eyes. "Got 'em, what else?'"

Whelan's eyes squinted while he scratched the back of his head.

"So, *not* an endless street!" Agent Jones jumped up and left the room a minute. Thomas was still shaking his head when she burst back through the door. "I've got seventeen pairs of fresh eyes, each taking one item on your list. We're going to start over like we never investigated any of those previously."

"You've investigated *all* of those previously?" Whelan thought surely a few were original to him.

"Of course. Remember, I've had three more weeks on this than you. We're going back to square one. Because, well, we *are* still at square one." She plopped into a chair and took a breath.

Whelan took a moment then asked, "Even Santa Claus?"

"From nine malls, the Red Cross and all the 'Santa suppliers' in the city."

"Wow," said Whelan, "I'm impressed. What else did I miss the first three weeks? You covered it briefly, but repeat it to me now, like it's the first time."

"Okay." Agent Jones stood and crossed to her corkboard. She scanned it before taking a breath. Tony had been added to the list.

JACKSON KENNY

      b. January 3, 1987 - Independence Elementary

PAUL DUKE

      b. February 18, 1987 - Independence Elementary

TRACY STAMFORD

      b. March 12, 1987 - Lee's Summit Elementary

SONJA CUEVAS

      b. April 6, 1992 - Raytown Elementary

TONY BALZANO

      b. May 25, 1985 - St. Vincent Elementary

"The first victim—Jackson Kenny—was discovered in Topeka. He'd been visiting his older sister. Local cops had it less than four hours before we got the call. He still lived in K.C., and they didn't want to deal with it. We focused on more intimate relationships. Friends, family, co-workers—the usual. We looked into his social groups, church, Facebook friends…bowling buddies… Paul Duke was found in his home in K.C. We now had someone to cross-reference. Commonalities were plenty. Same elementary school, as you well know, same junior and senior highs. They shared a lot of the same friends, sports, classes, et cetera. Then Duke went into construction, and Kenny went to UMKC one year before dropping out and joining the army. They didn't stay in touch from that point."

"Jackson went to UMKC? I never ran into him on campus."

"Then," Jones ignored his interruption, "Tracy Stamford was in Overland Park. She had a small townhome there. Neighbors heard her dog barking for two days before locals showed up to investigate and found her body. Here's where we were thrown. Different schools. Different friends. Different life. No one knew her from Independence. So now, we're looking at teachers, every student from either city who went to college and studied any of the sciences—specifically chemistry—and those who went on to pharmacology or are now working in pharmaceuticals anywhere within a two-hundred-mile radius. SAC Kendrick needed more manpower, and it was given. And I got you."

She stared at him bitterly, like he was supposed to stand and deliver the killer's name in the moment or be forever shamed.

Before he could speak, she apologized. "I'm sorry, Thomas. It's not you. I go through those same steps every night in my head when it hits the pillow. I go through the list of connections every morning in the shower. I go through it and through it, and *nothing* makes sense. No lead is panning out. Every time I think I'm on the right track, it dead ends. I'm frustrated. How do we catch this guy?"

"Or girl," he corrected.

"Or girl, you pompous prick. There it is, your dark side! I wondered when it would present itself. I mean, we all have one, but you, you throw it out casually like you're at a cocktail party." She released a chuckle. She hoped to break her discouragement by teasing him.

He graciously played along. "That's me. Party prick."

They enjoyed a moment of ease in their tension before Thomas sobered a bit.

"Party…" he started thinking out loud. "You know, I still can't shake the feeling that somehow our killer knew these people from a birthday party. Otherwise, why kill them in the order of their birth months? That *has* to be a connection."

Whelan rose and studied the list of names hanging on the corkboard. There were two photos of each victim—one with the bottle in their mouth, one with it removed—side by side. The first picture helped to keep track of the order of the killings. And to Agent Jones, it kept the atrocity of it all in the foreground. It was a reminder of the urgency to catch the killer before another such photo would make its way to the board.

"Okay," said Whelan, "we have a black guy, a white guy, a white girl, a Hispanic girl, and an Italian guy. Gender and race would seem a non-issue. Serial killers usually stick within their own race, so that's challenging. I'm guessing it's not a hate crime. Well…not in the *traditionally* defined sense. I mean, the killer must have despised these people for some reason."

Why did you hate these people?

"I'm pretty adept at profiling," said Jones, "but we did have the best in the bureau consult on this. We agreed. This is revenge killing. Not some unknown going around getting their jolly off. It's personal. That mix of races in the targets you mentioned makes it impossible to narrow down a race for the killer. Probably a male, but not definitely, as you keep reminding me. Likely age thirty to sixty, so that's no help. Educated enough to make an entirely new compound and administer an effective poison."

"In other words," said Whelan, "you got nothing."

"Nothing useful." Jones sighed. "So, back to *your* possible connections. What about Balzano? You didn't know Stamford or Cuevas. You remember seeing Balzano at any birthday parties?"

"No. I've searched my memories on that."

"You want to let the hypno-shrink give it a shot?"

"I'm pretty clear on it. But what else would trigger the killer to work in the order of their birth months? Did they specifically choose twelve people, each representing a month of the year? Is it a coincidence?"

"We don't know at this point."

"And," Whelan continued, "assuming it's not a teacher, what would connect kids from different cities together? Different schools? After Jackson and Paul, there are no other visible relations. None of the victim's friends' interviewed so far remember anyone on the list except one or two. No one can connect them all."

"That's why I'm still inclined to think it was a teacher. A teacher, especially a substitute, would have had the opportunity to meet all these children of varying ages in different cities."

"So would a sports coach, a scout leader, a Boys and Girls Club director... a pastor...."

"And Santa Claus. Yes, that's why seventeen of our agents are going to revisit all of those."

"Okay," said Whelan. "But I think the killer knew these kids more personally. Somehow, he or she was wronged by the people on the list."

"And that brings us back to where we started. How does one child wrong another so badly that twenty years later, they snap and go back and kill them? *Twelve* of them? And what causes the snap?"

Whelan shrugged. "That's the million-dollar answer."

An agent knocked on the door and came in. "Guys, the local news is breaking Balzano's death as a 12 Pills murder. Someone squealed."

Agents Whelan and Jones looked at each other.

Jones beat her partner to the punch. "Shit."

❦ ❦ ❦

Chapter 11

Assistant Special Agent Phil Cannon was fast becoming one of Agent Jones' most utilized team members. He was young and excelled at the academy. He was proving himself and wanted the chance to advance his career. He navigated the television in the bullpen to the breaking story. "It hasn't been picked up yet nationally. You want me to try and get a suppression order to silence Channel 5?"

Agent Whelan entered, carrying a sheet of paper. "Don't bother. The AP released it. Put it on forty-four. Anyone care to place bets on how many minutes before it airs? I've got one."

Everyone held their breath and looked at the screen. It didn't even take the full sixty seconds. The same cable anchor who first named the 12 Pills Killer popped up with "Breaking News," scrolling beneath his necktie. "We have breaking news, ladies and gentlemen. The 12 Pills Killer has struck again. This time, in Kansas City, Missouri. The latest victim…."

He rattled on about Tony's discovery and the Balzano Furniture stores for over five minutes. More consultants were already popping up to offer opinions, weigh in on the rumors about Balzano's mob connections, and suggest perhaps the killer was on a nationwide spree. No one in the country was now safe. It was no longer Floridians alone who needed to fear for their lives.

Whelan turned down the volume after a few more minutes. "Okay, folks. Nothing's changed. Back to work."

People scurried as Whelan and Jones returned to their office.

Agent Cannon was on their heels. "Should we issue a statement?"

"Yes," said Agent Jones. "Time to use the press to our advantage. Put out the usual blurbs. Offer ten-thousand dollars to any lead that results in the capture of the killer."

"And get that suppression order for the previous victims' names," said Whelan.

Agent Jones looked at her partner. "You sure? I think we should spill the whole bean-pot. I think it can help us from here on out."

"If the rest of the country realizes it's a Kansas City connection, they won't be much help to us."

"I'm fine with that. There *is* a K.C. connection, and I want the *locals* to know it. If they know it's in their own backyard, they're going to be more inclined to keep a lookout for unusual activity."

"Okay," conceded Whelan. "It's your show."

Agent Jones gave a "go-ahead" nod to Agent Cannon. He scampered away to make the necessary calls.

Around 5:30, Whelan's stomach prompted him to eat. *And a beer wouldn't hurt.* "Care to join me for happy hour? I'm headed to Slappy's."

"You go ahead," said Jones, "I've got some calls to make, and I'm still wound up today. We'll pick up here in the morning; unless Judy Ward surfaces before then."

Whelan nodded, grabbed his bag, and headed out in the direction of liquor, his mind not yet as tired as his body. *Somebody's birthday party. January, February, March, April, May... Who was born in June? Did I go to any birthday parties in June? Who's number six?*

He aimed his car toward the Plaza.

When he walked in around 6:00, George Beckford, the substitute teacher, was sitting at the bar, nursing a cold one and chomping down on a bowl of free bar-mix. Whelan tried to slip to the side without being seen, sitting at a table in the middle of the restaurant. When he glanced up to the bar, Beckford was staring straight at him, then stood and waltzed over as if they had an appointment.

"Hey detective! How are you? You catch your guy yet?"

Beckford moved a chair out to help himself to a seat.

"It's Special Agent, Mr. Beckford, and I'm sorry, but I'm expecting someone to join me in a minute. We'll have to catch up another time."

George Beckford frowned. "Oh. Well… okay then. Sorry to have bothered you." His shoulders dropped, and he moved back to his barstool.

Whelan dodged a bullet, but if Beckford was here much longer, he'd realize no one was joining him. He flashed his credentials to the hostess when she approached him about seating himself, and she obliged with a happy hour menu. He ordered a beer and some wings from the waitress who showed up and lost himself in his laptop's screen.

New notions and follow-up reminders were input into his software for the next ten minutes, and each time he peeked at the bar, Beckford was staring at him. Whelan was about to stand and approach him on the matter when the door opened, and someone he recognized from his childhood walked in. He waved to him as though he were expected.

The man turned his face to the side a minute, struggling to verify the familiarity. He decided to inquire.

Whelan beat him to it. "Aren't you Reggie Johnson? I'm Tommy Whelan. I think we had class together in fifth grade."

The man's eyes widened. "Oh my gosh. That's been... twenty-two years ago! I can't believe you remembered me. How are you?" He offered his hand.

Thomas shook it warmly and pulled out a seat. "I didn't mean to ambush you like that. I'm revisiting old memories lately, so you sort of jumped out to me when you walked in. What are you up to these days?" He glanced at the bar to confirm Beckford was witnessing the arrival of his "friend."

Reggie took a seat. He was well-groomed, with a short, uniform layered haircut complementing his multi-racial scalp. "Well, I'm working fifty hours a week, trying to pay those bills, you know? Went through a divorce a couple years back, so...that was fun. How about you? What's Tommy doing these days?"

"The same. More like working eighty hours a week, and I finalized my divorce about eight months ago."

Reggie laughed. "A newbie! Welcome to the club, cuz." He slapped Whelan on the shoulder and ordered a beer from the waitress.

Thomas realized the man likely had other plans when he walked in. "I'm not keeping you from meeting someone, am I?"

"No. I'm solo tonight. Popped in for a beer and some potstickers on my way home."

"Well, they're on me tonight. You saved me from having to deal with some undesired company."

Thomas explained the comment.

"So you're an FBI agent now? That's cool. James Bond and shit."

"Yeah," Whelan thought about the past two years. "Real cool. Took my family, my health...my sanity...."

Reggie's face expressed guilt for having broached the subject.

"I'm sorry," said Whelan, "I didn't mean to be a drag. It's all worth it in the end when I take the bad guy down."

"What bad guy you after these days?"

"Well, since you asked, the 12 Pills Killer."

"No shit? Shouldn't you be in Miami?"

"You haven't seen the news today." Whelan filled him in on the Kansas City details since it was officially out in the open now.

"Reggie," said Whelan, "how well did you know Jackson Kenny and Paul Duke? They went to elementary school with us."

"You think one of them's the killer?"

"No. They were both victims. The first two."

"Oh, that's terrible. I didn't really know them in elementary school, but I knew Jackson in high school. We had some classes together. Duke... I vaguely remember him. He hung in different circles than me. Why do you think they were killed?"

"Well, when I answer that, I should be able to figure out who killed them. Anything you can think of? Anybody you remember from school who'd want them dead?"

"Not really. I heard stories that Jackson's dad used to whip him a lot. You might start there."

Whelan smiled. His partner had already 'started' three weeks ago. "He has an alibi. Wasn't the dad, but thanks."

For over an hour, the two men caught up like they were indeed old friends, though they had never been before. It wound up being welcomed company. They stipulated no more 'shop-talk.' Instead, they talked baseball—namely the Royals—basketball, and fishing, before moving on to music and celebrities. They both agreed Scarlett Johansson was their dream date and sealed it with a toast from their fourth round.

Whelan couldn't remember when he shared an hour of downtime like this, with some quality male bonding and absent-minded laughter. It was before Eddie Morrison. He was still chuckling when he answered his phone. "Whelan."

It was Agent Jones. "Whelan, where are you? Uberto Ferretti showed up at Evelyn Ward's house. They have him detained 'til we get there."

"Shit," he sighed. "I'm not far. I'll meet you there."

He hung up and threw fifty dollars on the table. "My friend, duty calls."

Reggie's face expressed genuine concern for his new pal. "You okay to drive? You need an Uber?"

"I'm fine." Two years of blending in with Eddie Morrison's crowd built a substantial tolerance to alcohol.

"Well, be careful. And thanks for the drinks. This was a nice break from reality."

"Yes it was. Next time you get to treat."

"Deal," said Reggie Johnson.

Whelan walked out of the restaurant without ever setting a date for "next time."

He failed to spot George Beckford still sitting at the bar, staring at him the whole time he made his way to the door.

Chapter 12

When Whelan arrived at Evelyn Ward's, the door frame was splintered where the security chain used to be. *Those things are pointless.*

Inside were two local police officers who the neighbors called after hearing all the screaming and commotion, and the two federal agents who had been keeping an eye out for Judy. They felt obligated to step in when they saw a strange man kick in the front door. The two cops had him detained in cuffs and standing on the other side of the living room from where Evelyn was seated.

As soon as Agent Whelan entered, Uberto began screaming again at everyone, cursing in Italian and pressing his chest out like he was twenty instead of sixty-three. He tried wiggling free from the officers' clasp of his arms.

They all did their best to fill Whelan in over Ferretti's yelling. The homeowner was knocked senseless when the "perp" bashed in the door. So far, she was refusing to press charges. She was afraid it would cause her daughter more problems down the road.

"Mr. Ferretti," said Whelan, "please sit down and quit shouting at everyone, or I swear, I'll take you to the nearest station and have you brought up on breaking and entering, *and* assault, regardless of your mother-in-law's wishes. I will have those handcuffs removed as soon as I decide you're finished being a child and ready to start answering questions."

Uberto Ferretti spit in Agent Whelan's face as Agent Jones came through the door. "Fuck you! Fuck all of you!"

83

Jones gave Ferretti a tilted nod and took an admonishing tone. "Very couth."

Whelan looked at Evelyn Ward, sitting in her easy chair with her arms crossed. A bruise was starting to show up on her right cheek, where the front door knocked her as it was kicked in by Ferretti twenty minutes earlier. "You ready to press charges *now*?"

Evelyn stared down her son-in-law a moment. "Okay. Consider them pressed."

Agent Jones whistled low as the officers escorted Ferretti to their squad car. "That's quite the opposite of the cool and collected man I spoke with in Miami. I wouldn't have recognized him were it not for those eleven-hundred dollar shoes. Why is he so angry?"

"He's looking for Judy," said Whelan.

"We're all looking for Judy. Three days ago, he acted like he didn't care if she ever came home. Now...*this*? Doesn't make sense."

"It does if three days ago he was covering for her. He *cares*. You don't get that upset over someone you don't care about."

"Then why the about-face?"

Agent Whelan took a breath and held it while he pondered the possibilities. Before he could expel it, Evelyn Ward spoke up. "He said it was because Judy told him she was leaving him."

Whelan and Jones digested that for another moment.

"Please don't take this the wrong way, Evelyn," said Agent Jones, "but I don't think he loved her enough to be that upset. Unless he's upset at the impending divorce settlement. Money's always a motivator for anger."

"Money and embarrassment," said Mrs. Ward.

"What do you mean?"

Evelyn's eyebrows reached toward her hairline. "Nothing. I meant... well, I don't know how far back you dug on him, but this is going to be his fifth divorce. His earlier marriages lasted nowhere near as long as this one. In the circles he travels, another divorce equals another failure. Failure's not advantageous in business."

Agent Jones cocked her right eyebrow. "I'll have an officer take your official statement and you can sign the charges. I don't think you'll have to come to the precinct tonight. If we need more from you, someone will be by tomorrow. And again, please call me the moment you hear from Judy. It's vital we reach her in our other investigation." She patted Evelyn's hand then went outside.

Whelan and Jones spoke a minute with the arresting officers before taking Ferretti away and touched base with the agents keeping an eye out for Judy Ward.

They compared notes on the evening leaning against Whelan's car door.

"She's quick, that one," said Whelan, nodding back toward the house.

"What do you mean?"

"*Embarrassed* about a divorce? That was a lie. Bad for business? Every rich man I know has had multiple wives. They gossip around their single-malts about 'trophy-wife number seven or eight' being the 'best one yet.' It's like a game for some of them."

Miranda frowned. "You need to hang with a better selection of rich people. I've met some wealthy folks who were humble and happily married for decades."

"To the *same* people?" Whelan asked.

"Yes."

She shifted her expression to one of compassion. "You saw some real shit the past couple of years, huh?"

How could he begin to explain the scope of what he'd suffered to bring down Eddie Morrison? Some details would haunt him forever, and many others were blurring together. The last bit of evening sun lit Miranda's irises on fire; copper burnished into gold. Whelan smiled bittersweetly. "Yes. I saw my share."

He coughed and cleared his throat. "Sorry, I don't mean to sound jaded, but I think Evelyn's spewing malarkey. There's something else Ferretti's embarrassed by. She's covering again."

"Maybe that he's married to a serial killer?"

"Maybe."

"And I didn't think it was going to be a woman," said Jones.

"And I don't think it's a teacher any longer."

They sighed in unison, then said good night.

Thomas shut the light out in his hotel room and glanced at the clock; 9:48 p.m. He was exhausted, but it was early, and he wasn't able to drift off yet. The case was bothering him. Replaying every step so far in his head didn't open the door to new possibilities or jog any memories. He decided to check in with his mother. Perhaps Evelyn Ward reminded him in some way that he still had one.

Her name was Kathryn Elizabeth Whelan—Kate to her friends or Katie if you were closer—but to Thomas, she was just Mom. She was a third-generation Irish American.

When Thomas and his brother David were children, Kathryn tried to instill a respectable sense of ethics and work values in her boys. It stuck in Thomas. So much so, that Kathryn spoke a different message these days.

"You're working too hard. I hear it in your voice," she said on the phone after exchanging pleasantries.

Thomas snickered. "You got that from 'Hi Mom, how are you'?"

"That, and the fact I haven't heard from you in five weeks. And now you tell me you're *here*! I thought you were still relaxing at Gerrard's. What's going on that you haven't been able to come by and see me?"

Whelan took a moment before answering. If his mother knew the full hell he was struggling to overcome, she would constantly be ringing him. And telling her now he was working the most stressful and urgent case in the country? *No thanks.* He'd called to touch base for a quick minute and wasn't in the mood for an hour-long conversation this evening.

"It's a new case. I can't talk about it. How's Connor? You speak to him this week?"

"He's amazing. So smart that one. I think he takes after you. I'm going out to see him in a week. Why don't you come with me?"

"When I wrap this one up, I'll have time to get in a real visit."

"Horseshit! You'll be right on another one. You get your ass on a plane and meet me there. Unless you have time for dinner *this* week?"

Thomas' lips twisted upward. His mother was never one to mince words. He glanced at the calendar on his phone. "I will do my best to meet you there on the 4th. I'll even try to stay the night so we can go see the fireworks."

"I'm going to hold you to that. Are you sure you can't squeeze in even a quick lunch this week? Now that I know you're right here, I don't think I can wait another week and a half. And why can't you tell me about your case? You used to share them with me. Don't tell me you're going to let that bastard Morrison come between you and me now. That one's put to bed. Tell me what's going on. Maybe I can help."

Thomas pursed his lips. He knew his mother as well as she knew him. "Maybe you can. I'll fill you in soon. Night Mom."

"Good night Tommy. I love you. Stay safe."

"Love you too, Mom." He hung up the phone. He hated to admit it, but he felt a little better inside.

❀ ❀ ❀

Back in Westwood, another mother closed the curtains on her front windows as a tea-pot whistled from the kitchen. She retrieved it and poured the hot water into two cups waiting with bags of chamomile. She heard the creak of the basement door open behind her as she added a teaspoon of sugar to each mug.

"That should be sufficient time." Evelyn Ward spun around to face her daughter. "You ready to fill me in?"

Judy took the offered cup and swirled her tea bag around the murky water. "It's complicated."

Evelyn guffawed, then swallowed. "Sorry. But darling, you've never been anything but."

Sitting at the kitchen table, Judy looked directly into her mother's eyes. "You once told me you'd love me forever, no matter what I do. Unconditionally. Is that still true?"

Evelyn put her tea on the table and wrapped both hands around Judy's left, giving a gentle squeeze. She was instantly somber. "Of course. You've always been my everything."

Tears welled up in Judy as she fathomed the brevity of her mother's remaining weeks. She reached out with her other hand and caressed her mother's face where she'd been struck by the door her husband kicked in. The swelling from the bruise was starting to go down after an evening of ice-packs.

"I'm afraid that's my fault."

❀ ❀ ❀

Chapter 13

Tuesday morning, Agent Whelan walked into his office to find a laptop on his desk. He'd arrived early, well-rested, wanting to get a jump on the day. Agent Phil Cannon beat him there and was waiting with coffee for Jones and him.

"Thanks," said Whelan, taking both cups from Cannon's hands. "Agent Jones will be in late. She's …following up on a lead."

"The lead" was Derrick Domino and a private workout session. At home.

"This Balzano's?" asked Whelan, sitting in front of the laptop. He took a sip of coffee.

"Yes," said Cannon. "Tech recovered everything from the books, but so far, they haven't revealed any entries that pan out as a lead for murder. I know you said you wanted a look, so I brought it here instead of impound. They've already covered his Facebook and Instagram accounts, pulling all friends to investigate, cross-referencing any possible childhood school connections. Also, *your* tablet was updated with the batch of airline travelers from Miami to Kansas City. And there's a fresh list of students from '97 to '99 throughout the entire metro area, covering all the burbs and inner-city schools, K through twelve. We narrowed out a section of students who transferred from one school to another during those two years. They would have had a greater chance of knowing more people. There are two sub-lists from each with everyone who has a June birthday."

He took a breath before continuing. "Field agents are speaking with everyone who remembers knowing any of the victims from '97 to '99. Tracy Stamford was pretty popular, so her list is growing with each interview. Kenny and Duke's list of friends has pretty much been exhausted by now. There were a couple of possibles left. We're on it. Sonja Cuevas is proving to be a tough one. She wasn't here long, and the few people who even remember her weren't close to her. I think we have four leads there. She had a best friend with an older sister whose age matches the other targets. We're tracing their whereabouts now. And of course, every list of friends is being cross-referenced with each of the other lists of friends to narrow out a list of those who might have known multiple vics if not all of them."

Agent Cannon looked pleased with himself. "What else can I get for you?"

Whelan looked at his coffee cup. "More cream."

Phil Cannon's eyebrows shot up as his jaw fell. He mumbled a "yes sir" and disappeared out the door.

Thomas snickered. He began poking around Tony Balzano's files, skipping the accounting files. He doubted he'd catch anything the tech guys didn't already find there.

Right now, Whelan was more interested in who Tony was *personally*.

Recent browser history brought up a variety of sites, from online art stores and Italian imports to airline travel and Italian porn. And Japanese porn. And Hungarian. And Mediterranean, and African, and Californian, and Canadian and French... Tony Balzano might be the first person he'd seen browsing for Eskimo porn at 3:00 a.m. One video contained fat lesbians feeling each other up while wearing parkas in an igloo. For a few minutes, Whelan even had icicle envy.

He moved on to Tony's "Pictures" folder. There were a few family shots, lots of furniture and artwork shots, and some travel photos. Whelan unveiled a poorly disguised subfolder holding over two hundred video footage files from what looked like a Skype or Zoom account. Most of these contained a single naked woman on one end and a small thumbnail in the corner of Tony pleasuring himself while sitting at his desk. He'd been paying for online video sex and recording the exchange, undoubtedly for later viewing. *The guy knew how to stretch a dollar.*

At the end of some, Balzano forgot to end the recording. The main screen would go dark, and the thumbnail continued, usually with Tony working on what looked like journal entries from a logbook, staring up into his laptop's screen. He either forgot on many occasions to turn it off, or didn't know how, or perhaps thought when he opened up his accounting software, it ended the video recorder.

Sometimes there were a few minutes of extra footage, sometimes hours. Whelan grabbed a post-it and scribbled a reminder to make sure and notify the IRS to audit the Balzanos' stores. It looked like he was adding numbers from his "travel-log" book in the video clips. And the journal Gertrude Balzano handed him didn't match the one Tony was using.

Shit! Could it be...? Whelan didn't need to see more than a few of these "extra" recordings before jumping to three nights ago, the last such possible footage.

Sure enough, as usual, cybersex led to bookkeeping. Whelan sat glued to the little one by two-inch window in the corner. Tony kept sucking down his Italian Ice and punched around on his keyboard. Twelve minutes in, Balzano stood up abruptly and grabbed at his stomach. He braced against his desk for support, but his arm gave, and he toppled out of the frame.

Whelan turned up the audio as loud as it would go. Balzano could be heard moaning and cursing to himself. A minute of silence went by, and then Thomas had his first break in the case. A gloved hand appeared in the frame and sat down a second Honey & Sambuca beside Tony's. The video resolution was pretty decent, and even in the little window, Whelan could make out the color difference between the two Ices sitting side by side. More importantly, the gloved hand was large and exposed a wrist and partial arm. It was most likely a man's arm, with little hair and the color of caramel. The killer was either Hispanic, African-American, or... *Hell, could be a white guy with a tan. Could be anyone.*

Is that a man's arm? Or a large woman? He knew Agent Jones would jump his shit when she saw this. It *looked* like a man's arm. Adrenaline rushed through Whelan as he finished the video. The hand appeared again in a flash as it retrieved the cups of Italian Ice, then was out of the image. The footage did not reveal anything new. Sadly, no audio from the killer could be detected. *Maybe we just can't hear it!*

He needed a copy of this video—*after* the tech guys took a crack at enlarging it and enhancing it. Perhaps they could tweak the audio to see if the killer said anything the laptop wasn't playing back. Whelan looked at Jones' Board. He had five days before number six would be added. He was determined not to see any new names pinned to the cork. He raced to his office door and shouted, "Cannon!"

93

Chapter 14

"Son of a bitch!" Miranda was tickled and excited.

"I know," said Whelan, "you were right. I think that's a man's arm. I won't harp on you about gender-specific pronouns any longer."

"No," said Jones. "But you had a right to. I could have been wrong. I was beginning to think Judy Ward was the killer too. I suppose I should pull those agents off watching her house. We don't need to follow up on her domestic issue."

"Let's give it another day or two. We've invested so much time in her, might as well play it out." Whelan was generous to his partner, trying to make her feel better about her suspicions, even though there was clear evidence against them now.

"Yes, you're right. The first time I spoke with her husband, it occurred to me that she might have been *involved* with the killer. You know, back in the day. Maybe they were an item."

"Of course," said Whelan, "and now she comes home every week to cook up some new poison pills, and her old flame does the dirty work. It's a team effort."

Both agents laughed for a minute before processing the plausible truth of it. They looked at each other with big eyes.

"I'll make sure we keep those agents on the lookout," said Jones. She marched out of the office, presumably to give SAC Kendrick an update and file new requests.

The technology department turned up nothing new with the two hours they spent running the video through their software. Whelan had a copy on his laptop now, enhanced, with a finer, and larger image, but no more revealing than it was when he gave it to them.

He drifted out into the bullpen, eavesdropping on agents who were calling names on the lists. As he caught the eyes of those he passed, he saw many shaking heads with disappointed expressions. Nothing was panning out.

Whelan poured a fresh cup of coffee before sitting back down at his desk. He focused on his laptop screen. He'd made a still image of the killer's arm from the best frame of the video and put it as his wallpaper.

Agent Cannon popped in with an updated tablet. "These lists have all the men separated like you asked, with everyone who was anywhere from three to twenty between '97 to '99."

"Send that to my laptop, would you?"

Cannon obliged.

"Now," said Whelan, "cross-reference the STUDENTS sub-list with the airline logs."

Again, Cannon "clicked-clicked" away for a moment. "We're making progress. Eight names."

Agent Whelan took a long moment, staring at his computer screen. "You seeing what I'm seeing, or are my eyes playing tricks?"

Cannon's face lit up. "Number seven. Mark Whitfield! You think that's *our* Mark Whitfield?"

Whelan's head was bobbling. "Yes! I've got to show this to Agent Jones. I think she's in Kendrick's office. You're to keep silent about this for now. I don't want this to get out until we can speak to him. Not one word to *anyone*."

"Yes sir."

Playing golf Whitfield? In Miami? Agent Whelan couldn't stop shaking his head.

Thirteen minutes later, Special Agent in Charge Alan Kendrick sat silently in the corner of Whelan and Jones' office, as a frustrated Mark Whitfield, still remarkably tanned, was defending himself from an armchair. "Yeah, I was playing golf in Miami! That's not a crime."

Agent Jones was keeping a level head. "In June? You go to play at a course in Miami in the *summer*?"

"Yeah. The rates are off-season. And I know people there. People I enjoy playing a few rounds with and unwind with later on the water."

As Whitfield squirmed in the chair, Agent Whelan kept glancing from his laptop screen to Whitfield's arm. Tanned. Golden. *Caramel.* Little hair. It could be his arm. It could also belong to ten million other men.

Whelan spoke up. "Mark, why didn't you tell us you were in Miami at the same time Cuevas was killed? You have to respect it looks suspicious."

Whitfield stood up, practically spitting at Thomas in the face. "Because Tommy, I knew I was innocent. And your new partner had kicked me off the case. Why should I bother explaining anything? It would waste *my* time, *her* time... What would have been the point?"

"I feel you. I'm going to have Agent Cannon get some of those alibis from you so you can get on with your other cases and put this behind you."

Whelan shook his hand as he led him to the door. He looked at Kendrick in the corner. "Sir? Anything to add?"

"Not now." Kendrick stood and reached out his hand to Whitfield. "Thanks for your time, Mark. Until we get this cleared up, stay close and report directly to me."

"Yes sir," said Whitfield.

When he was gone, Whelan turned back to Miranda. "Well?"

"Well…" she began. "I guess we sort of have to follow up on it, but I don't think he's our guy."

"I don't know," said Whelan, looking once again at his computer screen. "Looks like a match to me."

Agent Jones looked at the image of the arm on the monitor. Then she looked at her own arm. It was practically a color match, but she decided she was a little darker. "That's not going to give us anything, is it? Hell, depending on which monitor you view it on, it's darker, lighter…more or less yellow…."

"Yep. Universal problem. You do have my concession that it's a man. *Probably…*"

Jones turned to SAC Kendrick. "I guess I'll have to stick a tail on Whitfield this Saturday. If we can vouch for his whereabouts for twenty-four hours and we have another killing, he'll be off the hook for good."

"Do it," said Kendrick. "Meet me in my office in five, so we can finish our earlier discussion."

Whelan shut the door behind him and whispered to his partner. "You want it to be Whitfield, don't you?"

"No. Well, it *would* wrap our case and save seven more lives. But I'm not *that* vindictive, Thomas. I'm not that person."

"I know."

He plopped into his desk chair and stared at his laptop.

Jones darted her eyes back and forth from the screen to Whelan's face. "Do *you* want it to be him?"

"No. But…it *would* wrap our case as you said *and* prove I can still trust my instincts. Whitfield is in the age range of the victim group. He fits and supports my theory."

Agent Jones released her sigh. She rolled her neck in circles for a few seconds, then pulled her shoulders up and left to meet Kendrick.

❀ ❀ ❀

Whelan worked on his computer for another two hours, pouring over names on lists. *I should have stuck with pharmacology.* When they are recruiting you for the FBI, no one tells you that the bulk of your time is spent doing tedious research. *If I wanted to do boring research, I could have done it at Pfizer and made three times the money.* After the nightmare of bringing Eddie Morrison to justice, Whelan had been looking forward to some boring time. But he'd had that; in Grand Cayman. His nature begged for more excitement now. It's why he so readily abandoned his doctorate and the lucrative income.

An agent stuck her head in from his doorway. "We've got a lead on Cuevas' friend's sister. You want to take it, or should I give it to Agent Jones?"

Whelan bolted for her hand holding the magical piece of paper. "She's busy. I got it, thanks."

An hour later, he was sitting at a coffee shop in Raytown. As he fumbled through his introduction in Spanish, he wondered if he'd made a mistake by not bringing Agent Jones along.

"It's all right, Agent Whelan. I speak English." Her maiden name was Tiana Presley—now Peterson. She was a lifetime resident of the suburb. Her mother was Mexican, her father of English descent, and she remembered her little sister, Charlotte—Charlie—playing with Sonja and bonding with her over their native tongue.

"My mother insisted we both learn Spanish first, and English we'd pick up in the school system. Charlie and Sonja were inseparable for about a year. Not too many other seven-year-old Spanish-speaking natives in the neighborhood back in the mid-'90s. There's more now. Mrs. Cuevas took a job in Independence in '97, so they moved there. Charlie and Sony—Sonja—managed to stay close. They were on the phone all the time and had sleepovers at least once a month."

"I believe Sonja, and maybe Charlotte, might have been a witness to something tragic," began Whelan. "An incident perhaps *you* were involved in? Around '96 or '97? Maybe '98?"

Tiana was taken aback. "*I* was involved in something tragic? Tragic how?"

"That's the question of the month. Do you recall ever being part of a group that might have traumatized someone around your age? Maybe someone you all made fun of, at say, a birthday party or other event?"

Tiana was five years older than Sonja, and *her* birthday was coming up in July. It was possible she was on the 12 Pills Killer's list, number seven perhaps. Ten days away. Whelan wondered if this woman had less than two weeks to live.

"No," she said. "I can't think of anything where I would have ever made fun of someone so much to have induced trauma. What is this about? Am I in trouble?"

Whelan didn't know how much to share but decided to spill the beans. There were no better leads at this point.

"The 12 Pills Killer!" shouted Ms. Peterson in panic.

Agent Whelan instinctively shushed her as others at tables nearby turned their heads.

"Should I be worried about my safety?" she continued. "Should I get a gun? Get out of town?"

"We can arrange for a patrol car to sit outside your house at night if it will make you feel safer." He couldn't tell her she didn't have to panic for another ten days, at which time she'd know for sure if she was on the list, in the worst kind of way. That would have been too much information.

"Yes. Please."

"Now," Whelan picked up, "do you remember anyone from 1997 to '99 who would have wanted to take revenge on a group of twelve people for anything? Take your time."

Tiana slurped on her coffee and nibbled at a cookie from the counter display case. Her eyes rove over the ceiling, around the walls, across the floor, and back to the ceiling, dozens of times.

After three minutes, she couldn't handle her silence. "No, nothing. I'm sorry. Well… unless you count poor Peanut."

"Poor Peanut?"

"She was a little Chihuahua—sort of this, neighborhood dog— that everyone took care of, feeding, watering, playing with. No one ever knew who the actual owner was. She showed up one day. And like that," she snapped her fingers, "one day, she was gone. Everyone missed her. We all asked about her, but no one knew what happened to her. Then two weeks later, she was seen dead in an alley trash can. She was a mess of fur, caked with dried blood."

"And how do you think that's relevant?"

"Well, there were about twelve of us who played with her in the neighborhood. I mean, give or take, about twelve. Maybe some sicko out there didn't like us playing with his dog? I don't know… I'm reaching here, but I honestly can't think of anything else we ever did to someone. We were pretty nice kids."

Whelan stood and handed his card to Ms. Peterson. The killer's twelve targets were not all from the same city, let alone neighborhood. "Thank you. If you think of anything else, please let me know immediately, day or night. This has my cell phone number on it. I'll have an officer reach out to you in a couple of hours to set up that nightly patrol car for your home. I appreciate your help. Do you know where or how I can reach your sister Charlotte—Charlie? I don't have a number for her."

"Oh, agent Whelan, didn't someone tell you? Charlie died a little over a year ago."

Thomas sat back down and gave a sincere, sympathetic pat on Tiana's shoulder. "No, I'm sorry. I had no idea."

He gave her a moment before proceeding. "How did she die?"

"Oh, it was self-inflicted, I'm afraid."

"Suicide? I'm so sorry."

"No, not suicide; she accidentally poisoned herself. She was living in Michigan and developed a hobby of making homemade wines and tea blends. She made lots of cherry wine, apple tea, dandelion wine, *and* tea. I didn't care for those. Oh, but in the summer, she'd make this amazing strawberry-rhubarb wine. Tasted like you were drinking a pie. Well, a year ago May, the toxicology report showed she'd gotten hold of some monkshood—that's a poisonous plant—probably while she was harvesting dandelions. She liked to be experimental. Who knew a plant so pretty could be so deadly? I looked them up online. They have a beautiful flower. I bet she thought they would taste like hibiscus and tried them in a tea." Tiana wiped the corner of her eyes.

"No," said Whelan, "nothing like hibiscus." The hairs on his neck stood up. He got out his cell phone and made a quick call before gathering information for another ten minutes. A patrol officer walked in the entrance, and Whelan flagged her over.

"Tiana, this is the officer I told you about. She'll escort you home and set up a twenty-four-hour schedule to monitor you. And again, please call me the moment you think of anything else. Sometimes the memory will trigger over something random once you point your thoughts in the right direction."

He gave her a warm handshake, patting the top of her hand like he'd seen Miranda do with her sources. It worked. Tiana thanked *him* for *his* time.

Whelan knew as he walked back to his car, this was the crucial break they needed. While not a botanist, he knew that monkshood was another name for aconitum or wolfsbane, one of the main ingredients in the 12 Pills Killer's unique formula!

Chapter 15

Charlotte Presley—Charlie—had ventured up to Michigan a few years back with a friend who wanted to start making homemade wines, teas, jams, and honey, to sell at craft fairs around the country. Charlie was a bit of a wild child and liked the game plan. Her vagabond attitude worked for a life on the festival circuit, and in their downtime, they'd manufacture organic products, selling them in local markets and online.

Whelan touched base with his partner before catching the last flight out to Traverse City.

"You should have notified me before running out to speak with Tiana Peterson," she scolded.

"You were tied up with Kendrick. Cannon was compiling—whatever Cannon compiles. Everyone seemed occupied. You were fine with it before."

"Uh-huh. But now I've gotten my ass chewed for splitting up on interviews."

"Oh. You want to come to Michigan with me? I can wait till morning."

"No. Go. Every minute counts on this one. That'll take a whole day. I wish we had another twenty agents. Kendrick's trying to borrow some from Omaha. And I'm having a hell of a time clearing Whitfield's name. Keep me updated."

"I'll be back before Kendrick knows I'm gone."

By 9:30, Whelan was renting a car at the Cherry Capital Airport.

Driving through town toward his bed and breakfast, he saw signs posted everywhere for the upcoming National Cherry Festival to start at the end of the month. But it wasn't cherries he was in search of; it was that deadly little flower.

No one was at the reception desk when he tried to check in. A small blackboard behind the counter held a chalk message for him. "Welcome, Thomas! Your room key was sent to your phone. There's a slice of pie in the fridge. Breakfast starts at 6:00. Nighty-night!" It was the perfect combination of old-fashioned and modern technologies that amused him.

He retrieved the pie—cherry, of course—and a glass of milk and made his way upstairs to his room. With a swipe of his phone, the door clicked open. The room decoration was tasteful, the right amount of flowery posh, mixed with transitional furnishings. The mattress' plushness enveloped him, lulling slumber.

He would have slept through his 6:30 a.m. alarm were it not for the smell of coffee and bacon that permeated the hallway and managed to creep into his room. Breakfast was to order and the best he could recall in years. He hated to check out from this respite, but duty called.

The address Tiana Peterson gave for her sister was on the outskirts of town. Whelan drove past the manicured lots, noting the quaintness of the city, all so pristine. It was a throwback to an era long gone you would be hard-pressed to find outside of Middle America, far removed from any major metropolises.

Inch-high grass and white picket fences fell away to larger lots, then small fields. Orchards and rows of fruit decorated the landscape. The smell of berries mixed with apples and traveled on the breeze.

Charlie's former home had a sign posted on the road: "Natural Honeys – Organic Jams and Other Treasures – Open 9-6". It was a five-acre lot with a small white house in the middle. Along the gravel road leading to the house were cherry and apple trees. Alternating fruit sizes dared you to indulge.

Not yet 8:00 a.m., Whelan parked his car in the "lot"—a space cleared for about ten cars—and made his way up the front porch to knock on the door. No one answered. The home was well maintained, and dozens of potted plants and flowers filled the scene, abundantly healthy and full of blooms. Several had price tags attached.

A small trail made its way around the side of the home to the back. Whelan stopped in awe. It was an organized jungle, a park built from nature. Massive oak trees had single and double-seated swings hanging from them. Benches carved from teak and acacia were scattered about, hiding in the shadows of still more, strategically placed cherry and apple trees. A man-made koi pond must have been over 20,000 gallons and zig-zagged beyond the tree line and out of sight. A rock waterfall, constructed fourteen feet high on the left end, fell into the main pool. Dozens of monstrous koi swam freely, a tiny ocean of orange, white, red and yellow moving swiftly without pattern.

Gravel paths cordoned off patches of strawberries, rhubarb, blackberries, and squash. Brick edging contained them, and various greens swirled around them, all looking edible and ready for harvest.

And filling all remaining areas were flowering plants. Some grew in pots, others in small gardens, and still more climbed tree trunks or hung from ropes in baskets. Willy Wonka's chocolate factory came to Whelan's mind. But it was all real and natural. Dozens of butterflies filled the air in at least ten species, every color Whelan knew existed and more. They competed for air-space with bees and a few hummingbirds, who dared to drift away from their feeders long enough to take a sip from an alluring pistil.

Thomas wiped away a tear he hadn't realized formed as he stood mesmerized at so much beauty. Never had organized chaos been any lovelier.

"This must be your first time here," said a voice to his side.

Whelan turned. A young woman was standing not five feet from him. He hadn't noticed her approach. She was short and a bit heavy, with no makeup. She removed her beekeeper hat and veil, revealing a mop of curly hair on the top of her head, falling over the sides, which were buzzed to a bare scalp. A boxful of freshly harvested honeycombs from the back of the property nestled her arms.

"We don't open for another hour," she continued, "but I suspect you know that. Something tells me you aren't here to buy my goodies."

"Well," said Thomas, "I wasn't, but now, I think I'm going to have to try some. This is amazing. I…I'm speechless. Truly."

The woman turned and looked at the yard. She smiled for a moment until her eyes landed on a few plants in one garden that were ready for pruning. "It's a passion, and it's work; a love-hate relationship. But it pays the bills, and I'm free to create. I let the primordial mother guide me."

"I'm Gaia," she held out her hand from beneath the crate.

Whelan took it and gave a firm shake. "The Greek Earth goddess? That's perfect. How long ago did you adopt it?"

He was afraid he might have offended her, but she smiled, "An educated man! Don't get many of those any more. I haven't been Jennifer since I turned eighteen. I'm thirty-four now, so, let's see, where did I leave my calculator?"

Whelan laughed. "I'm Special Agent Thomas Whelan with the FBI." He flashed his credentials.

"What makes you special?" she asked.

"I suppose all that training and education."

"Catch any bad guys lately?"

"Yes, but now I'm after another one. I could use your help."

"*My* help?" Gaia raised her eyebrows. "Okay. How can I help you, Special Agent Thomas Whelan with the FBI?"

"I don't think Charlie accidentally poisoned herself. I think the guy I'm after might have used her as a test subject for his chemistry experiment."

It had been over a year. While never a day went by that Gaia didn't think of her, she'd failed to realize it might be why Thomas was here. It caught her off-guard. Not typically one for crying, her cheeks were wet within seconds of his statement.

She composed herself a bit. "Would you like a cup of coffee?" She moved up the back porch before he could answer. He followed and took a seat at a small kitchen table while she fixed two cups.

Gaia sat next to him, quite close, and began spilling thoughts she'd locked away for the past ten months. They poured out in a whisper. "Everyone said I was crazy. They said Charlie was crazy. *We* were crazy—the Natural Honey girls—that's how we were known around town—we were crazy. We spent five years creating that." She motioned toward the garden.

"Five years making magic together." She stifled another sob before continuing. "The police didn't want to hear she'd been poisoned on purpose. I told them a hundred times, 'there's no way Charlie accidentally ingested monkshood. But they didn't want to hear it. They found some growing out back, off the beaten path, on the border with the property behind us. A nice little patch of beautiful blue monkshood. To anyone who's ever planted a flower before, you could tell it hadn't been there long. The soil around it was different. There wasn't a solid hold yet, deep in the dirt. Someone planted it and tried to make it look like a natural, wild patch of blossoms. But I didn't believe it. The cops questioned a few people, but no one around here would have had cause to do that to a pretty young woman, so they gave up and ruled it as accidental ingestion. Like she'd make a *tea* from monkshood! She loved her teas—hell, we sell some of her blends. She knew what she was doing."

Gaia choked up but continued through it. "Charlie was smarter than people gave her credit for. She was so sweet. Why do people confuse sweet with stupidity? Smart people can't be sweet? She knew her botany. She might not have had a degree in it, but I'll bet she knew more than any college-educated botanist ever knew. She did the flowers and plants; designed the gardens—the whole park, really. Look at it! *She* did that! I helped with the trees and can build furniture. And, of course, the bees were my thing. But Charlie created *that*. She would have known what monkshood was. And she wouldn't have turned it into tea!"

More tears flowed down Gaia's cheeks. "Damn. I'm sorry, agent. No amount of time will make this easier. And now… Now you've vindicated my testimony. It's too much." She wiped her face down again and filled the coffee cups. "So… How can I help you catch the evil bastard?"

"Well, *you've* vindicated my suspicions, so that's helpful already," he said.

"Where were you a year ago?" she asked.

For a brief flash, Whelan *did* remember where he was a year ago—mixed up with the wrong crowds in New York, Miami and Washington as he gathered evidence on Eddie Morrison. He'd never admitted it to his superiors, but to prove himself and get in tight, he'd snorted coke and shot heroin. It helped shield his subconscious from some of the more unscrupulous acts he committed in that final year to get close enough to Morrison and build his case.

Undercover work was never as glamorous as Sonny Crockett made it look. It wrecked him. He vowed never to work deep undercover again. He owed that much to his son. It would be impossible now, anyway. The Morrison case had too much exposure. In a world where every cell phone held a video library, his image would be forever stamped as a narc.

He answered Gaia. "Catching bad guys."

His emotions played out on his face, and she read them all. She put her hand on his arm a moment and made sure he locked his eyes on hers. "Thank you, *very* Special Agent, Thomas Whelan."

That simple gesture nearly made him lose it. He cleared his throat. "You're welcome."

Reaching for more cream, he got back on topic. "So, do you know who owns the property behind yours? Did you both get along with the owner?"

"Never met the owner. There's a small home on it, much like ours. It's been rented out for as long as we've owned this. Tenants sometimes stay a year, sometimes more, sometimes less. I don't keep track. Can't even see it over our jungle. My bee apiary is back there, so *I* see it all the time but can't bring myself to stare very long. Too painful. There's someone in there now. Moved in about three months after Charlie died. The police dug up all the monkshood, so…nothing to see *there*. I think the new tenant is single. At least, I've observed just one man in there."

"And when Charlie was alive?"

"Single man. Before that, a couple with little boys. And before that, a single woman."

"The single man who lived there when Charlie was killed; you have a name? What did he look like?"

"There's two acres of land between my bees and his house. Again, it's not like I was watching him with binoculars. I tend to mind my own business. I expect others to mind theirs. I wish I'd paid more attention now, but…I didn't. I could see a man, never any children or women. He wasn't there long. Maybe…three months? You think he's your fellow?"

"Possibly." Whelan nodded. "Quite possibly. Was he tall? Short? White? Black?"

Gaia's face looked pained. "Yeah. Tallish. Brownish. Maybe." She was kicking herself for not being more observant.

"Caramel?" asked Whelan.

"Yeah."

"He was questioned by the police?"

"They said they did. Came up with nothing there."

Gaia's head fell. "*I* should have gone over there and questioned him. I was grief-stricken and trusted they were doing their jobs. About a month later, I got the nerve to knock on the door, but he was gone. I went to the county sheriff's office to see if they would give me a name off the police report, so I could track him down. They didn't even have his name on the report! And the officers couldn't remember it. It wasn't a murder in their judgment. It was an '*accident,*' they kept saying. Well, *I* say it was damned sloppy police work!"

Whelan patted her hand.

Gaia wiped away a tear. "They didn't even write his name…."

"I'm sure they were convinced they knew what happened," comforted Whelan. "This killer is intelligent and well-planned. And

I think Charlie was his first victim. I'm sure there *was* no reason to suspect him at the time."

She shook her head. "I guess not."

Whelan stood. "Well, *I'm* going to track him down. Thank you so much for your time. I'll be sure to let you know when we catch the guy. If there's any way I can attach Charlie's death to the others, I'll work earnestly to make it stick."

"Thank you." Gaia handed him a card: *Gaia Presley – Natural Honey Girl.* Her contact information was on it.

Thomas cocked his head. "You took her last name?"

"Sure. Never liked my last name, either." She grinned at Whelan, and the pair instinctively reached in to one another for a long hug.

She sent him on his way with a huge basket of jams, honeys, homemade soaps and an assortment of herbal teas; sans monkshood. He tried to pay, but she wouldn't have it.

Pointing his car south, Whelan drove out in search of a name.

The police didn't get his name. Name.... What was his name? Gaia took Charlie's last name. Anybody can take anybody's name. I bet he didn't even give his real name to the police. How am I going to find his name? The realtor who had the rental listing! Hopefully, she ran a background check.

Chapter 16

Supervisory Special Agent Miranda Jones was growing irritable. "Whitfield, none of your Miami alibis are returning my calls."

Agent Whitfield glared from the other side of her desk. "They're busy people...with *lives*. Give them time. What about my local alibis for the nights Duke and Stamford were killed?"

"No proof. Your wife believes you were together the night of May thirtieth but can't verify it with phone records or receipts. On June sixth, your restaurant receipt buys you up until 10:30 p.m. at the latest. Your 'case informant,' that you *claimed* to have been with until the 'wee hours of the morning' can't recall for sure which night you were together, but *she* believed it was Friday, not Saturday."

"She's fucking with me 'cause I wouldn't sleep with her. Her info never panned out on the Everson case. I think she was hoping we were going to hook up."

"Of course." Agent Jones' face was expressionless.

Whitfield stood and stomped toward the door. "Let me know when you get confirmation."

"Mark," said Jones, standing, "I hate to do this to you, but I need your badge and gun. Kendrick is putting you on paid leave until we clear this up. He was going to tell you himself, but he got called away this morning."

The Kansas City Chief of Police was distressed, keeping the local media at bay. Everyone was demanding answers; the mayor, the papers, the public. Playing politics was half of the job for the head of a field office, and it was time for Kendrick to soothe city officials.

He could have handled Whitfield afterward, but Agent Jones suspected Kendrick wanted her to get an early taste of this side of responsibility. If Assistant Special Agent in Charge Henry Monroe didn't recover from his recent heart attack soon, he planned to move Agent Jones into that position, pending the Director's approval.

Jones felt genuine remorse for Whitfield. She didn't believe he was the 12 Pills Killer, but protocol dictated action.

Agent Whitfield slapped his badge and gun against the top of Jones' desk. "Fine! I guess I'll go *golfing* again."

"Make sure it's in the area. You try to sneak back down to Miami, I won't be responsible for what happens."

"I didn't *sneak* down there the last time! You didn't bother to get to know me at all when we were together. I'm an experienced agent, Miranda. Simply because *we* clashed doesn't make me an asshole. Or some damned psycho-killer." He stormed out of the room.

Jones sighed.

She went through an entire pot of coffee, staring at her board. Once in a while, she would move a post-it from one spot to another— sometimes back again—or it would be balled up and free thrown into the trash can in the corner.

Agent Cannon came bursting in without knocking. "We've got a strong lead tying together numbers three and five. Tracy Stamford's friend from Lee's Summit Elementary believes they met Tony Balzano in 1999. At a birthday party!"

"Good job Cannon. Grab your stuff, and let's go."

Never had a young agent smiled as wide.

"So Tracy's dead?" asked the woman. Her name was Rebecca Jordan. She took a sip from her diet cola. She was teaching middle school now. Agents Jones and Cannon cleared out the faculty break room so they could speak privately.

"I'm afraid so," said Jones.

"The 12 Pills Killer?" Rebecca questioned again. She was starting to repeat herself with her building acceptance.

Agent Cannon was not as patient as his mentor. "Ms. Jordan, we need to understand everything you can tell us about how well Tracy Stamford knew Tony Balzano. Were they friends? Were they more than friends? Were they enemies? How long after that birthday party did they remain acquainted?"

Agent Jones frowned at her protégé. He was a bit too aggressive. Sometimes aggression could work in one's favor, however. Rebecca seemed to snap out of her funk a bit.

"That party was strange—a strange mix of people. I don't mean to sound arrogant, but we were pretty well off, Tracy and I—our parents—financially. It wasn't unusual for a parent to spend ten thousand or more on their kid's party. They all wanted to impress and outdo each other, put on outrageous shows that would be talked about for weeks. We didn't even know Tony before that. Our parents knew each other from church. There must have been over a hundred kids at that party. Hardly any of them knew more than three or four other kids. If it weren't for the orchestrated games, there would have been little mingling."

"Orchestrated games?" asked Cannon.

"Old-school stuff. Pin the tail on the donkey, three-legged races, egg on a spoon races, musical chairs. You know, when I think about it, it was pretty spectacular. We need more of that now. These days the kids section themselves off, the girls staring at their phones and the boys shooting at a large-screen television. We need more 'old-school' games these days. Get children to actually talk to each other and get them moving." She sighed over the challenges facing teachers today, so different than twenty years ago.

Agent Jones patted her hand. "Rebecca, you said the parents all knew each other from church. Was that St. Vincent's?"

"Yes."

"And you'd never met Tony at church?"

"No. I didn't attend often, to be honest. My parents didn't force me to go. They figured when I was older, I'd go if I wanted. They were trying to be progressive, I think. My dad *hated* going, but he went for my mother. I typically went for a major holiday mass. And St. Vincent's had an enormous congregation. When I did go, if you didn't arrive thirty minutes early, it was standing room only."

"Did Tracy go there?"

"Yes."

Agent Cannon was perturbed. "So, getting back to my questions, Tracy's impression of Tony? Favorable? Not so much? Did they stay in touch?"

Agent Jones mouthed "I'm sorry" to her young tag-along for having interrupted him earlier. While Rebecca filled him in on the fact she didn't think Tracy ever saw Tony again after the party, she checked her notes.

Sonja Cuevas attended St. Vincent's Church in '99!

Waiting respectfully this time until Agent Cannon finished his questions, she asked, "Rebecca, did you or Tracy know a Sonja Cuevas? Cuban girl. She would have had a strong accent back then and would have been about five years younger than you and Tracy. Maybe from one of those few masses you attended?"

Rebecca Jordan pursed her lips and raced her eyes side to side as she ran the name through her memory bank. She paused, "Not from church. But I remember some younger girls at that party. I think Tony's dad opened up the invite to pretty much *any* kid from church. Had he considered some of the congregation was…less well-off—he would have amended his invitation."

"Less well-off?"

"There were a few boys and girls there who didn't belong." Rebecca paused a moment as she internally admonished herself. "Forgive me, I try to be a better Christian these days, but some of those kids I'm sure turned out to be crooks as they got older. In fact, one little boy was caught stealing at the party."

"And you think you met Sonja Cuevas *there?*" asked Jones. She showed a photo on her phone of Sonja when she was eight years old.

Rebecca studied it for a minute. "Maybe, I can't be sure. She definitely could have been one of those younger girls that day."

"Sonja's mother told me that a couple of her closest friends called her 'Sony,' like the TV brand, as sort of a nickname." She let that digest a moment.

"Yes." Rebecca grew excited like she'd won a prize. "I remember hearing that name called out. I thought it was such a cool name, Sony. It didn't occur to me that it was a nickname back then. I thought maybe it had a meaning in Spanish. 'Run Sony! Faster!' I remember a girl screaming that. It stuck in my head because she won the egg race."

Agent Cannon looked like he didn't believe her.

Rebecca caught his expression. "She wore a white dress with a pastel, rainbow-colored sash and a matching one pulling her hair back and woven into a wide braid. She was pretty. Her dress looked homemade. But it was lovely. She was noticeable. If you were noticing."

The agents collected a few more details before heading out. Rebecca Jordan's comment stuck in Miranda's head. *Someone else had definitely been noticing.*

Chapter 17

Agent Jones phoned Whelan from her car after dropping Agent Cannon at the office. "I've got Cannon pulling every congregation member who attended in '99. They keep their registers! I want to call those parents who attended Balzano's extravaganza and see what they remember. I think our killer was at that party!"

Agent Whelan tried to be graceful. "Okay... But Jackson Kenny and Paul Duke didn't go to St. Vincent's Church. Jackson was Baptist, and I read that Paul Duke was Methodist. I don't get the connection. I doubt they were at that party."

"No." Miranda's voice was deflated.

Thomas hated to burst her bubble. "That's a possibility for Sonja Cuevas, though. That might tie her and Balzano and Stamford together. Duke and Kenny were friends, so they're connected. Maybe we've been focusing on trying to correlate them all too much lately. Maybe a teacher is still the best bet. Take your congregation list and see if any of them were teachers or substitutes."

"I'll double-check," said Jones, "but we've been doing that anyway." It wasn't an encouraging suggestion.

"Hang in there, Miranda. We're getting close."

"Are we? I'm not feeling it."

"We've got three victims at one birthday party in '99. If we can figure out how the first two tie in to someone at that party, it should lead us to the killer."

"What if the connections aren't all the same?" started Miranda. "I mean, what if the killer didn't know them all the same way? Maybe he or she was a teacher to some, a coach to others, a minister to others…?"

"God I hope not. You've already been cross-referencing combinations of suspects for weeks. To think they might have been in each kid's life in a different way…the combinations would be endless. We'd never be able to connect all the dots."

"No." Miranda firmly reverted her theory. "I don't believe it matches the profile. There was a trigger of some kind. I'd guess around the time your girl Charlotte up there was killed, and it's taken the killer a year to perfect a plan. Something correlates these all more tightly!"

"So run with that teacher connection. *I* still can't shake the feeling he was around the same age as the kids in '99."

"So run with *that*. Where're you at with everything up there?"

Agent Whelan filled his partner in on his morning. "I verified with the police there's no tenant name attached to the report on Charlotte's death. So now, I'm trying to track down the *owner* for the house that had the monkshood. It's registered under M & S LLC. The division of corporations' website for Michigan has one managing member filed, Susan Jacobs. It can't be a coincidence that Sonja's childhood friend was poisoned last year with one of the main, plant-based substances traced in Sonja and our other vics. I'd bet a hundred bucks our killer was here."

"Not a thousand?" asked Agent Jones. "Then, you aren't too sure."

Thomas chuckled. "I'll be back in around 5:00. Meet me at Slappy's at 6:00, and we'll swap updates?"

"Sounds good."

❦ ❦ ❦

Questioning the current tenant in the home behind Gaia's didn't turn up any new names. He mailed his payments to an address in Ohio, made out to the LLC. Agent Whelan headed into town to find the real estate agent involved for the past few years. With any luck, she kept accurate records.

"I was sort of hired *not* to keep records," said the realty broker. "I run ads, field calls, and when someone has an interest, I turn them over to the owner to handle."

"*Not* to keep records?" Whelan repeated.

"Harder to file income taxes on a rental property if there's 'no income.' I'm paid a transaction fee up-front each time. No commissionable rental crosses through this office. Just paperwork. Or, the absence of it, if you will."

Whelan was silent.

"I'm not in any kind of trouble, am I?" asked the woman. "I don't think I've broken any laws. I put out some ads and passed names and numbers over the telephone. I'm careful not to pay too much attention."

"What's the owner's name?"

"Well, I always deal with Susan Jacobs."

"Deal with?"

"She has an investment partner. Going back many years. Never mentions him by name."

"What was the name of the tenant before the current one? The one that killed that sweet Natural Honey Girl." Whelan shouldn't have said that last out loud, but he was pissed.

"You think someone who rented that house killed Charlotte Presley?" She was shocked.

"You knew her?"

"*Everyone* knew her. Traverse City is on the grid for one week a year. For the other fifty-one, we're a pretty small community. Why did they kill her?"

Whelan debated whether or not to tell her for a moment, but she didn't appear to know anything useful. "I can't discuss it right now. What I need is the tenant's name."

"I don't know. I'm not sure who Susan picks each time. I always give her several names, and then she calls me and says to take down the ads; until she's ready for more tenants."

Whelan wanted to yell. His frustration was growing considerably. "Then give me all the names you remember."

The real estate agent took a deep breath and closed her eyes. "The men were... Trevor? Something... Renaldo? Something... maybe. Gosh. There were several. I think there was a George and a Howard. I may be missing a couple. And Ted Baker—*his* name stuck with me."

"How sure are you of those other names?"

"Pretty sure, not sure. I'm sorry. It wasn't Ted who rented it, though. He rented another property from a competitor of mine, one that would have made me some real money. Ingrate."

"Were the men white? Black? Hispanic?"

"Wouldn't know. I never met them in person. Any of them. None had an accent that I can recall."

"Any chance your phone still has call logs from sixteen months back?"

"Got a new phone for Mother's Day. Traded in the old one."

Whelan's head cocked to the side. *Thanks for nothing.* "Thank you. I'll be in touch if I need anything else."

What he needed was to track down the owner.

❄ ❄ ❄

When Whelan entered Slappy's at 6:00 that night, he ran into George Beckford coming out the door.

"Agent Whelan!" He was inebriated.

"Mr. Beckford." *That's the last time I ever meet a suspect at one of my favorite spots.*

"Catch your man yet?" he asked.

"Working on it." Whelan narrowed his eyes to mean, thin slits and whispered, "I'm getting real close."

Beckford's eyebrows shot halfway up his forehead. It was as if this was the first time he'd clued in *he* might be a suspect.

Whelan grabbed his arm. "Beckford, you ever live in Traverse City?"

"Michigan? No. Never lived in Michigan."

"Uh-huh. I'll be checking on that."

Beckford cleared his throat, "Well, 'night agent."

Thomas couldn't help but smirk as he moved toward the bar. As long as the rental house owner could confirm the tenant wasn't named George, he'd freed up his life from any more run-ins with Beckford. *I hope.*

Whelan's smile broadened when he saw Reggie Johnson nursing a beer over some potstickers and watching the Royals on the screen in front of him. There was no sign of Agent Jones yet, so he took the open stool next to his new friend.

"Tommy!"

Warm handshakes were exchanged, and they ordered more beer and some wings. They shared small talk until Agent Jones appeared alongside her colleague. Whelan made the introductions.

Reggie was immediately captivated by Miranda. "Tommy, you didn't tell me your partner was so beautiful."

"She's taken," he replied.

"And what do you do, Mr. Johnson?" asked Jones.

"I own a small landscape company. I've got four regular guys on the payroll, but I do most of the work myself. Keeps me fit with the exercise and pays the bills. I make enough to buy a beautiful lady dinner if she'll allow me."

Agent Jones tossed back her mane and giggled. "I'm sorry, Mr. Johnson, but I *am* involved with someone else. If it makes you feel better, though, your taxes *are* buying my dinner tonight."

"Well, I'll cringe a little less when I file my quarterly next week. And please, it's Reggie."

"Thank you, Reggie. Now, if you'll excuse us, we need to discuss business. It was nice to meet you."

The agents moved to a table.

"Quite the charmer," said Miranda. "If I ever get tired of Derrick, maybe I'll give him a call."

Thomas scowled. "Nope. I get first shot. As soon as all that money and amazing sex get old, you make sure and call *me*."

Miranda laughed. "You're on." She cocked her head and looked at her partner. "Will you wear a kilt?"

Thomas' eyes lit up. He put forward a thick accent, somewhere between Irish and Scottish. "Lassie, if it will entertain yer fantasy and bring ya joy, I'll wear a kilt fer ya."

They both howled heartily. The stress from this week needed a bit of unraveling.

More beer and burgers were ordered as they filled each other in on the past twenty-four hours.

"So, you think there's a chance Whitfield might be the killer?" asked Thomas.

"There's always a chance, but my gut says no."

"Your gut ever been wrong before?"

"Sure. But I've developed it over the years. It's better than it used to be."

Thomas looked at Miranda's stomach. Her blouse covered her abdominal muscles, but he saw them in his head, remembering how she looked in her halter top at the gym. "I'm sure it must be."

Miranda smiled and shook her head. "What am I going to do with you?"

"Anything."

They locked eyes for a moment, as both of them entertained thoughts they shouldn't.

Thomas had the propriety to snap out of it first. "Well, time to head out. A fresh night's rest will do us both wonders. See you at the office in the morning, Agent Jones."

"Good night, Agent Whelan."

A restful night was the last thing Whelan had as his mind wrestled his growing attraction to his partner with appropriateness.

❀ ❀ ❀

Chapter 18

By Friday afternoon, Agent Jones had three new suspects from the list of St. Vincent's churchgoers. She was able to visit the two full-time teachers at the same school. She put them on her mental backburner for now. They didn't seem likely. The third, a part-time substitute, was a man named Joe Mulligan. The school board listed him as "off" today. Agent Jones decided to pay a trip to his home. She asked Whelan to meet her there, and he was waiting in his car when she drove up.

It was a small home in Blue Springs, one of Kansas City's suburbs to the east. It was clean and comfortable looking but not impressive by any standards. He owned it outright and lived in it for the past twenty-four years. Miranda believed it to be of particular interest because three other suburbs separated Blue Springs from Kansas City: Lee's Summit, Raytown, and Independence—the three towns where the first four victims were from. While some substitutes would travel far for work, most preferred to stick within a thirty-minute drive.

Whelan was trying to peek in the front window as Jones rang the bell.

"Yes?" Mulligan asked, opening his door.

"I'm Supervisory Special Agent Miranda Jones, with the FBI," she began, holding up her credentials. "This is Agent Thomas Whelan. We need to speak with you, Mr. Mulligan. It's important."

After being invited in, she asked for her water so she could begin probing the place. It was a far cry from Uberto Ferretti's home in Miami. The entirety of it could fit in Ferretti's living room. Photos revealed little. A past wife, perhaps. Friends; new and old. Lots of kids. Some were students, some possibly his own. Activities like camping, basketball teams, high-school wrestling events, all played as reasonably typical for one in his profession. She observed an open door before the kitchen entryway, which led to the basement.

"Thank you!" She made an overt gesture of gratitude when he handed her the glass.

"Okay, agent. What's this about?"

"We're investigating a homicide. Your name popped up as a member of the congregation at St. Vincent's. Isn't that quite a drive for you? It must take you over an hour to get to church."

"Sunday mornings keep the roads pretty clear these days. I can make it in about forty-five minutes. Was someone at St. Vincent's killed?"

"Tony Balzano. Did you know him well?"

Joe Mulligan seemed taken aback. "I saw on TV that Balzano was murdered by the 12 Pills Killer!"

"Yes."

It took a few seconds to respond. "You think *I'm* the 12 Pills Killer?"

"I'm following leads, Mr. Mulligan." She looked at his fair, Caucasian skin tone. He was paler than she believed her killer would appear.

He felt obligated to state his position. "Well, I'm *not!*"

Agent Whelan stepped into the kitchen. "That's a relief. Thank you for your assurance. Now, how well did you know Tony Balzano?"

Mulligan took a loud slurp from his can of soda. He looked out the kitchen window, his eyes darting back and forth across the lawn. "Not well," he said.

"So, you *knew* him. Wonderful. Did you ever have him as a student?"

"Student?" The questioning utterly lost Joe.

"You're a substitute teacher, Mr. Mulligan."

"Yes."

"Did you ever have Tony Balzano as a student?"

"No. I teach locally."

"Fantastic! Then do you remember any students by the names of Jackson Kenny, Paul Duke, Tracy Stamford, or Sonja Cuevas?"

"No. Why? Why are you asking me all this?" He slammed his cola on the counter.

"You don't look well, Mr. Mulligan. Would you like to sit?" Agent Jones had a small red flag waving in her head. The man's reactions weren't quite 'right.' Her experiences taught her that not everyone behaves the same way, even when proven innocent. But she'd also learned to keep her guard up until that proof came through.

"I think I'm going to be sick. Would you excuse me a minute?" asked Mulligan. He walked to the basement opening. As an afterthought, he turned back to the agents. "The toilet up here isn't working. I'll be right back."

Agent Jones listened to his footsteps as he raced downstairs. She killed a minute by snooping through his cupboards. *Cheap glassware. Cheap dishes. He's earning a substitute's salary.* He also liked lots of cereal. Oat cereal, frosted wheat cereals—even two boxes of sugary 'usually reserved for five-year-olds' cereals. She wondered if he played with the enclosed toys.

A passing blur out the kitchen window caught in Jones' peripheral vision. She turned to see Joe Mulligan racing across his backyard and hop a privacy fence into an alley.

"Shit!"

❀ ❀ ❀

A twenty-minute search of the neighborhood left Whelan and Jones empty-handed. By the time they arrived back to Mulligan's home, the team of forensic agents Jones had called in was pulling up to the curb.

She left them to comb through the house and headed down to the basement. Her partner found her staring at an assortment of old memorabilia; baseball, Coca-Cola, vintage lunch boxes and tons of books. None of it looked particularly valuable, but then, Agent Jones wasn't a collector.

"There's a market for that Coca-Cola stuff, but his isn't in any condition to fetch more than a few dollars," said Agent Whelan. He noted the curtain covering the small window at the top of one wall. It came out at ground level. "He climbed through that jalousie?"

"Evidently. Fast fucker for a fifty-five-year-old. Good jumper too."

"I doubt he outran us. He must be holed-up nearby. Maybe a neighbor's? I've got men starting to door knock."

"Marvelous." Her tone was somewhere between sarcastic and jaded. "I saw his cogs turning. Mine were slower, or I'd have followed him down here."

"It's okay. We'll find him. He was merely another name on another list and a pasty one at that."

"Well, he ran for some reason…if he's not the killer, I wonder what he's guilty of," she asked.

"I think I smell it."

"Huh?"

Agent Whelan started sniffing more strongly, letting his nose guide him to a corner of the basement. There was a set of wooden bins stacked on top of one another. An odor was coming from them. Whelan lifted the lid off the top box. "Shrooms. The guy's been growing shrooms. I bet he's selling them to the kids he teaches. Gotta love our public education system."

"I don't want to ask how you smelled those from over there," said Jones, "especially over all this other mildew-covered crap."

Agent Whelan winked at her. "Exceptional training."

"Uh-huh. I'm sure you boys in the pharmacology program never decided to experiment when you were in college."

"What's with you and these stereotypically male assumptions? Did I go to an all-boys school, and no one told me? It would explain some things." Whelan teased.

Jones wasn't in the mood for his wit today. "Boys and *girls* in the pharmacology program…whatever." She marched upstairs, her locks swaying back and forth like a crowd at a tennis match.

Whelan followed close behind, catching the scent from her perfume along the way. It helped to desensitize his nose after opening the lid on the psychedelic mushroom garden.

No one upstairs uncovered anything else suspicious in the house.

An agent came running in from the back door, all excited. "I think I know why he ran!"

Jones and Whelan exchanged puzzled glances. They thought *they* knew.

Following the agent to a corner of the backyard, Whelan began sniffing again. This odor was more faint and would have been impossible to detect had the agent not led them straight to it. Hidden behind a vegetable garden, on the other side of an eight-foot wall of tomato vines, was a four by eight-foot patch of cannabis.

Whelan whistled.

Agent Jones' brain percolated. Mulligan was supplementing his low income. Substitute teaching was a cover for the creep. An opportunity to find eager clients. Young, impressionable, underage clients. *Bastard! No wonder he drove to St. Vincent's on Sundays. Why sell solely to the poor kids when you can also sell to the rich at twice the price!*

"I don't get it," she said to Whelan. "If he's earning extra cash, why live so poorly? What's he doing with the extra income? Saving for retirement?"

"I got the impression he was inherently lazy. He's not making a killing off sixty-four square feet of weed. The school board said he subs a couple of days a week. I think he's barely scraping through life."

The lead agents made a final sweep of the home before leaving. They would let the other agents confiscate the drugs and close up.

Whelan stopped in the living room, noticing a photo on a bookshelf. "Agent Jones, what made you follow this lead?"

"He was the one substitute teacher still in the area that came up in the 1999 congregation list from the church."

Agent Whelan picked up the frame holding the picture that caught his eye and squinted closely. "And do you happen to have that list on you?"

"Yes." Jones reached into her bag and pulled out a folded print-out.

Whelan made a mental note to encourage her to be more paperless in the future. "Did none of the other names on the list catch your attention?"

"No. But I didn't look at the *whole* list; there are hundreds of people who attend there. I was pursuing the cross-referenced list of the names who attended in '99 and were teachers. I have the complete list here, though; alphabetical. Who else you looking for?"

"Look through the 'W's."

Agent Jones ran her finger down the page, stopping it at a name. "Evelyn Ward. How'd you know?"

Whelan flipped the photo he was still holding around for his partner to see. He pointed to one of two men in the picture. "This look like Mulligan to you?"

She nodded. "I'd guess from the late '80s."

"Well, this guy," he said, pointing to the other man, "is James Ward. Judy's twin brother."

Chapter 19

Mark Whitfield swung his driver from the 14th tee box at Hilltop Golf and Driving. "Damn." He sliced it hard into the trees.

His lifelong friend, Patrick Kavanaugh, restrained his joy and slapped him on the back. "That's in some brush. You want to hunt for it or take a stroke?"

Mark grabbed another ball from his golf bag. "Whatever happened to practice strokes?"

Patrick snickered. "Not since junior high. And not with wings and brew on the line."

"I'd better go dig in the dirt," snorted Mark. He looked behind him. No one else was waiting. They arrived at 6:30 a.m., too early on a Saturday, in his opinion, though there were four tee times ahead of them. He would have preferred to sleep in, but his friend coaxed him out to cheer him up from his sour mood over the forced leave of absence. Mark's wife Jane had called Patrick the day before and urged him to get his friend out of the house. They were planning to play a round the following Saturday anyway for Patrick's birthday.

"Couldn't you play two weekends in a row?" she had asked her husband's friend.

"You bet."

Patrick's spouse understood.

And Mark *was* cheering up; by the third drink. At 10:30 in the morning.

When they tallied up the scorecard in front of their fourth beer, it was clear Kavanaugh out-played the former aspiring-pro player who had even toured a summer on the junior circuit his sophomore year.

"Mark, you're off your game. You want to talk about it."

"Nope."

Lunch was finished by 11:30. On the way to the parking lot, Kavanaugh suggested a matinee movie to sober up before returning home to their wives. The latest Vin Diesel movie was still playing.

"Sure."

About a quarter of the way through the movie, Whitfield was bored and wanted to return home. "You stay and finish it. I'm okay to drive. Really."

By 1:00 p.m., he was napping on his sofa. Jane took the kids to a ball game, and except for little Jeepers, the new family kitten who insisted on making a spot in the middle of Whitefield's belly to share a snooze, he had the house to himself.

At 3:35, his phone buzzed. He'd been ignoring it all day but decided to answer when his wife's name flashed across the screen. "Yeah."

"Honey! Where are you? Are you okay?"

"Yes. I'm home. I was resting." He rubbed his head and reached into a kitchen cabinet for some aspirin.

"Mark... Patrick's dead. They found his body at Truman Cinemas."

Whitfield didn't respond. *Am I still dreaming?*

"Mark! Are you there? Do you feel okay?"

"Yes. Stay with kids. I'll call you later."

"Mark, there's more. Are you sitting down?"

"No. I'm headed there now." He was already out the door and on his way to the garage. "Talk while I drive. Time's wasting." His training kicked in automatically. He'd process emotions later, but right now, he needed to find out what happened.

"Mark… "

He realized Jane was sobbing on the other end of the line. "I'm here."

"Mark, Patrick had an orange pill bottle shoved in his mouth! They told us the cap read '6 of 12'!"

❧ ❧ ❧

Whitfield barely parked his car before racing into theatre nine. The house lights were on, and a small group of agents huddled around the center of the seats, right where he'd been sitting four hours earlier.

Patrick Kavanaugh's head was tilted back in his chair. His eyes were open to the ceiling. A trail of diet soda left a drool mark down his chin and neck. Agents were collecting samples on Q-tips. Without asking permission, Whitfield approached from the side, elbowing a forensics agent out of the way. He placed his hand over Patrick's eyes and closed them, shielding them from the horror of his murder.

When Mark looked up to the group on the main floor, the one agent who registered in his head was Miranda Jones.

She was fighting a look of sympathy with one of speculation. "You were here?"

His chin absently moved up and down. "Twelve o'clock show. I left a few minutes in. Went home. Took a nap. Got the call. I leave my GPS on these days. You can verify my location."

"Perfect. We'll need to see everywhere you've been over the past forty-eight hours. Mark, come back down. They're not finished collecting prints and evidence around that area."

Seeing his life-long friend like this worked on Mark's nerves more profoundly than he'd expected. He wanted to yell at Jones but instead trudged down the steps and took a seat in the front row. It was too much. Tears started to flow.

Miranda approached her old partner with renewed sympathy. "Mark. I'm sorry. We'll get this cleared up soon. Tell me what you can about this."

She sat with him for a few minutes as he replayed in detail the events of the day.

Afterward, she went to the lobby to confer with Agent Whelan. He'd left after she started speaking with Whitfield, trying to be respectfully absent and give her space to do what she did best.

"You think that was all an act?" he asked.

"I don't think so. He should be on Broadway if it was."

"Please tell me you had a tail on him this morning," Whelan said.

"We were going to start it at eight this morning. Surveillance called in at 12:42, surprised to report Whitfield pulling into his garage. They assumed he'd been home all day. That's my fault. I should have realized he might be out golfing earlier than that. I'll take the heat on that one."

They returned five minutes later, in time to see Patrick Kavanaugh be baggied like an egg-salad sandwich. Mark Whitfield appeared to be in shock.

"Cannon!" snapped Whelan. "Get him out of here," he motioned toward Whitfield.

Agent Phil Cannon escorted Mark to the lobby and encouraged him to return home. He took the liberty of assigning another agent to follow him and report back when he arrived.

In the theatre, Kavanaugh was loaded onto a gurney.

"Mark's going to need counseling," said Agent Whelan. "We'll check his GPS, but let's assume he's not the killer—neither of us believe that—why would 12 Pills strike so early in the day? Doesn't he like to wait until night?"

"We think Stamford was killed in the morning. He's not been consistent—outside of the fact they've all been on the weekends. All on Saturdays, except Cuevas, who we think was around 3:30 Sunday morning. I think our killer's not so worried about the precise time. I imagine he trails them all day until the right opportunity comes to light. I believe the reason he even waits a week between is to toy with us. Strike fear in the public."

"Yes, he's playing a game. He's planned this for at least a year. Maybe his whole life. But still, this one was ballsy. Following a federal agent to a crime scene? He's either getting reckless or...."

"Or what?"

Whelan's mind was churning. "Or he intentionally wanted to frame Whitfield."

"I doubt it. That assumes he even knew who Whitfield was. Kavanaugh could have been playing golf with anyone this morning. Though... according to Whitfield, this was all planned in the past couple of days. It's not like Kavanaugh had the same routine every single Saturday morning. How did the killer know he'd be here at all?"

"He's been trailing him for more than a day. Or he is listening to calls made from within his home. Shit Miranda! Maybe he's planted listening devices in all their homes. Could have been weeks—months ago! We need to start looking for bugs."

"Well, that would be helpful if we knew who the next target was."

"Whitfield and Kavanaugh were lifelong friends—since grade school?" asked Whelan.

"Yes. Ahh… you think Whitfield's on the hit list?"

"Maybe. Can't hurt to check his house out. Let's get a team over there and see if they find anything. If my instincts are right, 12 Pills knows *exactly* who Whitfield is. Hell, if he *is* on the list, it would have been easy to take them both out today."

"Except that would go against the rules of his game. Whitfield's birthday isn't 'til August. He wouldn't be next on the list."

"No. And I bet that irked the shit out of our killer. Being so close, and yet having to wait."

"I doubt it. I'm sure it fed into the excitement, an early teaser of events to come. It's like getting a free sample of bourbon chicken at the food court in the mall. You know you're going to circle back around and get the chicken, but you take that little offering on the toothpick all the same."

Agents Jones and Whelan headed back out to the lobby. They both watched Whitfield climb into his car in the parking lot and speed off.

Poor little chicken on a stick.

Agent Whelan snapped out of his thoughts. "Cannon!" he yelled to the Assistant Special Agent.

"Yes sir," he said. He was quick to approach.

"I need a list of names for every license plate in the parking lot at Hilltop Golf this morning. And all the closest traffic cameras. Same for this theatre. Every name from 6:00 a.m. 'til now."

Agent Jones looked forlorn. "Street cameras? That'll be thousands of names. Tens of thousands."

"Then thank God for computer software. It shouldn't take long to cross-match them to any of our existing lists. Jones, if Whitfield *is* number eight, we can catch this bastard."

"Swell. But how do we prevent number seven in the meantime?"

❁ ❁ ❁

Toby Levinson was the "traffic-cam" guy at the Kansas City field office. "He wants *what?*"

"All the names, from all the plates, from all the cameras, from 6:00 to 4:00." Agent Cannon was confused as to why he needed to repeat himself. "Doesn't your software compile it?"

"Yes and no. First, it's not like the cameras you indicated are all top-notch, latest models, with advanced LPR software churning out a ninety-nine percent success rate of plate reads. The first one has been around for over seven years. That's like… a million years—in traffic camera years. And the other one, eight!" He was screaming into the phone.

"Okay?"

"We'll be lucky to put a list together with a seventy percent ratio of hits."

"I'll take it. Maybe we'll get lucky."

"And you can have that by a week from Tuesday."

"I need it before you go home today."

Levinson howled, "You've listed eleven cameras, with an average traffic count of forty-two thousand each, on a Saturday between 6:00 a.m. and 4:00 p.m. I can process about a thousand plates an hour if I'm lucky, with a thirty percent miss ratio for an eight-hour period across eleven cameras. That'll bring me to thirteen days, and if I pull Parkinson's computer in to help after he's done running the Levy and Jefferson cases, I believe I can shorten it down to nine. Give or take six hours."

Cannon was supposed to be intimidated, but he wasn't having it. "Start with the two nearest Hilltop Golf and Driving, between 6:00 and 12:00. Compile me a list of *those* names first and get them to me the *moment* they're done *before* continuing to the next camera. Run the rest of the cameras' footage from 11:00 to 4:00 first. Then, *again*, get me those names before proceeding. You can then finish the remaining time blocks for all the cameras after that. And, pause Parkinson's search. Put his computer on half the job, in the same order. We'll take the heat from the agents working those cases."

"Who's *we*? You don't have the authority to order this."

"Supervisory Special Agent Jones." Cannon went out on a limb using her name but was sure she'd back him if it came time to pay the piper.

Toby was silent for a moment on the other end. "Yes sir. I'll have the first list in a few hours."

Agent Cannon was pleased with himself. He turned around to Jones and Whelan. "Looks like at least several hours. For the *first* batch of names."

Whelan soured his lips. "Okay."

"And we'll have about a seventy percent hit ratio."

He sighed. "Okay."

Looking at his watch, Whelan perked up. "Well, at least we can go see Evelyn Ward now. She said she'd be home to speak with us by 6:00 p.m."

"I can't wait to see her face when we ask about Joe Mulligan," said Jones. "You suppose she'll remember her son's friend?"

"Definitely."

"Yeah? Why?"

"You were focusing on the congregation list from '99. I spoke with Father Cassidy last night, and he told me both Evelyn and Joe still go to St. Vincent's. In fact, he said they both attended the same service last week!"

Chapter 20

"I don't know a Joe Mulligan," Evelyn Ward lied to the agents in front of her. They weren't invited to sit and have tea this time.

Whelan showed her the photo of her son James and Joe together from the '80s. Evelyn looked like she'd burst into tears. "He looked so happy there! When was this taken?"

"We were hoping you could tell us exactly."

She studied it a moment. "I'd guess, '89, '90? Couldn't have been later than '91."

"You're sure?"

"Yes. That was the last year we had him."

Miranda mustered a bit of sympathy toward the elderly dying woman. Still, she was hardening up to her in light of all the recent evidence against her daughter and her own conspicuous lies. "Have you heard from Judy? I can't believe she hasn't reached out to you all week."

None of the surveillance teams had witnessed any sign of her.

"Not a word, dear. I hope Ferretti hasn't hurt her. You know he was out on bail in less than an hour after you arrested him?"

"I know. He cooperated at the arraignment, so the judge let him fly back to Miami with a promise to return in a month for the hearing."

"In a month, I'll be dead. Cancer dear. Remember?"

"Yes. It would have been difficult to keep him here with no priors. We're keeping an eye on him and the house. He's to notify us the moment he even *hears* from Judy. That was part of the bargain to let him return to Florida."

"That, and a pay-off to some district judge perhaps?"

Jones ignored her retort. She didn't know the specifics. It was handled locally.

Agent Whelan brought up Joe Mulligan again. "Mrs. Ward, we know you and Joe attend the same services together. You have since at least 1999. Twenty-one years in attendance, and you expect us to believe you don't know him?"

She shook her head.

"Bullshit. You saw him last Sunday at church! Father Cassidy told me the two of you were chummy at the pot luck following service."

"Well," said Evelyn, "wasn't he helpful!" She made her way to an armchair and took a seat.

The federal agents took up towering positions on either side of her.

"Mrs. Ward," said Agent Jones, "we can do this here or in a cell, but either way, you need to start telling us everything you know about Joe Mulligan. You know we're investigating the 12 Pills Killer. He might be involved."

"Oh. Well, why didn't you say that's what this was about, to begin with?" She gazed thoughtfully for a moment. "He's my drug dealer, dear."

Jones' brow furrowed. "Drug dealer?"

"Yes, dear. Every month after the potluck, I luck into some great pot. It helps the pain. I couldn't function at this stage without it."

Whelan spoke up. "*Luck* into it?"

"Well, lucky for *me*. I've known Joe so long, I get the St. Vincent's discount."

"There's a *discount* for St. Vincent's members?" Agent Jones' vocal tone shot up in pitch.

"Oh yes, 'family discount,' if you will," said Evelyn. "Twenty percent."

Agent Whelan whistled. "No wonder it's standing room only. Hell, I may convert."

"And he can make it there in forty-five minutes..." said Agent Jones. "Does Father Cassidy know? Does he put special envelopes in the collection plates?" She altered her voice, "One for me, one for you, one for me, one for you... what a racket!"

"Oh my," said Mrs. Ward, "nothing so elaborate, dear. It's all pretty hush-hush. There are perhaps ten others I've ever seen who approach him about it. And, no, Father Cassidy hasn't a clue. Goody two-shoes that one!"

"Well," said Whelan, "we might not catch our killer today, but we can expose and bust a drug supplier this weekend. At least that's a positive development."

"It's already been exposed, and I let our dealer get away!" Agent Jones was pissed. At herself, at the situation, and Evelyn Ward. "God, Whelan! What if he *is* the killer?"

"We'll find him."

Jones opened the front door and motioned for one of the agents sitting guard outside to come in. As the seconds ticked away, her foot tapping outpaced the shaking of her head.

"Get some shoes on, old woman. I don't care how sick you are; we're taking your ass in. You are going to give a formal statement—*dear*—on Mulligan, on Judy—all of it!"

Evelyn smiled wider. It was a little creepy—her new demeanor. "Sure, dear. Whatever you say."

✿ ✿ ✿

Agent Whelan came out of the interrogation room fifteen minutes after entering. Jones was pacing up and down in the hallway. She'd been asked to sit out by her partner, given her emotional investment at the moment.

"She clammed up," he said. "Asked for her attorney. Honestly, I think she's stalling, dragging this out to distract us from finding Judy."

Sipping a fresh cup of coffee, Agent Jones took a nearby seat and a slow, deep breath. She expelled it slowly and then repeated it all.

"Isn't that counteractive to the caffeine you're ingesting?" asked her partner.

She glared at him a second before continuing.

Whelan took a seat opposite her and waited for her to finish.

"It helps. And this is decaf." She lowered her voice and repeated her question from earlier. "Whelan, what if Joe Mulligan *is* our killer? It would explain how he knows people all over town. We need to ask all the victims' friends if they smoked pot or…worse. Drug-dealer wasn't on our list of possible ways to connect all the targets."

"No, it wasn't." It was Whelan's turn for a deep inhale, exhale moment. "But why would a drug dealer kill his buyers? He's killing his revenue. Doesn't make sense."

"Maybe they all refused to pay? Maybe they owe him so much money he has no choice. You know, to show his other buyers that they'd better not mess around with him."

Whelan locked eye contact with her and raised his eyebrows.

"Okay. I suppose that's pretty far-fetched," she conceded.

He nodded. "Mulligan was growing his own product to sell. He wasn't exactly importing from Columbia. It looked like more of a hobby."

"Well, maybe our jest about Judy being involved with the killer is more accurate than we knew. Maybe it really is a team effort."

"Maybe." They had nothing concrete to go on, and he wanted to give her something in the moment. "Mulligan and Judy Ward know each other at the very least. That photo with her brother made it look like he was part of the family once upon a time. Thirty years is a long time to build trust."

"It has to be connected to the killer somehow. It's *too* coincidental that our primary suspect goes missing, and this Joe Mulligan character shows up and knows the family, then runs on me when I start asking questions."

"Is it, though?" asked Agent Whelan.

"What?"

"Too coincidental. I mean, we've been pouring through hundreds—thousands—of names, cross-referencing them throughout the city for weeks—over a period of years. We're looking for connections. Well, we're bound to start making some. People *are* connected. Eventually, our lists are going to start making matches, whether they're related to our case or not."

Thomas was about to ask her if she still believed Judy Ward was her primary suspect. She certainly wasn't *his*. He hoped he was wrong. It would wrap all this up soon enough if it were true. If the first two killed had been St. Vincent's members, he'd be all in on Jones' suspicions. But it wasn't coming together for him in his head. *12 Pills isn't a teacher.* A text notification went off, and he glanced down at his phone.

Miranda broke her empty stare in his direction. "You're right."

She stood up and stretched. "I'm going home. It's been a long day. Let's meet here in the morning. Maybe sleep will give some fresh perspective."

"I have a better idea. Let's meet for breakfast near Evelyn Ward's home instead. While I was questioning her, I texted the magistrate's office. Her little stunt gave us just cause. We should have a 'search and seize' by 8:00 a.m."

Chapter 21

Sunday morning, the 12 Pills Killer opened the door to the basement. Steps were taken with leisure while eating a cup of yogurt. Fresh blueberries and a spoonful of granola rested on top. The light string was tugged before taking a seat at the table. The newspaper was left upstairs today. There were only thoughts for distraction.

Yesterday's timing couldn't have been more perfect. A dark theatre in the fifth week of a movie's outing? Child's play. There was no one else at the showing. And luckily, the back door was unlocked. Slipping in through the side curtain avoided any cameras that might have been in the lobby.

Success turned to a hunger to expedite the next killing. 12 Pills took the dust cover off the pill press and set it on the work table. Beakers were laid out. Burners were lit. A fresh root was extracted from the pot underneath the sun lamp.

I'll make a batch and see what the week brings.

Clean-up was completed two hours later as usual. The joy normally attained from cooking up the beautiful little blue pills was absent today. At the card table to the right of the stairs, an internal fight ensued.

Should I take the next bottle?

'7 of 12' called silently from its cubby hole.

Not today. Not Sunday. Today is the day we rest. And besides, it's too soon. I should wait at least a couple of days.

After returning the room to darkness, the stairs were mounted while patting the coat pocket with the pills, safely stashed in their little plastic pouch.

❈ ❈ ❈

The waitress set a ten-inch omelet down in front of Whelan. For $9.95, this diner served it with two slices of bacon and a large plate of crispy hash browns. Unlimited coffee was free with every entrée on Sundays, and the line went around the block.

Thankfully, Agent Jones didn't have a problem flashing her badge once in a while to get to the head of the line. They were "on the clock" after all.

"This would be $18.95 in D.C.," Whelan said. "Another three for coffee. It's nice to be back in the Midwest."

"See there," said Jones, "you don't need a raise. You just need to be reminded that value still exists in the world."

The sun was rising over the tree-line in the window behind her. It backlit her, providing a soft glow around the edges of her cheeks. Whelan almost reached out and touched one. *That can't happen.*

It had been at least thirty seconds since he'd checked his text for notification that the search warrant came in, so instead, he glanced at his lap.

"You gonna play with that all morning?" she asked.

He looked up from his crotch, curious. "Oh! Sorry." He set the phone on the table. "I have the volume turned up. Sometimes I miss hearing the beep. When it's in my lap, I can at least feel the vibration."

"Ahh..." She raised her brows and acquiesced.

Whelan turned red. It was easy for his freckled face to do. "Ah-ha... funny."

"When's the last time you got laid?" asked Jones.

"Excuse me?" Whelan went from beet to crimson.

"You clearly need some relief."

"Why, are you ready to break the fraternizing rule?" He put on his flirtiest expression. 7:30 in the morning with the full sun lighting up his face now wasn't the most flattering setting for him to try and work his charm. He'd lost his Caribbean tan and hadn't bothered to shave today.

Despite all that, Agent Jones examined her partner with some amount of temptation. "No. Not today." She smiled.

"Well," said Whelan, "let's get this one in the books, and I'll worry about my love life then."

"Agreed."

Whelan wasn't sure if she was still referencing his or her own.

They both looked at his phone on the counter. It loomed large with its silence.

After a few more bites, they asked for coffee to go. They steered themselves toward Evelyn Ward's home. It was 8:12 and no warrant yet.

"Should I call?" he asked.

"Give the clerk a few more minutes. Judge Chamberlain isn't an early riser. Though I do hear he's been rising for one little attorney lately."

"Oh? I didn't picture you as the gossipy type."

"I'm not. It's intel. If you're bringing criminals before the court, it's nice to know which way to steer them depending on which defense attorney's in which judge's favor."

"You have control over that?" asked Whelan.

"Not much, but depending on the crime, I've learned to 'hold' my suspect until a shift change at the courthouse."

"Ahh. I have a lot to learn about the local scene."

"Until you do, you've got me." She flashed her teeth at him.

Glorious. He looked out the window. *Maybe I do need to get laid.*

"You found a place yet?" She broke him out of his desolation.

"Haven't had a moment to look."

"*Still?* You know there's a little thing called the internet? You push some buttons, and houses for sale appear. It's really pretty clever."

"Well… I like Evelyn's. If we find a body in the basement, can I get it at a discount?"

Agent Jones grinned. "Maybe. Though she'd be under no legal obligation to disclose it in a sale."

"Damn. Always missing my opportunities."

They pulled up in front of Ward's home. For ten minutes, they visited with the surveillance team. Four other agents assigned had been waiting since 8:00 a.m. At 8:32, Whelan's phone went off. "We got it. Be here in another ten."

Phil Cannon showed up in under nine minutes and rushed the paper to Agent Jones's hand.

As customary, she knocked on the door first. Evelyn was held overnight on obstruction of justice charges. No one would be here to answer unless Judy herself surprised them by opening the door. She did not.

Agent Jones took a small battering ram out of her trunk and walked up the porch steps.

"Really?" asked Whelan. "Let me check if there's a window or back door open before you do that."

He disappeared around the side of the house.

Jones pursed her lips. She was still irritated with Evelyn's lies and misdirection.

She picked up her ram and was about to swing anyway when the front door opened. Whelan's lips couldn't hide his smirk from inside the entryway.

She evil-eyed him as she passed.

They both headed straight to the basement. Agent Jones was sure she was going to find a complete science lab. More disappointment. It was beautifully finished: painted drywall, carpeting, a full bathroom, and even a little kitchenette on one wall. There was a separate bedroom from the living area. Two small ground-level windows let in a bit of natural light. A fifty-five-inch flat screen was on the living-area wall, and a wine fridge held eight bottles, all fine labels.

"Okay," said Whelan, "now I *definitely* want this home. Anything in the morgue we can borrow and plant here?" He was only half-joking.

Agent Jones thought about her own basement. It was dirty and overcrowded, with boxes never unpacked. Her washer and dryer were down there, and she was forced to look at her mess every time she did a load. She vowed to take a weekend when this was over and make some effort on it.

For the next three hours, the seven agents scoured every inch of Evelyn Ward's home. In the end, there was nothing to indicate the 12 Pills Killer was operating here. There *was* plenty to suggest Judy Ward had been here. Evidence was discovered in the bathroom, not the least of which was her paper stub from her airline ticket, an exclusive private airline for the uber-rich.

"Ah, money…" Jones sighed.

Whelan walked up behind her. "Well, what now? There's nothing here that Judy has to come back for. Those clothes in the dresser are for winter. She must have her suitcase with her. I'll bet she's holed up in some hotel under a pseudonym."

Agent Cannon chimed in. "We've called every hotel in the area looking for her by name. I imagine she keeps a roll of cash bigger than my wrist to avoid using her cards. The most recent transaction on her Amex was over two weeks ago, in Miami."

He looked at Jones for guidance. She was the lead agent on this, after all. It was what she had wanted her whole life, a big case to prove herself at the bureau. She looked at Cannon. He was thirty, but at the moment, he looked incredibly young, a schoolboy awaiting further instructions.

"She's in this town *somewhere*," she began. "Cannon, get every available agent to start going around in person. Start with the most expensive hotels in the area, closest to here. She won't be staying at the 'Do Drop Inn.' Have them show her picture and flash badges. I'm tired of playing around with this bitch."

Whelan let her have her moment. He would give her some breadth today, but he would need to get her back on his page by tomorrow. Judy Ward was in some trouble. And it was possible she knew the killer. *Hell, it's still possible she* is *the killer.*

But every ounce of instinct was telling him they were wasting time chasing the wrong person. And they were counting precious minutes until number seven's number was up.

Literally.

He didn't know how precious. He wouldn't have a whole week between murders this time. He would have less than four days.

Chapter 22

By Monday morning, more dead ends surfaced. A three-hour sweep by the bureau revealed no bugs in Mark Whitfield's home. Either the killer wasn't bugging homes, or they were wrong about Whitfield being on the list. The latter half of Sunday was spent combing through Patrick Kavanaugh's home. Again, nothing.

"We need to search their cars for trackers," suggested Whelan.

"They did!" Agent Jones' tirade was escalating.

"And no sign of Judy Ward?" asked Whelan.

"No! And the hotels have been cleared. I'm going to move half the agents to start door-knocking in Evelyn's neighborhood. Maybe she has a neighbor who's hiding her."

"If they're *hiding* her, what would be the point? Are you going to get a search warrant for every house in the area? That'll never happen. Partner," Whelan approached her in their office, "it's time to move on to other suspects. We'll find Judy, but I'm telling you, it's not her."

Jones wheeled on him. She came close to yelling at him but checked herself before opening her mouth. Some amount of meditation and yoga was paying off. "Whelan, we have no other suspects besides Joe Mulligan. We can't find either of them, and I'm beginning to think they're working together."

"We have no other suspects *yet*. And they're going to be tough to find if all our resources are focused on Judy Ward."

She stared at him. "Okay…you're right. I didn't bring you in on this to be a 'yes' man. And I didn't bring you in *just* because you knew some of the victims and grew up here in the '90s. I brought you in for your insight, and experience too. If you say it's not Ward, I've got to listen to that. So..." she looked at her board before returning her gaze to him, "Fine. What do *you* want to do now?"

Agent Jones collapsed in her chair, rubbing her eyes until red and puffy.

"Whoever rented that house outside Traverse City last year is our killer. I need help tracking down the owner. No one seems to know where she is. The mailing address on file led to an empty house that's also for rent. In *Ohio*."

"So go to Ohio. Take Cannon. I'm not in the mood to reward eager puppies today anyway."

She put her feet up on the corner of her desk. "I'm letting you take the wheel for a day. I'm fried. My head..." She rubbed at her temples.

Whelan wanted to move in and massage them but stood frozen.

Jones looked at him. She was spent. "What can we do for you here, Agent Whelan?"

"Keep watching Mulligan's house. He's going to need to come home at some point. He ran out on his whole life. There's no way he doesn't try to sneak back in. Let's get those alibis for Whitfield so we can clear him from being the killer once and for all. It's a little challenging, not knowing whether to look at him as a suspect or a possible target. And we don't need additional suspects lingering in our heads. We need twenty-four-hour surveillance on him now, too, either way. And *if* you clear him, order some flowers sent to his home from the department. He's been through hell."

"Yes sir! Anything else?"

"Yes. Go speak with Father Cassidy. I think he's an honest guy and might know more if asked the right questions. And send Evelyn Ward home. Remove the surveillance team from out front. We received permission to bug *her* home, so with any luck, she'll call Judy the second she thinks we let our guard down. We've got hidden cameras now on every angle of her home, including the basement windows. Maybe Judy will even return to the house."

"You got it."

"Oh, and Toby's plate search matched two folks who attended St. Vincent's in '99. I don't think it will result in anything, but someone should ask some questions. If he gets any more hits, he's to inform you directly."

Agent Jones was relieved. Whelan once again validated her decision to bring him on board after chasing her tail in circles the past few days. "We'll get on all of it right away."

Whelan made for the door to find Cannon and get to the airport.

"Thomas!" said Jones.

He turned back, open-eyed.

"Thank you."

"We'll catch him, Miranda. I'm not coming home without a name."

❋ ❋ ❋

Agent Cannon chomped on a grilled chicken sandwich from one of the airport kiosks as soon as they took their seats on the plane. What he lacked in height, he made up for with a naturally muscular physique. Whelan looked at him with a bit of envy. He wished he could pack on more muscle himself, but he couldn't even find time to house hunt.

House hunt!

Firing up the wi-fi on his phone after take-off, Whelan started searching real estate sites for a home his budget would allow. *Maybe a little house near the plaza? Two bedrooms, two baths, a garage…*

Within three minutes, he was fast asleep.

Moments later, he was waking up to the plane landing in Toledo.

"Not sleeping at night?" asked Cannon.

"Not enough, I guess."

"Maybe you need to get laid."

Agent Whelan's brow shot up. "Excuse me?" It was one thing for his partner to kid him, but if this subordinate thought he was suddenly back in a frat house, he needed some correcting; and fast.

"My apologies," said Agent Cannon. "I meant, there's actual, scientific data which suggests it helps you get a better sleep; if you expend your energy before going to bed."

Whelan's face was blank. "Uh-huh." *Do I look like I'm wearing a toga? Do I have Sigma Nu tattooed on my arm? How many other agents in the office are talking about my sex life? Absence of a sex life?*

"Go rent us a car," he commanded as they deboarded. "A nice sedan. I need to be able to stretch my legs." He was afraid young Phil would choose either a sports car or worse, one of those intolerable tiny hybrids so trendy with the younger millennials. He realized he didn't know Agent Cannon well and perhaps was being overly judgmental. He was three years older than his fellow agent, but after the past two years, an eternity spanned between them.

"So…" started Cannon, "no Mustang then?"

Whelan growled.

Cannon grinned in return and headed for the car rentals.

Thomas decided he was being messed with and tried to shake it off. He'd made a promise to come home with a name, and it weighed on him more than he realized.

An hour later, they were knocking on the door of the small rental home owned by M & S LLC. No one answered.

"Agent Cannon," said Whelan, "could you please go around back and knock on the back door. We need to make sure this home is vacant."

The moment Cannon disappeared around the wall, Whelan slid a small case out of his pocket. He placed a deep hook tool and a flex tension rod from his lock pick set into the 1980s doorknob. It took less than six seconds for the click, and the door sprang open.

"Cannon!" he yelled to the side of the home.

Agent Cannon appeared shortly.

"I think we've been invited in."

"How?" asked Cannon. "It looks free of any occupants from what I can see through the windows. Furnished, but I don't think anyone's living here."

"Well, this door opened, and I doubt it was the wind. There might be someone inside in trouble." Whelan removed his gun from its shoulder rig and stepped inside.

Agent Cannon followed suit. "FBI!" he yelled upon entering. "Anyone home?"

Whelan's eyes rolled to meet his brow. His younger protégé was following procedure. *He'll learn in time. At some point, saving lives has to be more important.*

"I think the house is empty," said Cannon.

"Check upstairs, make sure." Whelan headed for the kitchen. He opened drawers and cabinets with a gloved hand. There was nothing with a name or address. No mail or magazines, no shipping labels; the house was clean.

"No one is here!" yelled Cannon. Two minutes went by before he yelled from the master bedroom. "Agent Whelan, you might want to get up here!"

Whelan took the stairs two at a time. All the drawers were open in the dresser.

Agent Cannon was staring into one. He looked up. "I think this house has ghosts. These drawers popped open when I walked by."

Good for you, you're learning. "I hate it when that happens." Whelan approached and looked inside. They were all lined with pages torn out of a magazine. The drawer Cannon was indicating had the back page, with a name and this home's address. It read Nancy Cartwright.

"Previous tenant?" said Cannon.

"Maybe." Whelan looked around the room at the nightstands and a chest of drawers. "Any other drawers pop open?"

"None with anything in them."

Whelan took the page with the mailing address printed on it. "Well, I'd hate for the next tenant to have this. Privacy concerns and all."

"Of course."

Nancy Cartwright's current address showed up on Whelan's laptop in the car. She moved to Cleveland in March. A couple of calls, and he soon had Nancy on the line.

"I'm sorry, Agent," she spoke from the other end, "I don't know where Susan Jacobs lives. I think she lived in that home before I did, but she didn't tell me her new address. I sent *my* payments to a P.O. Box in Kansas City."

Whelan's hair jumped on his arm.

"For what it's worth," said Nancy, "I couldn't reach her to get my security deposit back. She never returned my calls. But she also didn't cash my last month's rent check, so I figured it was a wash."

He took Susan's number. There was no answer, and her voice mailbox was full. He made a call to the post office. They had a physical address on file for the P.O. Box. He now had Susan Jacobs' address; in Kansas City. A quick property record search showed it belonged to yet another LLC, S & M LLC. Whelan smirked at the switching of her LLCs from M & S to S & M. What a difference two little letters could connote.

He did not have the name he wanted yet, but this was the step that would lead him to it. "Well," he said to Cannon, "no need to unpack. We're turning around and heading home."

Whelan contemplated the new information. *Son of a bitch. She's been in K.C. the whole time!*

It occurred to him, perhaps the killer wasn't the tenant in Traverse City. *Maybe it was the owner, Susan Jacobs. Or her mystery partner.*

Chapter 23

Father Cassidy was pushing sixty. He was portly and balding a bit in the back with graying, wiry hair. Sporting a chin strap beard that matched his scalp, he tended to pull on it at the bottom when he heard comments he didn't like.

He passed Agent Jones a glass of wine. His home was a few blocks from St. Vincent's. It was modestly adorned, and the furniture was all in decent shape, though at least two to four-decades-old, depending on the piece.

Scanning her eyes around the living room, Agent Jones couldn't believe he was skimming from the collection plates or participating in any kind of a drug ring.

"Drugs!" he exclaimed. "Being sold under *my* roof?"

"I'm afraid so." She took a sip. The wine surprised Jones. It was ambrosial—a word she'd picked up at a wine tasting event some years back. It was far better than she recalled having at any communions she had ever attended. She wondered if his parishioners were worthy of the expensive stuff on Sundays or was it squeezed from a five-liter box.

"How can I help?" he asked.

"I need to know where Joe Mulligan might go if he were hiding out from us. Friends? Family? Congregation members?" She made eyes toward Father Cassidy's back bedrooms.

He snorted. "My dear, you're welcome to look around. I assure you he's not here."

"Do you have some loyalty to your members? Not to reveal what they confess to you and such?"

"Yes. Some. It's a line I walk. But before I have to worry about crossing it, they have to confess it to me first. And Joe Mulligan never mentioned anything about drugs. Frankly, agent, if he's poisoning my flock, I'd rather have him caught and prosecuted." He stood up and paced about a moment before sitting again.

Jones looked at him with compassion. She hated to break horrific news to this man who seemed to be trying to work genuine goodness in the world. She stayed silent, watching him go through his physical and emotional processing of her news. He was animated; it was like a show—unedited and honest. She doubted he'd ever played poker or told a fib in his life.

"He has a sister—Geraldine—she attends service at Christmas Mass, maybe Easter if she's feeling guilty about something. Divorced three times and a child from each. I suspect she wouldn't have a problem hiding him."

"We've spoken to her. Says she knows nothing."

"Did you get a warrant? Did she invite you in? I'd check out her place well."

"I'll get on that, thank you. Anyone else?" Agent Jones wasn't getting anything useful so far.

Father Cassidy's head hung low. He was trying to clear away his anger and confusion to come up with a name. "I don't suppose you can tell me who he was selling the drugs to? I want to help them get counseling, or at least pray for them."

"Sorry, Father. That's a line *I* can't cross professionally. Personally, I'd tell you the whole scoop, but I'm not allowed. And it wouldn't be right to do a *dying* woman that way, anyway."

His face was blank for a moment, and then his light bulb went off. "Evelyn Ward? No! Really?"

The pair locked eye contact, daring the other to break with more information.

Agent Jones soon stood, tossed back the rest of her wine, and placed her card on the table. "Please call me, Father, if you can think of anything else useful."

"Yes, of course. And thank you, Agent Jones, for bringing this to my attention."

The moment she was out the door, he reached for his telephone. "Eileen? Are you sitting? I have news."

❉ ❉ ❉

The sun was setting as Agent Whelan's plane took off from Toledo. Like rocking a baby, Whelan was out cold in a matter of minutes. His dream from three weeks ago replayed itself.

"Come on, Tommy, throw the ball!"

Tommy was trying to read the arranged signals from the catcher behind the plate. None of the finger combinations were making sense. Tommy paused a moment. This felt familiar.

He looked into the stands. Recognizable faces were in the crowd. His mom, his brother, Paul Duke…Jackson Kenny… He looked to home plate. Jackson Kenny was there, too, holding his bat. He threw the pitch.

Jackson swung and knocked it far into left field. The runner on third came home, and the game was over. Tommy lost the game for his team. He looked back into the stands.

Friendly smiles replaced absent stares on new faces; Tracy Stamford, Sonja Cuevas, Tony Balzano, Patrick Kavanaugh. Jackson Kenny and Paul Duke were still there too. All of them were children;

their vacant eyes locked on Thomas. They were looking at him. Or through him.

He turned around to see if anyone was behind him. Mark Whitfield was there, shoulder to shoulder with his brother David. They were still fourteen. They turned around to look behind them.

The grass in the outfield was growing wildly; one foot, two foot, three—masking the fence and the street behind it, where cars were lined with angry parents. A lone kid sat in an old Subaru, looking through the window to try and watch the game. His eyes locked on Tommy's before filling with blue fire. The outfield filled with blue fire too. Soon the entire stadium was ablaze.

Tommy looked to the bleachers again. No one was moving. The 12 Pills Killer's victims were all motionless in the stands as fire whirled around them, burning everything to the ground. Orange pill bottles forced their mouths open, their white caps marked in Sharpie.

1 of 12...

2 of 12...

3 of 12...

4 of 12…

5 of 12…

6 of 12…

All faces he recognized.

7 of 12 was there also, the next target, a fiery blaze with a pill bottle protruding from the center. *Who is it?* Whelan couldn't tell. There remained only charred corpses littered about the grounds. Their ash swirled to become numbers written on singed post-its, falling silently from a corkboard, bursting into cerulean flames once again as they struck the floor.

Whelan snapped to, when the landing wheels skidded against the asphalt at Kansas City International.

He rubbed his eyes and jerked his body upright. He usually didn't retain his dreams, so he fought to remember the face of flames. Who was 7 of 12? *Who was it?* He still couldn't see it. He looked at their chest. *Was it a woman? A man?* He couldn't be sure. Soon it had escaped. His nightmare was gone, except the scorched earth with blistered bodies, a field of black with bright little pops of orange poking out of the cinders. That image would stay with him for the rest of his life.

Whelan relaxed back into his seat.

Agent Cannon was staring at him. "Anything?"

"No," said Whelan. "How long have you been watching me? Did I say anything? Sometimes I talk in my sleep."

"I've been reading throughout the flight, but you did mumble one word. I'm not sure what it was, but it sounded like—David?"

His brother's name triggered that part of the dream. David had been there. With Mark Whitfield.

Agent Whelan turned, looking at what little of the tarmac he could see in the night as the plane taxied to the gate. He hadn't spoken to his brother in over a year. They were never close. No "bad blood" was between them, but they had little in common, and when Thomas joined the FBI, his schedule made it impossible to stay connected.

He couldn't recall the last time he had a dream with his brother in it. Of course, he realized it was likely the connection to Whitfield that brought it to the forefront. But still… *Why were you in my dream David?* Did his brother have answers? Did he witness something when they were kids, something Thomas' subconscious recognized that his waking mind didn't? He wasn't a big believer in dream analysis. *Anything* could trigger *anything* in the dream world, and not all of it had meaning.

But if there's even a chance…

Whelan refused to focus on the other, ostensible connection as he dialed on his cell phone. Surely his brother couldn't be 12 Pills. *No way.*

The other end answered.

Thomas spoke up, "Hey, big brother. I need to see you."

Chapter 24

Whelan called his partner when they deboarded the plane and relayed Susan Jacobs' address in Kansas City. He wanted to help question her in person and search her home, but started feeling guilty for not phoning it in to Jones sooner. He'd allowed himself a bit of selfishness, and this wasn't the time for such nonsense.

"I can be there in thirty-five minutes," said Jones, hanging up the phone from her partner. She looked at the clock; 11:23 p.m.

Rolling over to plant a soft kiss on Derrick's forehead, asleep beside her in her bed, Agent Jones dressed and threw her wild locks into a loose ponytail. Derrick was a sound sleeper, even more so since dating Miranda, who often came and left at odd hours. He'd become accustomed to her irregular schedule.

She went to the kitchen, grabbed an iced coffee with one hand, and her car keys with the other.

Thirty-one minutes later, Supervisory Special Agent Miranda Jones was pulling up in front of Susan Jacobs' house on the south end of Kansas City, below Raytown. There wasn't much streetlight for the small row of ranch-style homes. Susan's was at the end of a cul-de-sac.

K.C.P.D. was waiting outside for Miranda when she arrived. She knocked on the door. No one answered. She rapped again and shook her head. "Either she's not home or doesn't want to be bothered."

Within minutes, the search warrant Whelan called for was handed off to her. Three other field agents arrived. She wanted to wait for Whelan but knew he'd understand the urgency. Kansas

166

City's airport was on the far north end of the city, and it would be a few more minutes before he could get here.

She rapped on the door once more. The knob was locked. Agents and officers were sent around the sides to see if any windows or doors could be opened. They all came back with shaking heads. She grabbed the butt-end of her battering ram and gave a pounding to the knob. It flew open without a fight.

The house took a breath, and when it exhaled, a wicked stench rushed out across the front porch. Officers and agents were quick to cover their noses, but the odor had done its damage. Two with the K.C.P.D. lost their dinner over the side of the railing.

"Everyone wait a minute," said Jones. She retrieved a package of new handkerchiefs from her trunk. A small vial kept in her glove box contained lavender essential oil. She put a few drops in the center of each cotton square and passed them out. The local officers took them gladly and held them up under their nostrils. It didn't kill the odor entirely, but it helped. One man's stomach turned again, however, and he barely made it to the bushes before losing his dessert too.

Agent Jones stepped inside and flicked the closest light switch. Nothing illuminated, so she tried a lamp. "The electric's not on."

She lit up the living room with a 3600-lumen tactical flashlight. It looked like daylight wherever she aimed it. No one was in the living room. She made her way toward the far left of the home. In the kitchen, with her back to Agent Jones, a woman hunkered in a chair at a small breakfast table.

Jones drew her sidearm and pointed it at the woman's head. "I'm Special Agent Miranda Jones with the FBI. Put your hands on the table in front of you."

Whelan's voice could be heard coming through the front door. "Jones?"

"Back here!" she yelled, not turning her head. The woman in front of her had not done as instructed.

Agent Whelan raced through the archway to the kitchen, Agent Cannon on his heels. Both had their weapons drawn. Whelan locked his sight-line on the woman as he walked around the table to face her.

He lowered his weapon and looked up at his partner. "I think it's Susan Jacobs. She's dead. About three months, if I had to guess."

❀ ❀ ❀

"Can we wait for forensics outside?" asked Phil Cannon. "It must be over 120 degrees in here. At least there's a mild breeze outside."

"Go ahead," said Whelan. "I want to get a few snapshots, at least."

"You," barked Agent Jones to an officer, handing them her car keys, "go to my trunk. I've got bolt-cutters. Cut the lock off the electric handle on the meter and turn the power back on."

Everyone was moving. Agent Cannon stepped to the front porch and saw several neighbors outside looking. He made the most of his need for fresh air by questioning those nearby. The standard questions were asked: Have you seen anyone coming or going? When was the last time you saw Susan Jacobs? Et cetera.

The community didn't seem to know her. She'd moved in four or five months back. Before that, there was a young family of renters who lived there. Everyone agreed they were ideal tenants and enjoyed their company for over four years. They moved on to a better school district, and the owner moved in shortly afterward. She kept to herself and then disappeared. Neighbors noticed a smell but decided a dead animal had crawled under the house and died. Locals were called to check on it, but with no one answering the door and no real reason to suspect suspicious activity, it had remained unbothered; shut up for the past three months.

The Evidence Response Team Unit showed and began sweeping the place. Once they cleared a room, Whelan and Jones opened drawers, closets, suitcases—anything which might reveal Susan's activities leading up to her death. There were hints but nothing useful.

With the electricity back on, they could see Susan was bound to her chair. Broken dishes on the floor indicated there had been a struggle. An empty glass was in front of her on the table.

Once all detectable evidence was collected, the body was bagged and removed. Whelan said a prayer on her behalf, then wheeled about in the middle of the living room. "I don't get it! I thought she might have been our killer. Now she's target practice? We need the name of that fucking tenant in Traverse City. I want every single piece of paper in this home piled in the middle of this coffee table. Now!"

People scrambled.

Agent Jones approached her partner. It was coming up on 4:00 a.m. "What about her 'mystery partner' you mentioned on the phone? Could still be him. How can we track that?"

"Unless she has documents here somewhere, it will be impossible. Anyone can register an LLC online these days and file any names they want as managing members, presidents, secretaries… janitors… there's so many registered now that there's no accountability by the states. No, follow up. *And*, there are hundreds of businesses out there right now that are shells for purposes of fraud and corruption, but where do you start?"

"So a silent partner can really stay silent," Agent Jones concluded his thought process.

"Yep."

Assistant Special Agent Phil Cannon made his way back inside after they cleared the body. He overheard the exchange. "Follow the money."

Both Jones and Whelan turned to him.

Whelan grinned. "Give that man a raise."

❀ ❀ ❀

They planned to go home and rest, and then meet at the office at 10:00 a.m. Whelan steered his car toward his hotel when a call came in. He looked at the clock on the radio; 4:32.

"Whelan," he answered.

"Agent Whelan, this is Agent Domburg. I'm monitoring the cameras for Evelyn Ward's home. I'm sorry to bother you so early, but sir, someone crept into the basement window on the side of the home two minutes ago."

Whelan barely avoided wrecking his car doing a high-speed U-turn on a two-lane road.

"Are you there, sir?" asked the other agent.

"Yes! I'm heading there now. Get local officers there ASAP until I can get there. Make sure they know to stay quiet and not alert anyone to their presence. And make sure they know not to let anyone leave! If anyone walks out of any door—or window—they're to be caught and held 'til I arrive."

He hung up and dialed his partner. "Miranda, head to Evelyn's. Judy Ward surfaced!"

Chapter 25

Judy Ward had indeed shown up. Whelan stared at her for a full minute. *Are you a serial killer? Are you pure evil?*

He asked K.C.P.D. to take her to the nearest precinct. He would question her there. This home was too safe. She didn't deserve to be safe right now.

Agent Jones arrived and jumped out in time to see her driven away. "Local precinct?"

"Yes."

"You get the bitch mom yet?"

Whelan pursed his lips a moment. "I was saving her for you."

"Gee, and it's not even Christmas." She bolted through the front door. A couple of minutes later, she escorted Evelyn to her car and threw her in the backseat.

"Wasn't that a tad rough?" asked Whelan.

"Why, did it get you excited?"

Whelan's face wasn't sure what expression to make, and it wrestled with several. "Maybe…?"

Jones laughed, then hopped in her car and sped off toward the police station, leaving Whelan in the middle of the street. As he opened his car door, he looked up at the local officer. He opened his mouth to explain. *Fuck it. I'm too tired.*

Pulling away from the curb, he realized he had no idea where the local station was. He lowered the passenger side window and shouted to the cop still staring in his direction. "Uhmm… Any chance you need a lift back to the station?"

"No, I'm good."

Whelan put his car in drive and dialed Agent Jones. He mumbled to himself as he waited for her to answer, "It's going to be a long-assed day."

❀ ❀ ❀

Mother and daughter were separated into two different interrogation rooms. They'd spoken with Evelyn enough. Judy was at bat, and Whelan was determined not to let her make it to first. He watched as Agent Jones tore into her.

"You *know* we have a search warrant out for you. I know your mother told you!"

"No, sorry, I was unaware. Am I in some kind of trouble?"

Jones got in front of her face. "You expect me to believe you haven't been filled in by Evelyn? Judy, we have your conversations on recorded audio. And before you open up your mouth in protest, here's the judge's signature for it!" She slammed down a piece of paper on the table.

She neglected to mention that the recorded audio was for the last twenty minutes she was in the home. That was all they obtained. And they could barely hear anything the women said. The Wards were smart enough to whisper with music turned on loudly. Sometimes the stuff you see in movies *does* work.

Judy Ward was a broad woman but thinner now than the photos Jones saw at her home in Miami. And not in a healthy way. She looked stressed. She'd been on the run for over a week. Her cash roll was bound to be running low. The one thing going for her was her tan. Agent Jones was comparing it to the still photo of the arm that "iced" Balzano.

"Nice tan, Judy. Are you enjoying your vacation?"

"Not so much at the moment. I keep a pretty dark tan all year. I do live in Miami."

"Uh-huh."

"If I'm in some kind of trouble," Judy said, "I think I'd like to ask for my attorney."

"You'll get your fucking attorney when I'm ready. I've got questions you're going to answer first! How well do you know Joe Mulligan? When was the last time you had contact with him?"

Judy glared at her.

"I've got all day," said Jones.

Whelan was a bit troubled that his partner ignored the suspect's request for an attorney. Perhaps because he still believed they had the wrong person. *12 Pills is cunning—cool under pressure. This woman's distraught.* She'd been dealing with a lot and not handling it well. This wasn't the same person who less than forty-eight hours ago followed Whitfield and Kavanaugh from the golf course to the movie theatre, then managed to make her sixth kill.

Unless she's a master actress or has multiple personalities.

Agent Whelan decided to intrude before his partner made a statement that could get her badge suspended or worse. "Mrs. Ward. Let's both put our cards on the table. You know you're a suspect in the 12 Pills Killer case. You know we've been trying to find you for questioning. If you truly knew nothing about that, you wouldn't have tried to evade the agents watching your house by slipping through a basement window. I have to believe you would have used the front door. You're not a fifteen-year-old sneaking in after curfew. That stunt certainly makes you look guilty of *something.*"

He let that digest a moment. Judy stayed silent.

"We're trying to catch a killer. That's all we're running here. Anything else you've done or are hiding from, we don't care. That's between you and the local authorities."

He looked at Agent Jones. "But my partner here has you in her sights. And you're not helping me prove your innocence by avoiding us. We're on the clock. We have less than five days before we think the killer will strike again. Now, Agent Jones wants to arrest you and hold you for that entire time. Granted, it's not a bad idea. I mean, if you're guilty, then we shouldn't have any more killings this weekend. But if you're innocent, you're going to spend much of the last couple weeks of your mother's life sitting in a jail cell awaiting an arraignment instead of being there for her in her final days. I think you would never be able to live with yourself if she died alone when you had the opportunity to be with her."

Judy hung her head. "No. Of course not. This is insane." She looked up at the agents. "You're both insane."

Whelan took a seat opposite her. "No. But we're tired, and if you had come by on your own to answer our questions this week, we wouldn't have gotten to this point."

He took a deep breath and exhaled it slowly. "Let's start fresh. First, do you know anyone named Susan Jacobs?"

There was no reaction on her face. "No."

He slid a piece of paper to her with the names of the six who were killed. *So far.* "Do you know anyone on that list?"

Her eyes filled with moisture as she read. "These are the victims?"

"Yes."

"I knew Jackson Kenny and Sonja Cuevas. Sweet kids."

An attack of goosebumps ran from Jones' wrist to her shoulder. She was ready for a denial. "How? When did you see them last?"

"Not for over twenty years. I taught them."

"You expect me to believe you remember two kids from twenty years ago you taught as a *substitute teacher*? No way!"

"You've never taught children, have you, Agent Jones? I'm guessing you don't have any of your own, either. Well, I couldn't *have* my own. The children I taught were the closest I'd ever come. And I remember the good ones. Lots of them." She took a swig of water before continuing.

"One of the benefits of being a substitute was that you didn't get locked into one grade. I subbed for kids of all ages, in all grades— K through twelve. I wasn't too picky where they sent me. I needed the money back then. I kept track of Jackson Kenny until he graduated high school. He had a big heart. He was afraid to show it to his friends. It wasn't *cool*, being nice. I'm glad the world's changing now—waking up to the idea that bullying shouldn't be tolerated. When Jackson wasn't busy 'fitting in,' he was sweet and funny. An amazing student. I think his regular teachers didn't give him much of a chance. He performed for me. His grades improved when I was around. Most of my students' did."

She looked at Jones under squinched brows. "I was a *great* teacher Agent Jones." She couldn't hold off the tears any longer as memories flooded her. She looked at the list of names in front of her again, and the drops fell freely.

Whelan spoke up. "Mrs. Ward, what about Sonja Cuevas?"

"Sweet, shy girl. Not the best student, but she was always happy; enjoyed her friends. Always wore a smile. I had fewer classes with her. Her teacher didn't miss much time. And then she disappeared after about…a year?"

"She went back to Miami with her mother."

"Ahh…well, we suspected."

Agent Jones was calming down some. "What about those other names?"

Judy wiped her eyes and reread the list. "No. Didn't have any of the others, or at least they weren't memorable. I think I've seen Balzano on those awful commercials for their stores? I think I'd have remembered a blowhard like that if I'd taught him. Where did he attend?"

"St. Vincent's."

"Never taught at St. Vincent's. Public schools; a couple of charters. Why were these kids killed?"

"They aren't kids now," said Whelan. "And we don't know why yet. Mrs. Ward, what can you tell us about Joe Mulligan? Your mother claims he sells her dope."

"She did?" Judy seemed skeptical.

"I think she thought it would divert our attention from you."

"Oh… well, God bless her. She's always tried to protect me."

"What did you need protecting from?" asked Jones.

Judy reflected for a moment before speaking. "All the things kids need protecting from in this world. Are you arresting her for possession?"

"No," said Whelan. "We didn't find any. She must have smoked it all."

"If she didn't get any on Sunday, then she's in a lot of pain by now." Judy Ward was suddenly more concerned for her mother, locked away in another room somewhere. "She looked awful this morning. That must be why. Agents, I don't think she'll make it through the week. Please, can't she go home and rest? Die in her own bed?"

Jones hardened up again. "That depends on you. Joe Mulligan? He's been friends with your family going way back."

"Yes. We were friends in school. He was nice."

"Did you date him?" asked Whelan.

"We... decided it was best just to be friends. I think he liked me more than I liked him. I wasn't feeling any real attraction."

"Any idea where he might be hiding out?" asked Jones.

"No. I'm sorry. Well, his sister Geraldine might be hiding him. I think she still lives in the area. Look, I know he sells my mother pot, but honestly, I haven't seen him in years. I've been coming here a lot this past year, with her being sick, but I don't *live* here."

"No. You live in Miami. With Ferretti. Nice house, by the way."

"Thank you."

"So, what's the deal with you and Ferretti? Why's he so angry with you? He thinks you're having an affair. Why doesn't he buy that you are here to see your dying mother? Which reminds me, if that's the case, why didn't Evelyn know you were in town a week ago last Friday? Why did you tell her you were arriving on Tuesday? What were you doing last weekend in town that even your mother couldn't know about? Are you sure you didn't know Balzano from more than the TV?"

Judy Ward looked directly at the agents. "I'm sure I didn't know Tony Balzano. As for the rest of it... the *deal* with my husband is I'm leaving him. I told him that two weeks ago and then got the hell out of Miami. He's furious. I snuck into my mother's home through the basement window because I thought your people might have been *his*, looking for me. I embarrassed him, and I'm concerned about retaliation. You've seen his temper in person."

Whelan tilted his head. "It's been my experience that men like Ferretti don't get too upset or embarrassed over a divorce. Won't this be his fifth? That's what your mother said. She tried to sell us on that *embarrassed* crap too."

Judy looked back and forth between the agents before settling on Agent Whelan's face. "He's *angry*, agent, because I *have* been having an affair here in Kansas City. My mother didn't know I was in town early the week before last. I hadn't told her. I was enjoying some downtime from the stress of everything. And Uberto's *embarrassed* because I'm leaving him for a woman."

Chapter 26

Susan Jacobs' autopsy later that afternoon could not determine a cause of death. She was far too decomposed to obtain anything. The killer's mystery pills were problematic enough to trace in *fresh* bodies.

"I did find some dried blood under two of her nails," said the pathologist on the other end of the phone. "We ran a DNA and put it through the records. No match. But I can tell you it's from a male. We believe she scratched her murderer before he could get her to succumb."

"Thank You." Agent Whelan hung up the phone. He looked at Agent Jones. "Judy Ward's not our killer. You've been right all along. It's a man. They found a Y-chromosome under Susan's nails."

"So... Evelyn and Judy? Ferretti? That's simply been a domestic marriage issue this whole time?"

"Appears that way. Unless Judy really is in cahoots with Joe Mulligan—cooking the cocktail, and he delivers it." Whelan shook his head.

They released the Wards but asked Judy not to leave town without notification. All of the surveillance equipment on and in Evelyn's home was removed. They stationed an agent out front to keep an eye on the house until they located Mulligan and could rule them out as suspects entirely.

Agent Jones told the "watchdog" to make sure and position herself so she could see the basement's bedroom window.

"What about the back door?" she asked.

"We'll have to take our chances from there. I'm out of resources. I wanted to leave the exterior cameras in place, but SAC Kendrick wouldn't allow it. Grounds for a suit since they've been temporarily cleared as suspects."

"You know that basement has windows on *two* sides, right?"

"Yep. Do your best." She went to find Whelan.

He was giving Cannon charge over several agents at the office to read through all the papers brought back from Susan Jacobs' house.

"I still don't trust the Wards," Jones said to her partner. "Judy should have been thrilled we released them. Instead, she clammed up. Wouldn't give me her girlfriend's name and address, no more info on Mulligan, nothing about her plans to return to Miami. She stared at me like I was some sort of monster instead of someone sworn to protect and serve her civilian ass. Ingrate."

"If they're innocent, and it appears they are now, then...yeah, I'd look at us like we were monsters too. We've been one hell of an interruption in their lives. And Evelyn...she looks like she could go any day now."

An agent popped his head up from his monitor and interrupted, "We've got the approval to pull Susan Jacob's bank records."

Jones retreated to her office with Whelan, and they both jumped on their computers.

Online, her bank account covered the past two years. Nothing helpful presented itself. They grabbed their second warrant of the day and headed to the branch of one of the local banks, where they kept older records. At a small table in the basement, they began pouring through physical copies of canceled checks and bank statements, going back ten years.

After two hours, Agent Jones threw a set of papers on the table in disgust. "I've got several names now of people who could have been her mystery investor. More names. You know, I haven't even had a chance to follow up on the two new names from the license plate search—the ones that went to St. Vincent's. More names. Damn it, Thomas! When is this going to end?"

"We're getting there, Miranda. Susan's the key. Whoever killed *her* is the 12 Pills Killer. Has to be. It's the only way it adds up. Charlotte Presley didn't accidentally ingest wolfsbane from an adjacent property to a house Susan owned, twelve months before her childhood friend from '99 was poisoned with it by our killer. Either it was the missing tenant or the missing investor partner. One of those men is our guy. I'd say we're getting *real* close."

Agent Jones reached across the table toward Whelan. She touched the back of his hand. "Thank you, Thomas. You're right. We are getting somewhere. I wish we had more agents on all this. Kendrick's working on it, but bureaucrats and politicians dictate our funds. At the public's expense. *Figuratively* as well as literally."

She looked at the mess in front of her. "After this, let's grab some rest. If I've slept six hours the past two days, I'd be surprised."

"Except for two quick plane naps, I haven't slept at all. And I wouldn't call those naps restful."

They sorted and poked through papers and statements for another thirty minutes. Susan owned multiple LLCs. At least five they could track on sixteen rental properties. The paper trail was quite large.

"There's a lot of people living rent-free at the moment," commented Agent Jones.

"Leave that to the family to settle," said Whelan.

As they took the cover off the last box brought into them by the clerk, Jones thought this whole effort was simply going to result in more follow-up, more time. *More names equal more time. More time equals more murders.*

Five minutes into his final stack, Whelan exclaimed, "Holy shit!"

"What?"

"There's a payment here from Susan on one of the dissolved LLCs from five years ago. It's made out to Mark Whitfield! The memo line says, 'Traverse City.' Mark Whitfield is her mystery partner!"

"Holy. Freaking. Shit."

Chapter 27

Agent Jones tried to ring Mark Whitfield's cell phone all the way back to the office. Two agents were dispatched to his home to keep an eye out. The GPS signal was not transmitting on his phone. Mark was *not* keeping it on everywhere he went as promised.

She decided to try his home number for the third time in twenty minutes.

Whitfield's wife answered the phone. "He's not here. He went out for lunch today, and he's not back yet."

"Jane," said Miranda, glancing at her watch. It was 5:42 p.m. "I hate to even bring this up to you, but I need answers; fast. Do you know a Susan Jacobs?"

There was no answer on the other end of the line.

"Jane?"

"I'm here."

"Mark was receiving rental income from a woman named Susan Jacobs. What do you know about that?"

Again, there was no answer. Jones thought she might have heard sobbing on the other end, but she couldn't be sure. Then the call ended.

She stared at her phone in disbelief, unsure if she'd lost the connection or been hung up on. There was no answer when she tried again.

An affair? What the hell has Whitfield been doing?

She looked across her desk at Agent Whelan. "She hung up on me!"

Whelan shouted toward their open door. "Cannon!"

He appeared, looking tired from all his work on the case. His energy was waning.

"Cannon," started Whelan, then stopped himself. This guy had been doing backflips for two weeks. "Go home. Rest up. Be back here in the morning."

Assistant Special Agent Phil Cannon gave a mock salute and disappeared without any resistance.

Agent Jones looked at Whelan. "Softie."

"Yeah…well… Hey, what's that other eager beaver's name out there, the woman in her early forties who came late to the party?"

"Baker? She's not field-ready. Not for this case."

"Don't need her in the field. Baker!"

Assistant Special Agent Tamara Baker poked her head in. "Yes?"

"Get two more agents over to Mark Whitfield's house. Get them to go inside and sit with his wife. Tell her it's for her and the kids' protection. She's not to leave the house. The second they're in place, I want a phone call for confirmation. Two out front. Two inside. Got it?"

"Got it."

Jones and Whelan exchanged looks.

Whelan broke first. "I need a drink and some rest, in that order. If Whitfield shows up tonight, we can hold him 'til morning. Miranda?"

"What? I'm learning your faces. What is it?"

"Miranda, how many agents are on this case, who were on it when Whitfield started working it with you?"

"Most of them… twenty? Twenty-five?"

"If he's our killer… we may have a mole inside, still active with our case file."

She pondered that a moment. "I don't think anyone here would knowingly be in on these serial killings. Those murders wreak of a sociopath; one, not two."

"They wouldn't *knowingly* be helping a sociopath necessarily. They might think they're simply updating an old buddy who perhaps they still have loyalty to."

"You think?"

"Maybe. I don't know. I'm thinking out loud here. It's possible. Let's see how tonight plays out, but if he's brought in, I don't want anyone alone with him until we can get here."

"Of course."

"You said socio*path*, not paths," said Whelan. "Are you ruling out the Judy Ward and Joe Mulligan collaboration?"

"Not at all. They're the possible exception that proves the theory," she kidded.

"Well… Mark Whitfield has jumped to the head of my suspect list. Let's hope I'm wrong." He stood to leave.

Jones grabbed his arm a moment as he walked by. "You headed to Slappy's? I'll join you."

"Can't tonight. I'm supposed to meet my brother. In Raytown." He looked at his watch. "I'm already late."

"Then I'm crashing for the night. I'll see you here in the morning. Sleep tonight. That's an order."

"Oh, you're back in charge?"

She laughed on her way out the door. "Like I ever really gave it up!"

❄ ❄ ❄

12 PILLS

David Whelan, like Mark Whitfield, was a "forever member of the old boys' club." Unlike Whitfield, he'd let himself go. He was overweight, went through two marriages, and was working part-time at a home improvement store.

He answered Thomas' knock on the door of his Raytown apartment in his underwear. "Tommy. You're late." He left the door open and walked away.

Entering the one-bedroom unit, Thomas remembered that divorce could be financially devastating to some. Piles of unpaid bills were stacked on a table nearby, and empty soup cans lined the kitchen counter.

"You want a beer?" David asked.

"Sure."

They sat on opposite sides of a table in the dining area.

"I hear you joined the divorcées club," said David. He raised his bottle. "Welcome."

Thomas took a sip and stayed silent. What response was proper? *Am I being goaded?* His brother could often be an ass.

"Why are you here, Tommy?"

"Mark Whitfield is a suspect in the 12 Pills Killer case." He was tired and didn't have time to beat around the bush. Being delicate and hiding details at this point would needlessly delay the investigation.

His brother whistled. "You're working the 12 Pills Killer? Impressive Tommy. You must be a big shot."

"Not at all."

"Gosh, I haven't seen Mark in… ten years? Maybe longer?"

"That's okay. It's not recent news I'm after. Something happened when we were kids. The killer's targeting those from the metro area who were in school when we were; K through tenth grade—so far. *That's* why I'm on the team. We might know helpful information."

"Like what?"

"You tell me," said Thomas. "You remember anyone when we were kids who we might have wronged so terribly they'd want to reach out and kill us twenty, twenty-five years later?"

"Someone wants to kill me?" David seemed interested for the first time. "You here to warn me?"

Thomas looked at his brother. *Are you the killer?* It was possible. "I don't know David. Anyone could be on the list. And anyone could be the killer. That's our problem. We can't link all the victims to any one person."

"Why someone from our childhood? Maybe it's someone *now.* Maybe we all used the same divorce attorney. I know mine wants to kill *me.*" He glanced at the stack of bills burying his lawyer's third letter demanding payment.

Debating for a moment whether to explain how he knew it was not David's divorce attorney, Thomas' head sank. *This is a waste of time.* He looked around the apartment. It bordered on disgust. David couldn't be the killer. The profile called for someone much more meticulous, a neat freak.

He stood to leave. "It was good to see you, David. Thanks for the beer."

"You just *got* here. I know we're not real close Tommy, but can't you visit for a while. How's Connor?"

"He's well. David, we'll have to catch up another time. I'm on the clock, and I haven't slept in two days. I was hoping you might have some insight. You and Whitfield were close growing up. You guys liked to play a bit rough too. BB guns led to shotguns. That led to handguns… You guys ever threaten anyone who would want revenge?"

David cast his eyes on Thomas' gun, tucked into its holster at his waist. "You're one to talk. Look at you now."

"Yeah-yeah, I'm a real tough guy now. David, you're not helping."

"Well, sit and finish your beer and let me think a minute. Geesh."

David reached up and scratched his head. Thomas wasn't sure if he was trying to dig out a memory or a flea.

"We flirted with a lot of girls. That wasn't always welcomed. Is the killer a man or a woman?"

"We're not sure." He didn't want to share there was evidence now with a man's DNA.

"There was a girl in high school—she was a bit crazy. Used to follow Mark around all the time. Went out with me a few times too, but she had it bad for Mark. When he brushed her off after they had sex the first time, she sort of went all 'fatal attraction' on his ass."

"How?"

"Sent letters, emails, photos of herself naked…some of those she mailed to his girlfriend—anything that could draw his attention back to her and cause him problems."

"She went to Independence?"

"Yep." David felt like he was on to something. "When he went to college, he got rid of her. Then one day, she shows up in his dorm room bed, buck-naked with her ass in the air—after not a word for over two years!"

"What did Mark do?"

"He fucked her! What would you do?" David guffawed.

All Thomas could do was shake his head. "I think we're looking for someone who knew us all when we were in grade school, maybe up through early high school."

"I don't know, bro, that girl was pretty whacky. Got back into Mark's life for a couple years, convincing him she was sane. Then one day, she pulls a shotgun on him and accuses him of cheating on her."

"Was he?"

"Yeah. But to pull a shotgun! That's nuts, man. Women are crazy."

Thomas had enough. Women weren't crazy. Men were. "Sure."

He stood to leave once more. This was the complete waste of time he'd feared it would be. "David, I'll reach out to you in a few weeks. We'll catch up for real." He reached for the front door.

"Aren't you even going to look into that crazy bitch?"

"Fine," said Thomas. "What's her name?"

"Susan Jacobs."

Thomas looked at his brother a moment before continuing out the door. "Thanks, David. I'll look into it."

Thomas hopped in his driver's seat. The pieces were coming together. "I'm coming for you, Whitfield."

Chapter 28

The ten o'clock news ran an update on the 12 Pills Killer. Kavanaugh's name hadn't been released yet, but the fact that another murder occurred in the Kansas City area was mentioned. The details were kept hush, but residents throughout the entire metro area were to be on high alert and report any suspicious activity.

Like golfing and going to the movies.

12 Pills turned off the television and shut out the lights. Turning in earlier than usual, teeth were brushed, PJs were put on, and a final check of all the doors and windows was conducted before lying in bed. *Mustn't make it easy for the bad guys to get me.* The lamp on the nightstand was turned off.

Ten minutes later, another click illuminated the room again. Twenty-three minutes of pacing the home did little to relieve the restlessness. Boredom led to thoughts that led to cravings.

Tennis shoes were put on, with several layers of duct tape wrapped around them.

Tromping down the basement steps, an internal debate surged about whether or not to cook some more. Cooking brought joy and peace. Cooking partially satiated a hunger. Cooking was fun. *It puts the chickie in the pot.*

12 Pills yanked the light string and removed the dust cover from the pill press, looking at it for a minute unmoving, before returning the cover. *It's too late in the evening to start. I'll be tired soon. I have medicine ready. I don't need more now.*

Releasing a sigh, 12 Pills darkened the basement once again. As always, light from the top of the stairs spilled down the steps and highlighted the table at the bottom. The killer stopped and stared at the six remaining bottles, each with a numbered "name" scribbled in sharpie, titling it. Perfect circular cut-outs in a large sheet of cardboard swaddled the little orange canisters.

The names of the first six victims were printed next to their vacant slips: Jackson Kenny, Paul Duke, Tracy Stamford, Sonja Cuevas, Tony Balzano, Patrick Kavanaugh. 7 of 12 was picked up and stuffed inside the shirt pocket of the pajama top. The killer looked at the name beside the now-empty hole: *Frances Moffett.*

❧ ❧ ❧

Thomas Whelan made it through the door of his hotel room. He almost fell asleep before he could shower, but he didn't want to crawl into bed this filthy. On the drive, he'd called in a "Be On the Lookout" for Whitfield, who had yet to show up at his home.

Hot water beat on Thomas' neck, his first moment of relaxation in the past three days. *It's nice to be alone. No one else. Silence. Me and my thoughts. Me... and my shadow... walking down the list of suspects.* His mind sang the song for a minute. Until it didn't. *Shadowing... Is someone at the bureau shadowing us? Leaking info to Whitfield?*

Suddenly it occurred to Thomas that if Mark Whitfield *was* the killer and had been recently involved with Susan Jacobs, he could be orchestrating the whole operation from a rental home in the area. *For that matter, so could anyone else.* Was the killer *still* a tenant of Jacobs, here in Kansas City? *If so, he's living rent-free now too.*

Whelan fell into bed. The nightstand clock displayed 10:47.

He blinked. It read 8:04.

Oh shit! He'd slept over nine hours straight.

"Jones," he said into his phone, "I just woke up. I'm sorry. I'll be in ASAP."

"Don't worry about it. You weren't going to be any use to me in the condition you were in. Anything from your brother?"

"Not much. I'll fill you in at the office."

"I'm heading out. Mark Whitfield never came home last night," said Jones. "Meet me at his house. We filed for a warrant, but Jane's invited us in. She's worried and scared. I think she wants some answers herself at this point."

Jane Whitfield opened the door. She had a fresh pot of coffee ready and a roll of refrigerated cinnamon rolls, hot out of the oven. They were arranged on a tray of delicate china, with matching coffee cups. She even had little sugar cubes in their coordinated bowl. If not for the circumstances, you'd think Jane was hosting welcomed company. It was merely in her nature to put on "airs." One might think she'd attended a finishing school instead of obtaining her nursing degree at St. Louis University.

Whelan couldn't recall ever being served sugar cubes in his life. He picked one up with curiosity and rolled it across his fingers.

Agent Jones watched Jane, willing her to break and divulge every detail she knew about her husband. Jane gawked back, bewildered and possibly afraid. Her eyes were searching for answers, not hiding them.

"Jane," said agent Whelan, "what can you tell us about Mark's whereabouts this week?"

"He's been sleeping little. I wake to find him pacing the floor or the car gone. He says going for a drive helps tire him. At three o'clock in the morning." She looked like she'd burst into tears. Apparently, she didn't believe his stories.

"Walk me through it," said Whelan. "He comes back home Saturday, and...?"

"And I fixed dinner. Neither of us ate much. We sat there pushing peas around the plate, like we were five again. He had a couple of beers and stayed downstairs while I went to bed. I got up around three, and he was gone. The car was gone. I went back to bed. He was here for breakfast. This time we pushed eggs."

"We had surveillance on this house!" Whelan snapped at Jones. "I wasn't told he left!"

"Neither was I," said Jones. "I'll get names, and someone is going to get their shit reamed."

Poor Jane's eyes were wide—and red. "Sunday," she continued, "we stayed in all day. He watched golf on television. I tried to give him space. He doesn't like to talk much when he's in a sour mood. Quiet type."

"Mark?" said Jones. She hadn't meant to interrupt, but quiet was not a word she would use to describe him. Some people displayed two personalities; one for work and one for private life.

"When he's angry. He's often angry. Especially lately. You know, when we met, he was charming and handsome. Truly romanced me—flowers, candy, new golf clubs. I was dating someone else—not serious—but Mark didn't care. He still did everything he could to work himself into my life. It worked. I fell hard, and well, that was 2005. We had Matthew in 2008 and Jeremy in 2010. Everything was wonderful until..." she looked at the ceiling, "I'd guess about four years ago. He started distancing himself from us. Slowly at first. This year, he's rarely been present. Says he's working a lot." She looked at Agent Jones.

"Yes, we've stayed pretty busy. I know it's tough, living with an FBI agent. We're gone a lot and work odd hours. It can be exacting on children." She was trying to be compassionate.

"Well, at least twice," said Jane, "I caught him in a lie. Said he was working on a case, but when I called to relay some important information, they said he was supposed to be home with me. I was stupid enough to believe him when he said he was working undercover, and not everyone at the bureau stayed updated on his entire schedule. It made sense." She stopped talking.

"But?" Whelan encouraged her to continue.

"But, I'm a woman. With instincts. And mine said he was having an affair. I had no proof. Just…my gut."

"Jane," said Whelan. He tried to take her hand and pat it like Agent Jones usually did when digging for sensitive information. Jane whipped her hand away and took a sip of coffee.

Ouch.

"Jane, you previously stated you were with Mark on May thirtieth. Was that true?"

"Yes."

"I need you to look at these other dates and see if you can recall whether or not he was home." Whelan brought up a list of the victims' names and dates killed on his phone. He handed it to Jane.

She was a bit numb to it all. Seeing their names didn't do much to shake her. "I can't remember May twenty-third. He was with me on June sixth, June fourteenth he was out of town on a case. June twentieth… I'm not sure. Was that a Saturday?"

Whelan nodded.

"I think he was working all weekend. And of course, this last Saturday was Patrick. Poor Patrick. We have dinner with him and Betty all the time. Had. We were all close. I'm closer to Betty than I am my sister." Jane let a few tears fall. "And now her kids are fatherless! It's all so tragic."

"Jane," said Jones, "I wish I had time for you to process more of this, but the clock's running. Mark wasn't working a case on June fourteenth. He'd been let go as my partner, and he took a week off and went to Miami. He played golf and went boating with some friends."

For a minute, Jane's face was a host of different emotions, digesting Miranda's comments. She stood and walked into the kitchen.

Whelan tilted his head and raised his eyebrows at his partner, questioning whether or not they should follow her. Jones shook her head. In a couple of minutes, Jane returned with a bottle of cognac. She dispensed a sizeable portion into a fresh coffee cup and took a large sip.

She pushed the bottle toward the agents. "Help yourself."

Agent Jones spoke up, "We're good, thanks. What is it, Jane?"

"More lies." She looked at Agent Jones. They'd met a few times the past couple of years since she partnered with Mark. "You're extraordinarily beautiful."

The comment caught Jones off guard.

"I was always jealous of you," said Jane. "I half-believed he was sleeping with *you*."

"I can assure you," said Miranda, "he was not." She wanted to tell the woman in front of her how much her husband repulsed her, and the idea of having an affair with him disgusted her in multiple ways. But she remained courteous and silent.

Jane sighed. "No, I suppose not. He didn't tell me you were no longer partners. First I've heard that. And he went *golfing* in Miami? *Boating*?" She sighed again. "Bastard."

12 PILLS

She drank the rest of her cup and slammed it against its saucer. "Sunday night, he was downstairs all night, as far as I could tell. Sleeping to the TV in the recliner. Monday, he was on the phone a lot. We went to Betty's for a while. Talked about funeral arrangements for Patrick. Last night, he was out for a long time. Left around 11:00, and I don't think he came in until after 5:00 a.m. Ate breakfast with the kids. He left again around noon, and I haven't seen him since. Haven't heard a word from him either." She leaned back into her chair, absently gazing in Whelan's direction.

"Jane," he said. "Please take a look at those dates again."

She complied.

"Notice the locations each of the bodies was found—the cities."

Jane ran her eyes down the list a third time. "Sonja Cuevas, Miami Florida, *June fourteenth*. Oh my God. You think Mark is the 12 Pills Killer." She dropped Whelan's phone on the floor and fell back again into her seat. She was out cold.

Agent Jones was doing her best to muster more sympathy, but that well was drying up. "So, I'm guessing Jane here had no idea about any of this."

"Agreed," Whelan said. He reached out and jostled Jane's shoulder.

She woke in a flash. "What happened?"

"You fainted," said Jones.

"You think *Mark* is the 12 Pills Killer?" asked Jane. She was quite shaken still. "He'd never kill Patrick! They were best friends. For years. Since elementary school!"

Whelan didn't mention that, under the circumstances, something might have happened in elementary school which made Mark harbor ill feelings all these years until the right trigger went off and he snapped.

"Jane," he said, "was there anything you can think of that happened in Mark's life about a year ago, maybe twelve to fourteen months back, which would trigger him to go on a killing spree?"

"No!" she responded. "What do you mean a year ago? I thought these killings were all in the past six weeks? A *year* ago?"

Agent Jones stepped in, "These killings *are* from the past few weeks. We have reason to believe the killer has been planning this for a while, if not a lifetime. But around a year ago, we believe he set his plan in motion and started perfecting the poison that he would use for killing."

"Perfecting poison?" she was trying to keep up. "The pills? Poison pills? You're making him out to be a villain. You think Mark's making poison pills?" She steadied herself by clutching the arm of her chair, then reached for the cognac and took a sip straight from the bottle.

Jane half-mumbled as she ruminated. "He always enjoyed it when he spotted a dead rat in the attic from the poison he placed up there…it's possible."

She grabbed her stomach and turned another shade paler. "Have I been living all these years with a psychotic killer?"

It was too much.

Agent Whelan read her face. "Jane, we're not sure if he's the killer. We have to pursue every possible suspect, and right now, Mark's on that list. With your help, maybe we can clear him off the list."

"Okay."

"Do you know a Susan Jacobs?" he asked.

"Yes. Well, no, I don't *know* her. But I know *of* her. Mark dated her in college. I've come across a few envelopes from her to him over the years. He said they were casual friends now and not to worry about it. He never showed the letters to me, and I never asked to read them. I trusted what he told me. We haven't received any for a few months. That I know of. Why? Is he still sleeping with her? Is she the one he's having an affair with?"

"He has some investment properties with her. At least three we've uncovered now."

"Investment properties?"

"Rentals. She was sending him rent checks—those 'letters' you intercepted."

"Rent checks?" Jane was lost again. It was becoming more apparent to her that she didn't know her husband at all anymore. "He was making money with Susan Jacobs?"

"Yes."

"I never saw a dime of it. I had no idea."

Her mumbled rantings took over again. "I bet that's where he's at; Susan's. I'm sure he's still sleeping with her. Rolling around in twenty-dollar bills on an uncovered mattress…full of more twenty-dollar bills…used condoms all over the floor…."

She looked up at the agents. "You know the last time he made love to me, he wore a condom? Said it was for birth control even though I'm on the pill. Probably didn't want to give me his STDs!"

"We found Susan Jacobs dead in her home," Jones interrupted. "We believe she was murdered about three months ago and by the same man who we now call the 12 Pills Killer."

"So, he's not over there right now? He didn't slip out the past two nights to go fuck her?" Her thoughts were becoming more volatile. "Who's he fucking *now*?" she yelled at them.

Agent Jones moved to her and grabbed both of Jane's hands. "Jane, I'm going to have a counselor come and speak with you. It's important you don't wildly speculate without having more facts. I'm so sorry we had to burden you with all this, but if any of it triggers a memory or idea that can help us find Mark and get some answers, then it will have been worth it. In the meantime, get some rest. Put this out of your head as best you can, and for God's sake, if Mark calls you, let us know immediately. In fact, we'd like to put a listening device on your phone. The faster we get answers, the faster we can clear his name, and your life can get back to normal."

Jane looked at her like Miranda was crazy. "Back to normal?" She pulled her hands from Agent Jones'. "We're going to be redefining normal in this house. Starting with a divorce."

Agent Whelan stood to leave, pushing the end call button on his phone. "I've phoned in for new officers to relieve the agents out front."

Whelan and Jones looked at each other with the same conclusion. Several of the agents in the current surveillance team had to be on Whitfield's side. No reports were submitted of his leaving multiple times over the past three days and nights. Not one. There would be new hell to pay, but in the meantime, they needed a watch team they could trust.

"Local cops?" asked Jones.

"Yes, I requisitioned some. Made sure none of them ever heard the name, Mark Whitfield."

Jones moved her head in agreement. She turned to Jane. "If you recall anything that might help us clear your husband, call me."

"What if I recall something that makes his case looks worse?

"At this point, it can't look any worse."

Jones looked to her partner. "Come on. It's my turn to go push some peas around."

They took their leave. One agent out front who Jones trusted was put in charge until the local officers arrived to take over the watch.

On the drive back to the field office, Whelan received a call. Someone reported seeing a 12 Pills Killer victim through his neighbor's window.

Chapter 29

The body had a 7 of 12 bottle shoved in her mouth. She was lying on the floor of her kitchen. A glass was on the counter, about a quarter full of Kool-Aid. Testing that afternoon would reveal it contained the custom compound the killer created and used on his victims. It was the first time they collected such a pure sample that hadn't run its course through a body and mixed with blood and been filtered by kidneys.

Her name was Frances Moffett. The neighbor happened to be cutting the hedge between their homes and saw Frances on the floor. He called 911 and rang her bell to no avail. No one else was home. There was no husband, no children. She lived alone in a higher-end community in Lee's Summit, east of Longview Lake. The town was in the southeast quadrant of the greater Kansas City metro area—below Raytown and Independence.

She reminded Agent Jones of the singer, Rihanna. "Beautiful girl." She recovered Frances' drivers' license from her purse on the hall table. "Born July twenty-first, '92. She's on the younger end of our nine-year scale."

Whelan looked through squinted eyes at his partner. "Say that again."

Jones obliged. "She's on the younger end of our nine-year scale. Cuevas and Kavanaugh were nine years apart in age."

"You know, we've been focusing on '97 to '99 so much, what if those years happened to fall into a nine-year scale? I think our killer experienced what he believed were atrocities against him over a period of several years. It makes more sense. There wasn't necessarily one singular, inciting incident!"

Miranda's eyes grew. "Shit. I don't know if that's better or worse."

"It's better!" said Whelan.

"How?"

"We've been trying to connect the victims to each *other*, from some event. We've been limiting ourselves to a two-year window to find that event, which I don't think defines this case any longer. I think there's a nine-year window now, maybe more. Our killer could know these people from lots of places over many years. Let's say it *is* Mark? If we can tie *him* to each of them, there's no need to tie them all to each other."

"I'm glad that makes you happy," said Jones. "It scares the hell out of *me*. We should be at the point where we are narrowing in— not broadening—our parameters. *Nine* years? Shit..."

Whelan gazed at the dead woman in front of him. She wore a nose ring. One ear had two piercings; the other six. She was dressed in hip, well-tailored clothes. She looked like she belonged in Paris or Madrid. "Oh my God."

"What?" asked Jones.

"It's Franny. I knew her. She grew up in Independence. She was a freshman when I was a junior in high school. She was in theatre. I saw her in a play once. She was amazing—talented. Always well dressed—ahead of the curve. She was in my speech class."

"You waited 'til junior year to take speech?"

"Yes. I dreaded speaking in front of people back then. I've gained some confidence over the years. It's funny how the tables turn between high school and college. In high school, it's the jocks who get all the attention. Those with brains over brawn don't get their dues until the former football players get beer bellies and jobs managing fast food. Us nerds start looking a lot better then."

Jones smirked. "And you're not the least bit bitter."

"Not at all." He returned her grin for a moment before casting his eyes back on Frances. "She would have been six years behind Whitfield. I'm not getting it. If it's Mark, how did he know *her*?"

"Did she have an older sibling?" asked Jones.

"I'm not sure. I don't think so. We'll find out. He's taking revenge on younger siblings?"

"Well, that's sort of been our working theory for Charlotte Presley, and through her, Sonja Cuevas."

Whelan was out of ideas for the moment.

Forensics agent Joe Cusack spent a minute with the deceased, then looked up to agents Whelan and Jones. "I'm guessing she's been dead less than an hour. She's warm, and there's no lividity. Forty-five to sixty minutes."

"The neighbor must have seen her within minutes after she was dosed. Shame he didn't see anyone else near the house. I'm sure the killer is gone now." said Jones.

"Could have been gone much longer," said Whelan. "No one makes just one glass of Kool-Aid."

He opened the refrigerator. Indeed, a pitcher stood half full.

Agent Cusack inspected it. "Not *too* much longer. It looks like a hint of sugar's still on the bottom of the pitcher. That would have dissolved if made yesterday. I would say she used cold water and made it fresh this morning." He took his voice to a whisper. "Don't let anyone drink the Kool-Aid."

The body was bagged and sent for autopsy, and the Kool-Aid was sent to the lab. A team scoured the house, dusting for prints, looking for signs of a struggle—the usual. None would be detected, *as* usual, with this killer.

The home was cleared, and by late afternoon, Cannon headed back to the field office, leaving Whelan and Jones. Whelan spent the day combing through her laptop.

"What are the odds it's just a coincidence she recently bought a living room set from Balzano's?" he asked.

"Pretty high. I bought a dinette set from them last year. They're the big name in town. I bet at least a quarter of the population have bought furniture from one of their stores over the past two decades."

Whelan chuckled. "Yeah, I think our set when I was in high school came from them too. So… What now?"

"Well, the lab called," said Jones. "Confirmed that our Kool-Aid is indeed *the* Kool-Aid. They're breaking it down. Frances Moffett had a large amount in her. She was small. I think it hit her fast. I think the killer *wanted* her to go down fast—here—before she had a chance to go out for the day. She was a mortgage broker. Kept odd hours, sometimes nights and weekends. Our killer's been quite the voyeur. He's known everyone's schedules pretty damn well."

"Yes," said Whelan. "He's had a year to prepare… We need a bug unit here. He has ears on this house."

"I'll call it in. Right now, I've got Cannon organizing some teams. Susan Jacobs owned seven rental properties we know of in the K.C. area. The warrants I asked for should be in by now. I know it's getting late, but I want every rental home searched before we call it a day. Even the ones with tenants in them currently."

"Did you catch Jane's comment earlier about Mark? She said he was acting differently for the past four years, really distancing himself this year."

"Yes, I caught that. The timing's right. I think it has to be him."

"It's certainly possible." Whelan's face went blank. "Now, where do we find him? He knows we're on to him. How many do you think are helping him? At the bureau?"

"At least six by my count—maybe more. It's sad. They think they're helping an old buddy—being loyal. I doubt they're even aware they are impeding an active investigation to the degree they are. That ole boys' club is about to get a shakedown. While you guys are searching homes, I'm meeting with SAC Kendrick. My little peas are going to get pushed around like they don't know what hit them. We may have a whole new team by the time I'm done picking off the rotten ones.

Chapter 30

No one was answering the door at the last rental house assigned to Special Agent Thomas Whelan and his team of three. The first two on their list revealed nothing unusual, and it was now well into the evening. Windows were checked, along with the back door. There was no basement. It was tenant occupied from the looks, but no one was home. He picked the lock within twenty seconds. One of the assistant agents whistled their awe.

"Yeah, yeah," said Whelan. "It's a gift."

After an hour, the four agents ruled the house clean. On the way out, the tenant was pulling in the driveway. Agent Whelan let the others go for the evening and approached the renter's car alone. He proceeded to explain the FBI's presence.

"Criminal investigation?" asked the woman. She had two young children in the back seat, dressed in little league gear.

"Not to worry, though. We don't suspect this home has anything to do with the case now. You're free to go in." He handed her a card. "We left it as we found it, as much as we could. You're getting free rent as payment for the inconvenience," he joked.

"Free rent?"

"Uhmm… your landlord is part of the case. She's deceased."

"Susan? She's dead?" The woman began tearing up.

"I'm sorry. I didn't know you were close."

"Kids!" she yelled toward the car. They came running. "Get inside! Get your showers. I don't want to see any dirt on you at the dinner table."

They disappeared without any words. Whelan wished he'd had that kind of discipline with Connor when he was younger. He was afraid he'd spoiled him a bit much. It was rough, not seeing him often—even before the divorce. Who wants to play disciplinarian when you have quality time with your child three or four times a month, if you're lucky? He felt sorrier for his ex-wife staring at this presumed single mother of two.

Angst played havoc with the tenant's face.

"Did you have something you wanted to tell me?" Whelan asked.

"Susan and I weren't close. But she's done a lot for me this year, for those boys. I've been so busy lately. I haven't even talked to her in over four months. We had a falling out a few years back, and we've been tryin' to pick up the pieces."

"You hadn't realized your rent checks weren't being cashed lately?" he asked.

"I'm not paying any rent. Susan's letting me stay here while I get back on my feet. I've been through rehab and got my kids back eight months ago after a long fight with my ex-boyfriend. I've been sober for over a year now."

"Congratulations. So, if you'll pardon my directness, if you and Susan weren't close, why is she helping you out."

"Because our mother asked her to, and she's afraid she'll be cut out of the will down the road if she doesn't make all nice now."

"*Our* mother?"

"Yes. Susan's my sister. I thought you knew."

❀ ❀ ❀

Special Agent in Charge Alan Kendrick was in a sour mood. He'd been with the bureau for over thirty years, and never had he seen such a divide within the department before. By the time Agent Jones got done unwinding on him, he was equally upset.

"You know, I'm too tired to deal with it. I'm planning on retiring in four years." He wagged a finger at Agent Jones' face. "That's between us!"

"Got it," she said.

"I've been looking at you as a possible replacement."

"At thirty-eight? I don't think I've paid enough dues. Don't I need to be an Assistant SAC first?" she joked.

"You'll be forty-two then," he corrected. "May of 2024. I've decided to hold out that long. You're going to solve this case and a few more in the next couple of years. That'll give you eleven with the bureau, six with the local P.D., and four in the Navy. That's a strong resume—on top of your college degree. I'm planning to make you my ASAC in June 2022, when Hank retires. If he decides to hang it up early after all this heart nonsense, I'm going to try and move you into that role now. All this is hush-hush! There are a lot of us old dogs going to be leaving in the coming few years. Time for a new generation to sweep in and keep up with the tech—and rookies. It takes a lot of energy. You're ready. I can't guarantee *any* of this, of course, it has to be run up the ladder, but you'll have my endorsement."

Agent Jones was beaming inside. This was what she'd been busting her ass for.

"Thank you sir. I'm up for the challenge, and I appreciate your recommendation."

"You're welcome. You've earned it."

He turned, motioning her to take his chair at his desk while he sat in the adjacent chair. She tested the cushion, a bit pensive, then took in the view from behind the wheel. She smiled.

"Cute, but I wasn't trying to give you an early taste," he said. "I want you to pull up our agent list and tell me who you want off your case so I can start re-assigning."

"Oh!" Jones' ears reddened. Thankfully, her hair covered them this evening. "Yes." She began pulling up every agent she knew or suspected had been helping Whitfield by covering his whereabouts.

She spent the next two hours going through them one by one with Kendrick.

When finished, there would be eleven agents removed from the 12 Pills Killer case. Four would be terminated directly. Four others would be investigated while under suspension. Three could be transferred to new cases without any serious interruptions.

"So now what?" she asked. "How do I replace eleven agents? We're down to eighteen."

"We can start that in the morning. I can get four right away, and I've got three more here I can pull over who I trust. I'm working on more. It's a busy summer. Every office across the country seems short-handed, but the Director will also shift some folks our way soon. And when this case is over, you can go with me to Quantico, and we'll look at some rookies. I think you'll appreciate the loyalty and energy fresh recruits can bring."

"Thank you sir." Agent Jones' spirit was renewed with the support and encouragement of her superior.

"You're welcome. Now go. Figure out how to find this fucker so we can all get some sleep."

"Yes sir. Good night."

A few bites of yogurt and a hot shower were all Miranda needed before turning in. She thought of her partner, sure he must be in bed by now. She couldn't wait to share the news with him. They were going to make some immediate changes that would lead to finding Whitfield and wrapping up their case.

She was about to drift to sleep when she felt the other side of her mattress give with the weight of a body sliding up behind her. His hands were on her, rubbing her legs and then lower back. He grabbed her buttocks and tried to slide his finger between her thighs. She squeezed them tightly, her muscles blocking the intrusion any further.

"I'm tired, Derrick. I really need some sleep."

He kissed her behind her ear. "You got it, boss."

She liked the sound of that. In four years, she'd be the boss. Her hard work would pay off. She drifted into a dream state with random comments of "yes boss" floating in and out of her head. One of them had Whelan's voice attached.

※ ※ ※

"Can I offer you any more coffee?" asked Tammy Jacobs, Susan's sister.

She had invited Agent Whelan in to stay for dinner; boxed pasta with jarred sauce—always a convenient and inexpensive staple that can be on the table in ten minutes. The boys were allowed to watch a half-hour of television before bed.

"No, thank you, Ms. Jacobs. I won't sleep if I have any more."

"I can't believe she's dead." Tammy shuddered. "I figured we'd have time to make up—for real—for once. Have you called our mother?"

211

Whelan shook his head.

"Good. This will kill her. I want to be the one to break it to her. Susan was the favorite. The "pretty" one. The one who was supposed to go far and make a name for herself. I was the loser. I was supposed to already be dead by now."

"That's a bit harsh."

"Yeah? Well, the truth hurts," she commented. "Can we go to the front porch? I need a smoke. There's a couple of chairs."

"Sure," said Whelan. It was time to get the dirt.

Neither woman ever married. Tammy was two years younger. Both were raised by a mother who also never married.

Tammy turned on a mosquito zapper in the corner of the porch. Every few seconds, Whelan would hear a slight "buzz," followed by a "pop."

Once seated and Tammy was two puffs in, Whelan asked the fundamental question he'd stayed for. "What can you tell me about Mark Whitfield? I need to know everything—past and present."

"Ahh...Mark... he was special, that one."

"How so?" asked Whelan.

"In high school, Susan had it bad for him. I think he was smart enough to recognize her as trouble. She wasn't the respectable girl our mother thought. But, compared to me, she was a fuckin' saint, I guess."

"You started getting high in school?"

"High. Low. Far out..." Tammy giggled with unshared memories. "Mark dumped her. Then after school, she convinced him she was drug-free, and she took the money our grandfather left us and bought some houses. They were makin' money; Mark seemed impressed."

"Your grandfather didn't leave *you* any money?"

"He did. Smoked most of it, shot up the rest." She frowned with regret.

"So... Mark and her get back together..." he prodded.

"Yeah. I think it lasted a couple of years. He gave her some money to go halfsies on some rentals. At one point, she asked him to marry her. He put her off a while, then he bailed."

"But he kept in touch? Collected rent checks?"

"Sure. He wasn't stupid. It was easy money. I don't know how many she owns now. Owned." Tammy teared up a bit. "I think twenty-three—four? She told me when I moved in here. This was her crappiest place in the K.C. area. She said I could stay a while before paying rent. Our mother said she'd make it up to her in the will. They didn't think I'd ever get sober and get the boys back. She's doing it for those boys, but I'm grateful. I'm workin' hard. I should be able to support us and pay rent soon. Got two jobs. Not great, but I have time for the kids, and we're all home for dinner together every night. Even if it is at 9:30 sometimes." She looked at her watch. It was after ten now.

"So," said Whelan, "why did Mark end it with her? Why weren't they compatible?"

"Because Susan couldn't keep up that sweet 'normal' act forever. She *was* crazy. Not many saw it. You had to know her, more than casual-like."

"Your mother doesn't see it? Didn't?" he corrected himself.

"Nope. She was exactly like her. And no one wants to believe their own shit stinks."

"How was she crazy?"

Tammy reached for the right words, "Obsessive...and... insecure. That's a dangerous combination."

Whelan nodded. "In school, do you remember Mark ever acting odd in any way?"

"Odd? Like?"

"Like…dangerous, evil maybe. Ever see him killing small animals? Being 'normal' one minute and cruel the next? Anything you might reflect on now as sociopathic behavior?"

"Killing small animals and shit? No." She snickered a bit at the visual. "He was normal. If he ever got mean with *me*, it was 'cause he was defendin' Susan."

"He got mean with you?"

"Just yelling. Not physically. Susan had what I dished out comin', though. She was super aggressive back then. You practically had to hit her to get her to leave you alone some days."

"Did *Mark* ever hit her?"

"Not that I saw. But no one would have blamed him if he did."

Tammy Jacobs took a final drag and stomped on her cigarette butt. She looked directly at Agent Whelan. "Did Mark kill her?"

"We don't know yet. I'm sorry. He may or may not be involved, which is why I'm trying to get as much information as I can. At the moment, we can't find him."

"I see. Well, I'm sorry I don't know much about him in the *present* like you asked. After school, I sort of went my own way. Didn't follow the *'Susan Soap Opera'* any more. I turned that channel."

Whelan sighed. He handed Tammy a card. "If you think of anything else that might be relevant about Mark Whitfield, please give me a call."

"I will."

He made it to his car before turning back. "Tammy, what month were you born?"

"April. Is that important?"

"No. Thanks. Good night."

I'm making sure I don't have to set up a patrol car to protect you. He climbed in his car and drove to his hotel, no wiser than when he began the day.

Chapter 31

Agent Jones was already getting updates in the bullpen from everyone on the 12 Pills case when Whelan made it to the office. No one had any solid leads on Whitfield. It didn't appear he was holing up in any of Susan's rentals in the area. Kendrick called other field offices and coordinated agents in other cities to investigate her properties in Michigan, Nevada and Ohio.

"I thought we were cutting people. There are over forty in here," Whelan whispered into Jones' ear.

"We're about to. Kendrick and I decided to let go of eleven."

Whelan whistled.

It was made clear to all, Mark Whitfield was the number one suspect. Agent Jones watched the facial expressions of those she knew were helping Mark. *Fools.* Some were sacrificing their careers for him.

When everyone finished sharing their status, they were all told to sit tight. Eleven names were called and separated into three conference rooms. Twenty-seven of those who remained looked to each other with puzzled expressions.

The first group was let go by Kendrick personally. He gave them termination notices. No prosecution was planned, but he expressed that their negligence could be construed as criminal activity, and they were lucky. All four understood and left without question.

The four up for suspension and investigation didn't take it as lightly. Their loyalties and who they took their orders from fell in a "gray area." They defended their actions. Kendrick wound up firing one on the spot. The other three fell in line and agreed to suspension.

The final three, after hearing the screaming match from the previous group, all took their re-assignments without questions. They left the room with a clearer understanding of the hierarchy in this division office. Mandatory refresher courses on procedure, leadership and structure were ordered.

Agent Jones came back to the bullpen after twenty-eight minutes. That was all it took to alter the course of eleven lives. *If there are any Whitfield supporters left in the room, they must be getting a kick out of my "agenda" now.*

Kendrick followed her in and walked to the center of the room. "All right, everybody, listen up. You all know Agent Jones has more or less been "Acting ASAC" since Hank went into the hospital. That hasn't changed. She's on top of this case and will continue to take lead moving forward."

He looked at Jones and raised his hands like he was presenting a gift. "Agent."

"Okay," she started. "Here's the deal." She spelled it all out for them. She wanted full disclosure for those left on the case. "I don't want anyone leaving here and questioning anything that occurred. If you have questions or concerns, express them now. Or never again."

She paused. No one moved or spoke a syllable. "Okay. By the end of the day, we'll have new—*temporary*—partner assignments. Some of you may have discerned seven new faces here today. Please welcome these agents to the team. If you're paired with them, get them up to speed ASAP. When this case is over, we'll revisit everyone's partnerships, and those with a successful history will be put back together."

Everyone stayed mute. She looked at their faces, some younger, some older. New and experienced agents spread out around her with overt concern on their faces.

Agent Jones couldn't afford to worry about how this looked to them all. "I know some of you have notions in your head. This is a *good* thing, people. Stay positive and give this a chance. Please know that my top priority is finding the 12 Pills Killer and closing this case. I need that to be *your* top priority. Put away all petty notions and concerns. The thirty-four people in this room are the best chance we have at catching this bastard. I have complete confidence in your ability to handle this shakeup with professionalism and dignity. I promise you, when this is over, I'll listen to every concern and request you have. In the meantime, Agent Cannon will hand out your updated assignments following lunch. Dismissed."

A couple of agents came up to Jones and gave her kudos for shaking out some of the rotten seeds. Most disappeared into their computer screens.

By 5:00, everyone was on the same page. A sense of hope and revitalized energy was beginning to fill the air.

Agent Jones took a break from playing cheerleader and went to the office she temporarily shared with Whelan. A photo of Hank Monroe with his family adorned a bookshelf nearby. She stared into it, pondering his heart attack, the toll it took on him and his children. She didn't want to fill his shoes early because of that. It didn't seem fair somehow. She put her back against a wall and released a deep breath.

"Putting away your pom-poms?" asked Whelan.

"I have a new respect for ASAC Monroe. He made all his upbeat, motivational speeches seem effortless."

"They'll get easier," offered Whelan.

"They'll have to. Where are we at?"

"Frances Moffett had no siblings. Her mother never heard of Mark Whitfield. She's flying in from Florida tonight."

"Miami?" asked Jones.

"West Palm Beach."

"Okay. And?"

"And she didn't know Jackson Kenny or Paul Duke, so odds are, Franny didn't either. I mean, they were in *my* class, and we weren't hanging out with many freshmen when we were juniors. Kavanaugh had six years on her, so doubtful she knew *him*, but I haven't run her name by his parents yet. She wouldn't have known Sonja from elementary school. *She* went to Raytown, and Frances was in Independence, K through twelve. And Frances went to a small Baptist church in Independence when she was younger. So, no St. Vincent's connection. But she could have known Tony from her furniture buying."

"I don't think he made it to the sales floor much. No… you can say it. There's no evident connection to the others. Again."

"None of them."

"Okay. So I'm buying in more and more to your notion that this wasn't a singular event everyone attended that traumatized Mark."

She took a seat and put her legs up on the desk. She looked at her corkboard. She'd added Frances first thing that morning.

JACKSON KENNY

      b. January 3, 1987 – Independence Elementary

PAUL DUKE

      b. February 18, 1987 – Independence Elementary

TRACY STAMFORD

      b. March 12, 1987 – Lee's Summit Elementary

SONJA CUEVAS

b. April 6, 1992 – Raytown Elementary

TONY BALZANO

b. May 25, 1985 – St. Vincent's Elementary

PATRICK KAVANAUGH –

b. June 30, 1983 – Independence Elementary

FRANCES MOFFETT

b. July 21, 1992 – Independence Elementary

"You know," said Jones, "it occurs to me looking at this… What are the odds that Mark was wronged by *exactly* twelve people, each born in a different month? I mean, *really*? I think there's a larger picture developing here. There have to be a lot more people, and he's simply picked out twelve, each with a different birthday month, to fuck with us."

"My little bell rang in the back of my head when you said 'Mark was wronged,' instead of 'our killer.' I'm starting to think it might not be him."

"You're kidding! Why?" she snarled.

"I don't know. My gut instinct again, kicking in..."

"Well, your gut was right about Judy Ward. But Whitfield would have been one of those 'peers' you referred to. '*Instead of a teacher connection,*' you said. He's in the age range…." Jones stopped herself mid-thought.

"What?" asked Whelan.

"You were born in December?"

"Yes."

"What about David?"

"My brother? February. Your reaching now… Mark and David were four years older than the oldest victim. You think some fourteen to sixteen-year-old kid is going to be forever-traumatized by twelve-year-olds? And seven and nine-year-olds? The more I think about it, the less sense it makes."

"Well, why did *you* think Mark was the killer?"

"Because he owned that house in Traverse City with Jacobs. And if it wasn't her, that left *him*. Or whoever rented it a year ago, which we may never track down now."

"Well, if it's not him, why is he on the run?"

"He's only on the run in our imagination at the moment. Hell, he may simply be out screwing someone else behind Jane's back. He may be unaware we're even looking for him."

"I'm aware," said a voice from the doorway. "And I'm not out screwing anyone."

Whelan and Jones both cocked their necks in disbelief.

Standing not seven feet from them was Mark Whitfield.

Chapter 32

Agent Cannon was standing behind him. "The cat coughed this up on our doorstep."

He marched Whitfield in and sat him in an empty chair. He stood behind him, like some guard at Alcatraz on his first night watching over Al Capone.

Whitfield looked back and forth between Jones and Whelan. "I'm not the 12 Pills Killer. Here." He plucked a hair from his head and held it up to Cannon. It was a ceremonial gesture. A cheek swab would be performed shortly, yielding faster results.

Jones nodded to Cannon, and he left to retrieve a kit.

"Where've you been, Mark?"

"Not screwing around behind Jane's back!" he barked at Whelan.

"Hey," Thomas defended himself, "that was Jane's suggestion. Why did she think you were cheating on her?"

"That's not any of your damned business. I made one mistake. Once! A long time ago. And now she thinks I'm out whoring around every time I'm away overnight."

Whelan decided he had nothing to lose. "She knows about Miami."

"You told her that? You son-of-a-bitch. What gives you the right?"

Whelan tapped on his badge, clipped to his belt. "This. And a murder investigation where you've become the prime suspect."

"Well, in two hours, you're going to find my DNA doesn't match the sample collected from Susan's nails."

"How'd you know about that, Mark?" asked Jones. "Oh yes... you had some little birdies working for you. Well, we cleared out your little birdies today. You'll be getting no case updates from now on. You may even be charged for willfully interfering in an active investigation. I'm leaving that up to Kendrick. *I'm* biased against you."

She stood up, coming within inches of his face. "Two years we worked together, you sick fuck. So help me, God, if you're the 12 Pills Killer, I'm going to ask to pull the lever at your electrocution."

Mark laughed at her. She slapped him across his right cheek. He thought to retort or stand and deal her a physical blow, but he was smart enough to restrain himself.

Jones looked to Whelan. "I can't right now. Would you take him downstairs and make sure he's swabbed then locked up?"

"Yes *ma'am.*" He used the word for Whitfield's benefit. He knew it would piss him off.

Jones was alone. She marched circles around her desk for a minute, willing herself to calm down. She stopped and focused on Patrick Kavanaugh's name on the board. "Shit."

With Mark's surrender, she realized Whelan's gut was right. Whitfield wasn't their man.

❈ ❈ ❈

"Look, Tommy, you know I'm innocent. I've been set up!" said Mark.

"Who would want to do that?"

"I don't know!"

"Well, you'd better come up with somebody, 'cause right now, you're suspect number one."

"Look, I'm here! I'm cooperating. I didn't realize you guys *really* believed it was me until this morning. I called Jane, and she filled me in. Not on *all* of it, but that you think I'm 12 Pills," said Mark.

Whelan squinted his eyes. "You *knew* we had you on our suspect list."

"Yeah, but not...*really*! I haven't killed anybody! I figured you'd catch the guy and realize how silly it was for you to have wasted time on me. Tommy, Patrick was my closest friend...forever. I didn't kill him. I'd like the chance now to help solve this thing and put the bastard behind bars."

"Okay. Start by telling me who rented out the house you owned with Susan in Traverse City eighteen months ago."

"I have no idea. Susan never told me who rented *any*thing. I rarely spoke to her. I haven't seen her in years."

"Why hide that income from your wife?"

"Because... I don't know. It was *my* money, from before we met. It was my extra golf money...my *play* money."

"Your 'run down to Miami and boat with friends I don't tell my wife about' money?" asked Whelan.

"Yeah. Fine. So there might have been a little fling in Miami. Last time was the last time, though, I swear."

"Uh-huh. So, Susan Jacobs... '*Rarely*' ever spoke to her? When was the last you heard from her?"

"About a year ago. *She* ran those rentals. She sent me a check every once in a while, and I didn't question it. I figured she was pocketing more than her fair share, but I didn't care. Management expenses and all. We got them on a steal before the market took off. We've more than doubled our money on the value, and they're paid off now."

"I couldn't trace you as the owner on any deeds. How exactly *are* you a co-owner?"

"There's a farm we own in Nebraska, outside of Lincoln. It's owned by an LLC that Susan and I set up after our third purchase together. Marsan Properties. We used that as a tax shelter. It's a parent corp for another company that's a parent corp for our three rental properties. The rent is driven to the middle company, a property management company, with every possible expense deducted, then if there's profit, it's claimed under Marsan, which runs dairy at a loss."

Whelan thought he'd followed all of that. "You own a *dairy* farm? In Nebraska?"

"Yeah. Well, twenty-five percent of it. There are four of us now, each owning a quarter. Susan has other real estate investments with the other two partners. Everything's funneled to the cows. And they're not great producers. Truly. It's all legal. We take advantage of tax loopholes that are in place."

"No doubt. I'm going to need those other two partner names for…Marsan?"

"Susan's idea. Mark and Susan—Marsan. We started it before selling off half to the other guys about eight years ago. As I got busy with the bureau, I wanted less involvement. The market hadn't recovered yet, and I wanted to be less hands-on anyway."

"Mark," asked Whelan, "any chance these other two owners of Marsan might know who the tenant was in Traverse City?"

"Doubtful. I never knew *their* business; they didn't know mine. Susan kept all the books and ran the show. She knew about not commingling funds. Actually developed quite a head for business. I'm telling you, by the time the last penny was sent to the IRS for Marsan, it was all legit."

"Uh-huh. So you keep stressing." Whelan reflected on Gertrude Balzano. She'd sworn the same thing about their furniture stores. *I should have done some investing...*

"Okay, Mark." He handed him one of his cards. "Call me the moment you think of anything useful. You *can* help us solve this case, but you're going to be doing it from a holding cell. Not on the ground running."

"Thanks, Tommy. Thanks for not being a dick."

"Oh, I thought about it. If that slap upstairs had come from me, it would have been balled into a fist."

Chapter 33

Whelan and Jones' first beer went down like water at Slappy's. They'd taken seats at the bar. Whelan flagged the bartender down for another round.

"Keep them coming," he said. "And bring us two shots of tequila. Top-shelf."

"Tequila?" asked Jones. She digested that for a moment. The past thirty-six hours had been hell: another corpse—not even four full days since the previous, Mark's appearance and DNA offering—which indeed ruled him out—and eleven agents kicked off the team. It was the most significant shake-up at the division in over a decade.

"Sure," she agreed. "Make them doubles."

"Whelan," Jones revolved her stool toward him, "we may as well be on the first day of the case. We know nothing. Seven people are dead with five more to come, and we know nothing."

"Stop that. We know the killer rented the house outside Traverse City. We know who *isn't* the killer... Yeah, okay, we know nothing." He was too tired to give a pep talk.

Twenty minutes later, tension was fading as alcohol ran its course. Whelan turned toward the door when he heard a familiar voice.

"You guys must have had a rough day—you beat *me* here today!" It was Reggie Johnson.

Whelan smiled and extended his hand. The corner of his eye caught George Beckford looking through the window from the sidewalk. He turned and stared, making direct visual contact with the man. Beckford puckered his lips and kept walking up the street. Whelan let out a raucous laugh.

Reggie turned in time to see the back of Beckford's head bounce out of view. "Man, I don't know what you said to him, but every time I'm here, he peeps through the window to see if *you're* here. Creepy. He actually sat next to me a couple of nights ago and struck up a conversation like we were friends. Two minutes in, he made a racist comment—didn't even know he'd made it. To my *face!*"

"What did he say," asked Miranda.

Looking at *her* face, a little darker in tone than his own, Reggie shook his head. "Doesn't matter."

"Oh, I'm a big girl." She beamed at him.

He couldn't help but glance at her breasts. "Yes you are… We were talking about Steven Spielberg movies, and quickly he took it to like…how the country would be better off if the *Amistad* and all the other boats *like* her had sunk in the ocean. I mean, I know I'm not exactly Djimon Hounsou, but hello? Asshole…"

Whelan shoved a shot of tequila toward him. "Here. They make this wonderful stuff now, imported from magical far-away lands. Helps you to forget all about assholes."

Reggie chortled. He raised the glass in toast, then shot it back. "Oh, damn. That's nice! You're drinking the good stuff. You know that's not on happy hour, right?"

Whelan opened his mouth in an O shape. He turned to Miranda. "What do you say, partner? Taxpayers buying us the good stuff tonight?"

"Taxpayers aren't buying us *any* stuff tonight. We're off the clock."

Whelan motioned the bartender over. "Another round of beers, please."

For the remaining hour, the threesome cheered and joked their way through *Thai Chili Pot Stickers, Better Than Buffalo Hot Wings, Southern Fried Cod Sliders*, and ended by sharing a giant slice of *Caribbean Inspired Cheesecake with Guavaberry Rum Sauce*.

Miranda found Reggie attractive and funny. She dared to ask him the question that no one is supposed to ask someone, "How are you still single?" She'd missed the conversation three weeks back about his divorce.

"Ms. Miranda, if you're looking to rectify that, I'm all yours."

She realized she had set herself up for that. "If I were available... No, I was thinking of a friend of mine from the gym. I think you'd like her. She's cute and outgoing. I can pass her your card if you'd like."

Reggie's eyes twinkled. "After you, everyone else would fall short of my expectations."

"Flattery won't get you anywhere, but you can dish it out all you'd like," she smiled back. She didn't mean to flirt, but too much alcohol had flowed.

"Well, in that case, here's my card. But you keep it for yourself," he said. He handed her a card from his wallet. *Johnson Landscaping—Creating Dream Lawns and Gardens since 2001.*

She tucked it into the top of her blouse, sliding a corner into her bra. "Thank you. If I ever change my mind and decide my bush needs trimming, I'll know who to call."

Reggie's eyes grew as wide as they could, and his mouth fell open.

"Okay!" said Thomas. "You're cut off." He slid the beer in front of her out of reach.

"Could you call us a couple of Ubers, please?" he asked the bartender. "Reggie, you need one?"

His friend couldn't take his eyes off Miranda. "Uh-uh. You guys had quite a head start on me. I'm good."

"Enjoy the rest of your evening." Thomas paid the bill, threw down a considerable tip, then ushered Miranda to the sidewalk.

"Night," said Reggie. His mouth was still open as the door closed behind them.

❀ ❀ ❀

Agent Jones was on her fourth cup of coffee and fifth aspirin when she walked into the office the next morning. Whelan had beat her there for once.

"So…yeah…that happened. Remind me to drink a glass of water every other drink in the future, deal?" She rubbed at her temples.

"Deal. And, because I care, are there problems between you and Derrick?" He hoped his voice didn't show too much optimism.

Jones' pupils expanded as she narrowed her glare. "I was letting my hair down for an evening. Not my pants. Don't read anything into it."

"Yes ma'am!"

"No. Stop that. Not your *ma'am*… Don't make me out to be my mother yet."

Whelan acquiesced. "Never."

Agent Jones looked at her board. "So, where are we at?"

"We're following up on all the info Whitfield gave us—his companies—Susan's—trying to track down any connections to Traverse City. I've got calls in to the other two owners of Marsan.

It's a long shot, but I want to visit every rental in every state like we did here in K.C. the night before. I want them to look for any record which can be traced back to Marsan, and I want all the properties searched for monkshood. Our killer travels. Maybe he's living in one of her other properties still."

"I doubt it," said Jones.

Whelan sighed. "Yeah, me too. But… it *is* free rent now. Hard to pass up."

"Maybe, but I don't think he's that stupid. He's already cleaned up those ties. He killed Susan off before he started on his list of twelve. He's miles ahead of us."

Staring at Jones' board, Whelan stood and went through the names in his head. He looked at birthdates and cities.

"What?" asked his partner.

"Nothing. I don't know. There's something here. I can't jump the gap to make the connection yet, but something…is here."

She stood and leaned her shoulder into his while staring at the same list. "Do you think he knew I'd wind up bringing you in on this case?"

"I don't see how. Am I the only FBI agent in the country that attended Independence Elementary with the first two victims?"

"That's the best question you've asked all day. The answer is no. There are two others. One a year behind you, one a year ahead. But they didn't know Jackson Kenny like you did. Both of them remembered your little league career, however."

"My little league career? I wouldn't have even played if my mom hadn't forced me. I'd have rather been inside building models, but she used to rag at me, 'Get some exercise, get some fresh air,' so I did. I don't know how anyone would have remembered me. I was horrible."

"Yes, that's what they said." Miranda tried to stifle a snicker.

"Oh." Whelan's chin fell.

"Remember, I had three weeks on this before I brought you in. When interviewing Kenny's and Duke's families and friends, some of them remembered your friendship with Jackson. I knew you would be the closest agent to this."

"How'd you know *I* wasn't the killer? Hell, I'd be a more logical suspect than Whitfield."

"Well, before we knew of his involvement with Susan Jacobs, that might have been true. But I knew you were fresh off the Morrison case. I knew the killer had to have been planning this for a while, and I figured you didn't have time while you were involved with that to also be planning for this. I mean, I think you're amazing, but come on." She smiled at him.

"Yeah, that would have been some feat."

"Records also showed you were in Grand Cayman during the first three homicides as well, so... I felt pretty confident."

"Well, if *I* could have been a suspect, what about those other two agents? Who were they?"

"Doesn't matter. They were vetted and have solid alibis. Definitely not our guy."

Whelan looked at her. The creases in his forehead deepened with his raised eyebrows.

"Three weeks Whelan," she explained. "I wasn't sitting on my ass."

He looked back to the corkboard. *What am I not seeing? How do I make the leap?*

❁ ❁ ❁

Chapter 34

After lunch, a call came in. "Put it on forty-four!"

Whelan went to the bullpen and obliged. National news was repeating the story. The third video of Sonja Cuevas' body lying in her courtyard was playing on live television.

One of the new agents typed away at her desk, then raised her head. "It's on YouTube! Posted twenty minutes ago. Four million views and counting. It's got two ads! One's a damn cola company. This guy was smart enough to secure his advertisers before he released it. I'll guarantee you he's made over a million dollars in twenty minutes."

"Thank you...?"

"Nadine."

"Thank you, Nadine. Make a copy, then get a suppression ordered ASAP. He knew he'd have a short window. He's going to secure another mil before we can shut it off."

Whelan looked at Jones. "I don't understand. Why the middle of a Thursday?"

Jones took a guess. "It's summer. Nights and weekends, kids have plans, but right now, they're sitting there bored on a hot day with nothing to do. Perfect time to tune in and share."

Nadine spoke up again. "Three Twitter feeds I've found so far, blasting it to everyone. Pinterest has it. There's a Facebook page, Tumblr, Instagram...he's launched on at least ten other social media sites I've identified, all in the past hour. He's been pushing a five-second trailer, all with links to YouTube. He had over a million lined up waiting. Oh! It's growing exponentially. Over ten million views now!"

"Get it off there, now!" Whelan shouted at her.

"I have them on the line. I'm on hold."

Whelan marched to his office and slammed the door. *Some sick fuck is making millions on a poor girl's death! What is the world coming to?*

Agent Jones came in and shut the door behind her. "I know. It's disgusting. What's more disgusting is that we have to watch it now."

"Yeah…" Whelan plopped into his chair and pointed his browser toward YouTube.

They watched the video five times. It caught Janine Cook crying over her friend and looking terrified at the crowd around her. She scooped up little Lorena and disappeared from view. The screams from Victoria—Sonja's mother—were nonstop. Too much to take, by the third viewing, Thomas turned the volume off.

"I think I might be sick," he said.

Jones was standing behind him the whole time. She absently twirled her hand around his back.

Whelan felt her warmth and leaned into it before coming back into the moment. His face grew red. "Thanks," he excused her.

Miranda smirked at herself. Her head bobbed her curls as she plopped down for another viewing of the video.

Every person in the video was scrutinized. She watched it again. And again. On her twelfth time through it, she caught what she'd been missing. "Whelan!"

She pointed to a frozen image on the paused screen. "Who's that?"

An older woman neither of them had seen or spoken to before was standing between two other people, about ten feet back from the crowd. She looked horrified—terrified.

Jones let the clip resume for thirty seconds, then paused it again. "Look, she's going into that apartment. Didn't we speak to everyone who lived there? What the hell?"

"Maybe she was visiting?" Whelan looked at his partner, reading her thoughts. "You want to go back to Miami? For her?"

"She's scared."

"They're all scared. They're looking at a frightening scene involving a neighbor in the courtyard of their own home."

"She knows something."

"You got that from a one-second glimpse?"

"Yes."

Whelan stared at Jones for a few seconds. "Okay. Let's go. We've got nothing to lose, and no leads here at the moment. Let's stop by my hotel so I can pack an overnight."

"No, I've got it. If we weren't spread too thin before, we certainly are now. I'll get Mansilla to assign me an escort. I'll be fine. Follow up with the other field offices that are supposed to be looking at Susan's other rental properties. Jackson Kenny was killed in Nebraska. Push those teams to hurry. I need reports by the time I return tomorrow."

"You bet."

She stood to leave. Her partner looked apprehensive.

"What?" asked Jones.

"I had a call a few minutes ago from a hospice nurse. Evelyn Ward died this morning. Her funeral's tomorrow at 10:00."

"Wow, that's fast."

235

"Yeah, well, they've been on 'stand-by' for weeks. I figured I'd go. Pay my respects. After that, if you don't need me in Miami, I'd like to fly out to D.C. for one night. I've been putting off my mother, but she might be able to think of something that can help us. Her memory is tack sharp, and she used to shuttle Davie and Mark Whitfield and their other friends around all the time before they got their own cars. I'll be back first flight Saturday morning."

"She's in D.C.? Visiting your son?"

"Yes."

"I look forward to meeting him one day."

"That would be nice." Whelan's thoughts wandered. He was excited by Miranda one minute and accepting it would never happen the next. *Must never happen.* Not if they were going to stay an effective team.

"Have a safe flight," he said.

"You too. I'll see you Saturday."

She raced out the door. As she passed him, he caught a scent he hadn't noticed in a while. *Why does she always smell so amazing?*

"Put that out of your mind, buddy," he mumbled aloud to himself. "*Not* happening."

He sighed and sat down at his computer. The mystery woman Jones discovered was still frozen on his screen. She did look frightened. *I think she's scared because she realized she was caught on video.*

❄ ❄ ❄

By 8:00 a.m. the following morning, Jones was knocking on an apartment door in Miami. She held her credentials in hand.

A man, about twenty-three, opened the door. He recognized her. He spoke in Spanish. "What do you want. I answered all of your questions."

"I'm Supervisory Special Agent Miranda Jones," she re-introduced herself, matching his language and dialect. "You're Yosvani Malave?"

"Yes."

"I need to speak to her." Agent Jones held up her phone with a still image of the unidentified woman in the video.

Yosvani's eyes gave away his recognition. "I don't know her."

"Look, it's been a long week. We can do this here or downtown—your choice. But if you make me drag you downtown for interference in an active criminal investigation, I'll throw you in a cell for as long as the law allows me. I'm in that kind of mood."

"It will be worth it."

"No, it won't," said a feeble voice behind him. "Let her in."

"Grandma, no!" Yosvani turned to the woman. "What are you doing?"

"You're not going to jail for me. And I'm tired of being scared. My heart can't take it." She put her hand on her grandson, and he moved out of the doorway.

"You want some Cuban coffee? I have a fresh pot," she said to Agent Jones.

"Thank you. That would be lovely." She stepped inside and followed the woman back to the kitchen.

Yosvani was on her heels. They all took seats at a small table. The woman even set down a small plate with toast and some scrambled eggs in front of Agent Jones.

"Eat. Young people forget to eat. I'm Maria Herrera-Malave. My friends call me Frecita. Are you my friend?"

"I hope so." Agent Jones flashed her the photo on her phone. "*You* weren't being very friendly three weeks ago when we went door-to-door. Why did you hide? What did you see?"

Maria looked at her grandson. She slapped the top of his hand, resting on the table. "I told you, Vani! They found me from that video!"

Agent Jones turned to Yosvani. "Did *you* record that video?"

"I wish. Did you see he had over thirteen million views before they took it down? Instant millionaire man... lucky bastard. He set that up real sweet."

"Do you know him? Does he live here?"

"Yeah. Did. But lots of luck getting to him. His name's Mike Boliver. He lawyered up and left town a week ago. A few of us knew he had it. He was shopping the networks, but they weren't offering him enough. So he went to the internet. It's all about the net these days. Screw television."

"Do you know where he is now?" Jones asked.

"No. You think he's foolish enough to tell us that? No one knows. He'll never be back. I know he got top pay from those sponsors. Thirteen million views? I bet he made over three million in one hour."

"That doesn't sicken you on some level?" she asked.

"Sure it does. I should have had *my* video camera out. I wasn't even here that morning, or I'd be sitting sweet right now."

"I meant," Jones said, "doesn't it sicken you that a poor girl's death was broadcast to millions of people for entertainment value and profit."

"It's reality TV. Why should only the Kardashians make money for that shit?"

Maria Herrera-Malave stepped in. "He's young. He doesn't get it. You can't expect him to. He's a product of the generation before him. They forgot to instill morality in their children." She slapped him again, this time on the back of the head, as she took her cup to the sink.

"It sickens *me*, Agent Jones. It sickens me that I should have spoken up sooner, but I've been afraid."

"Why? What did you see?"

"I saw your killer."

Chapter 35

Whelan cinched his belt tighter to hold his suit pants up. He was supposed to be putting on weight, but he feared he was going in the wrong direction.

He could hear his mother in his head, "You're too skinny. You're not taking care of yourself." She'd be right. Well, he'd be getting her special kind of hell that few but a mother could give around 4:00 p.m. when she picked him up at Dulles International.

But first—a funeral. He wasn't sure if he should go but felt obligated somehow. He'd put Evelyn and Judy through the wringer this week, all for nothing. He wanted to apologize to Judy and deliver a nice floral arrangement for the service on behalf of the bureau. It was the least they could do.

Forty minutes of prayers and songs were read and played throughout the service, concluding with, *To Where You Are*. Everyone was in tears as the last notes echoed off the cathedral walls of St. Vincent's.

Evelyn packed a full house. It took Whelan another thirty minutes to make his way to Judy Ward to express condolences.

She was surprised to see him. "Agent Whelan! I didn't realize you were here. Thank you for coming."

"I wanted to say how sorry I am for your loss. I can't believe you put all this together on such short notice."

"Not so short. Everyone's been ready for days, waiting for the call. I have to fly back to Miami right after this. I haven't taken even a moment to process leaving my husband. It's time to deal with all of that."

"We asked you to check in with us if you travel."

"I did. I called the number given."

"Oh. Well, thank you, and again, my condolences. I'm sorry your mother spent her final days in so much pain and turmoil."

"She wasn't that disturbed by it, Agent. I think she garnered some pleasure and fun in tormenting you all a bit. She had her ornery side."

"Yes. I could see that," Whelan chuckled.

"And she wasn't in that much pain. I made sure of it."

"Oh?"

"Have a nice day Agent Whelan." Judy excused him and stuck out her hand to the person in line behind him.

Whelan took his cue and started walking back up the aisle. *What the hell did that mean?*

He looked up, admiring the stained glass high on the walls, lit up from behind. He caught a man staring at him from the balcony. The man's face seemed familiar. He raced through names in his head for a few seconds. *Shit! That's Joe Mulligan!*

Evelyn's marijuana dealer disappeared below the balcony's front wall.

Whelan's adrenaline level rose high. He bolted through the main doors and stopped in the lobby, staring at two staircases on either side of him. He took the left. At the top, a central door was open to the balcony seats. He flew through the doorway and directly into Joe Mulligan. Both men tumbled to the floor.

Joe recovered first and headed back down the steps to the bottom of the balcony. He looked to each side, but there was no way out. He turned around.

Whelan blockaded the doorway. "Joe Mulligan? There's a warrant out for your arrest. We met briefly at your home. I'm Agent Thomas Whelan with the FBI."

Mulligan was frantic. He looked over the ledge. It was about a fourteen-foot drop. A few parishioners were beginning to watch them from below.

Agent Whelan began a slow descent down the steps of the middle aisle. With five rows left, he raced toward Mulligan. Joe fled to the right and then started climbing back over seats, working his way up.

"Come on, Joe. Don't make this any harder on yourself," said Whelan. *Or me...*

Mulligan started to work his way back to the middle of the aisle, but Whelan beat him to his row before he could get there. They were a few feet apart.

"I can't do prison. I'll die first," said Mulligan. He climbed to an armrest and began walking on the upright seat cushions. Each step forced the seat to fall, his steps pushing on the front end of the cushions. He was down all of them in less than five seconds and back at the bottom of the balcony.

Joe was panicked. He glanced down again. There was quite an audience now, watching the spectacle above them.

"Joe..." Whelan took a couple of steps down.

Mulligan turned and flung himself over the balcony, holding on to the railing. His feet were now nine feet above the floor. He should have no problem landing from this height. He let go.

He misjudged the distance of a pew underneath him. He'd meant to land on the seat but caught his left leg on the backrest. He was split in two, a leg on each side. He screamed in agony.

Whelan's face appeared over the balcony after witnessing the unfortunate landing. His groin hurt in empathy as he watched Mulligan topple to the floor.

"Someone hold him!" Agent Whelan shouted to the crowd.

None of them moved. The scene before them was surreal.

It took forty seconds for Whelan to run back up the aisle, down the lobby staircase and back into the cathedral. Mulligan was gone.

"Which way?" he screamed at his audience.

One man pointed to a door at the head of the church, left of the altar and the choir grandstand. Whelan raced through the doorway. He threw open two doors to small chambers, but Mulligan wasn't there. A back door was open to the rear parking lot. Blinded by the sunlight, Whelan paused a moment. Three men were standing around the hearse. An elderly couple was getting into a car at the far end of the lot.

"Did you see a man come through here?" Whelan screamed at them. "Joe Mulligan!"

They shook their heads. *There's no way he made it out of this parking lot.* It was clear of anyone else. Whelan went back inside. Again, he poked his head into the two chambers. *Still empty.*

He came back into the sanctuary, ready to raise literal hell with the membership. As he opened his mouth, a moan was heard behind the choir. Whelan lifted a curtain around the side of the three-tiered bleachers. Joe Mulligan was on his side, doubled up in pain.

He looked at Agent Whelan while clutching between his thighs. "You know, I just came to pay my respects…hell of a day."

"Pay respects? Or deliver product orders? Thought you'd slip in and out with the crowd?"

Hell, he almost did! Whelan phoned in for backup, standing guard over Mulligan. He was winded and fighting a bit for air.

243

Judy Ward approached the pair. "Agent Whelan, thank you for making this service so memorable. Would you kindly take Mr. Mulligan and go?"

"I think he's leaving on a stretcher. Sorry for the racket. If you'd informed me your mother's pot dealer was hiding out in the gallery, we could have avoided this fiasco."

"I didn't know he was here!" Judy bent over and looked at Mulligan. "Thanks for coming, Joe. I'm sure you scored some brownie points in heaven with my mother."

Whelan and Mulligan looked at each other. Despite the circumstances, they both shared the same thought.

Brownie points indeed!

❀ ❀ ❀

Paramedics arrived, and thirty minutes later, Mulligan and Whelan were alone in a private room inside the emergency department at the nearest hospital. Agent Cannon showed up in Jones' absence.

"Mulligan," said Whelan, "you're in about as much trouble as it comes. If you cooperate, I'll ask the locals to go easy on you with your little farming career."

"What do you want?"

"For starters, some DNA. If you don't give it willingly, I can have a court order here in two hours, so you might as well cough it up."

"Okay, take it."

A nurse was called in. She drew a blood sample and handed it to the pathology field agent, waiting to take it to the lab.

"So what I can't figure out," Whelan said, "is how you know Jackson Kenny and Paul Duke."

"Who?" Mulligan's face was blank.

"And Patrick Kavanaugh and Frances Moffett," said Agent Cannon.

Both he and Whelan scrutinized Joe Mulligan, willing him to come clean on the spot.

His face registered nothing. "I don't know who any of those people are. Are they from St. Vincent's? They're not *my* clients. And don't ask me to give up my clients. I have a reputation to uphold, and since I'm headed to prison, I'd like to keep my odds of staying alive in there as high as I can. Stool pigeons get shanked."

"You've seen a lot of prison movies?" asked Agent Cannon.

"A few."

"Wonderful. They're not nearly as realistic at representing the actual, total shit-storm you're about to face. You'll be lucky to survive a week. Why, a small thing like you? Get used to stocking up on K-Y from the commissary, or you'll bleed for days from all the tearing. You'd better start cooperating, or we'll show no mercy at your trial." Phil Cannon's eyes were tiny slits of red, and he spit a bit with that last sentence.

Whelan looked at the agent, a protégé no more. He bit his lower lip, watching the show.

Three more minutes and Mulligan caved. "I'll write down my client list! But I don't know those people you asked about. Why are you so insistent I should? Who are they?"

"For starters, they're all dead," said Cannon.

Whelan weighed in, "They went the same way as Tony Balzano."

"Balzano was killed by the 12 Pills Killer!" snapped Mulligan before remembering he was accused of being the serial killer by this agent's partner a few days ago.

Whelan and Cannon stood silent while the full implication hit Joe Mulligan.

"You mean—you genuinely think *I'm* the 12 Pills Killer? Are you *crazy*?"

Mulligan looked a little crazy at the moment. "I haven't killed anybody! I'm not a killer!" He was pleading for their belief. "And I don't cook custom pharmaceuticals! Honestly, you've searched my place. Did you find a lab? No! If it can't be grown naturally with sunshine and God, I don't dabble in it."

Cannon cocked his head. "You'll be praying to see both of those soon." He left the room. Whelan was on his heels.

The two men stood in the hall, looking through the window of the door at Mulligan. He was pulling at his hair and pouring his face into his hands.

Whelan spoke first. "Well? What does your gut say?"

"No. I don't think he's our killer. Can't rule it out yet, though. Should we mention to him our theory that he partnered with Judy Ward?"

"I don't know. I don't think that's plausible now. *She* cooked, and *he* delivered? I mean… I'm not buying that myself anymore."

"Well, if Whitfield's innocent, and Judy's innocent…and Mulligan's innocent… we are out of named suspects."

"Exactly. I think our murderer's unknown and still at large."

"Then we have nothing to lose…" offered Agent Cannon.

"Okay, but ease up a bit. You've scared him. Now let's show him *we* can cooperate if he does. No more comments like, 'It won't just be the lips on your face that scar from all the puckering.' Agreed?"

"You got it. I'm still wound up a bit. Why don't you take the lead?"

Whelan smiled. "Yeah. I think it's time we showed some lenience.

The two men returned to the room. They brought Joe Mulligan a soda.

"I'd offer you a cigarette, but you know…hospital and all," said Whelan.

"I don't smoke."

Whelan's face expressed incredulity.

"*Cigarettes*," Mulligan amended. Of course, he smoked something else.

"Mr. Mulligan," Whelan began, "how well do you know Judy Ward? Was she a regular client?"

"No. Just her mom."

"But she bought Kush from you in the past couple of days to help ease Evelyn's pain. How did she get hold of you?"

"Evelyn called me."

"Evelyn wasn't in any condition to meet you, and the house was still being watched, which I'm sure they told you…so…technically, Judy's the one who bought it from you. We could go after her for that."

"The woman's mother died, and she's going through hell right now with her ex… you want to cause her *more* grief at this time? Why don't you cut her some slack? Haven't you guys put her through enough?"

Agents Whelan and Cannon exchanged looks.

Cannon spoke up. "You're much closer to that family than we realized. You've known Judy her whole life?"

"Pretty much." Mulligan realized he'd overspoken.

"You knew James, too, didn't you?" asked Whelan.

Mulligan nodded.

"Were you and Judy's brother close?"

"We knew each other in school."

"I don't know. You looked pretty chummy in the photo you keep in your living room," said Whelan.

"We were friends. What of it?" asked Joe.

"I'm trying to connect all the dots that led you and Judy to go on a killing spree together." Agent Whelan hadn't intended to put it out there like that, but there it was.

"What?" Mulligan screamed.

"You two partnered up on this. Why? For what reason?"

"Judy's not a killer! Do you think *she's* the 12 Pills Killer? No way!"

"I don't know. Maybe she cooked and you delivered? Evelyn said you were sweet on her once upon a time. Are you still harboring feelings? Unrequited?"

"No. That was a long time ago. Until this week, I hadn't even seen her in…at least ten years."

"So…ever since she married Uberto Ferretti?" said Whelan.

"Yeah. Pretty much."

"Well, she's leaving him now. Perfect time for you to step back into the picture."

"She's seeing someone," said Mulligan.

"Yeah, she told us. A woman. I wonder what pushed her that direction." Whelan was trying to push Mulligan.

"To each his own."

"Sure. I get it. Look, Joe… remember we told you we'd ask for the D.A. to go easy on you if you cooperated? I don't feel like you're cooperating."

Agent Cannon puckered his lips toward Mulligan. When Joe turned toward him, he blew them out with a kiss and a wink.

Whelan sighed. They weren't getting anywhere. If he *was* in cahoots with Judy, and together they were the 12 Pills Killer, now was the time to bring it out in the open. They needed to shake him. And hard.

"What's Judy's new girlfriend's name?"

"I don't know. She didn't tell me. I didn't ask."

Whelan found that impossible to believe. Wasn't he curious?

"So take me back to high school," said Agent Whelan. "You and James Ward were friends. You got on with Evelyn nicely. You had the hots for Judy…then James dies, and Judy rejects you. Say, how did James die anyway?"

Mulligan sat silent.

"That was in '91, right?" asked Cannon.

There was no response. Mulligan pretended to read his can of cola.

"Car wreck?" asked Whelan. "Was he driving drunk? Was Judy in the car with him? Were you?"

Mulligan's eyes began to tear up a bit. His buttons were being pushed all right.

"Was it a drug overdose? Did you play with stronger—what did you call them—pharmaceuticals—back then? Did James die because you injected him with more than he could handle?"

"No!" Mulligan raised his head.

"Leukemia?" pushed Cannon.

"Suicide?" pushed Whelan.

"Did you drive him to kill himself?" pushed Cannon.

"Did he hang himself? Carbon monoxide?" pushed Whelan.

"I'm sticking with overdose," pushed Cannon. "You helped him kill himself, and now you can't live with it! Look at you. You're a wreck!"

"What was it, Mulligan?" asked Whelan.

"Yeah, what was it, Mulligan!" demanded Cannon.

"What was it?"

"What was it?"

"What was it!"

"She didn't kill herself!" screamed Mulligan.

Both agents were wide-eyed and all ears.

Joe Mulligan wiped away at his cheeks. "James didn't kill himself," he corrected.

Whelan's eyebrows couldn't travel any higher on his head. "*That's*—not what you said."

"Have you ever seen photos of Judy prior to '91?" asked Mulligan.

"Holy shit…" mumbled Whelan.

Cannon wasn't quick enough. "What?"

Mulligan spelled it out for him. "Judy never had a twin brother. James never died. In 1991, James Ward went into the hospital, and five days later, Judy Ward came out."

"Holy shit…" echoed Agent Phil Cannon.

Whelan hopped up, pulling out his cell. He looked at young Cannon. "We've got to get over to the church! Judy was flying out immediately after the service!"

"Okay…but…?" he was still catching up.

12 PILLS

"Judy Ward has a Y-chromosome!"

Chapter 36

Five hours earlier in Miami, Agent Jones was still staring at Maria Herrera-Malave, who confessed to seeing the killer.

"Tell me what you saw," she prompted.

"It was about 4:30 in the morning—I get up early. Our air wasn't working that week, so I had the window open. I heard a noise."

"A noise? Like what?"

"It was a strangled sound. Like someone choking, perhaps? I'm not sure. And then it cut off. It was… odd. I looked out the window to see if the lamplight showed anything. Nothing at first, but then I spotted a figure in the shadows. He was in the bushes of the courtyard, against the wall. I think it was a man, but I can't be sure. The shoulders were broad. I think he was looking down, at the center of the sidewalk. He was watching something, but I couldn't see what, not from my view."

"What did he look like? Was he white? Black? Hispanic?"

"I don't know. He was a shadow. We're all black in the shadows."

"Tall? Short? Fat? Skinny?" Agent Jones persisted.

"Tall, maybe. Not fat. Let me finish."

"Oh! Yes, I'm sorry. Please."

"So, I figured he was a burglar. I kept watching. After a few minutes, he steps from the shadow, but he's bent over. All I see is a flash of orange coming from the darkness. And then he looked up. Right at me! Ay Dios mío! I jumped back quickly. He saw my face!

I shut the light out and hid the rest of the morning until the screaming started."

"Then you saw *his* face!" Agent Jones pounced.

"I did…and I couldn't tell you what it looked like now to save myself. My memory is a terrible blank. I was so scared he was going to come after me. I have tried for three weeks to recall any details of what I saw. I'm sorry, Agent Jones. It's all shadows in my mind now."

Jones hesitated a moment. She felt sorry for the old woman, living in such horrible fear the past few weeks. "Maria… Frecita… You had the overhead light on? In the ceiling?"

"Yes."

"Then, from the vantage point of the courtyard, looking up this direction, you were backlit—shadowed—yourself—from him."

"Eh?"

"I don't think he could see who you were. He saw *your* silhouette like you saw his. Except you saw more than a darkened head in that split second. I'd like to bring you in this afternoon for hypnosis therapy to help you remember."

"No! I don't want to remember."

"Frecita, that man has killed seven people now, with five more on the way. Please, I know you are frightened. I can get twenty-four-hour security for your apartment until we catch him and put him behind bars. But we may never find him without your help. Please, Frecita… five more people will die."

The woman chomped on her nails while she pondered the request.

"You don't have to do this, grandma," said Yosvani. He'd suddenly come back to life after hearing his grandmother's story for the second time in three weeks. "It's not your problem. Let *them* find this killer. Why should you risk your life?"

Her grandson's resolve to stay on the sidelines helped reaffirm Frecita's resolve to do the right thing. She slapped him for the third time in twenty minutes. This time across the face. "Because it's the right thing to do, Yosvani. Am I not teaching you to do the right thing? If I had gone to the police three weeks ago, three more lives would have been saved!"

"And you'd be dead!"

"No, Yosvani, I don't think so," said Agent Jones. "I believe the killer didn't recognize your grandmother, and anyway, it doesn't matter. We can't go back in time. We can do the right thing now, though, and stop five more!"

Grandmother and grandson looked at one another—afraid. Frecita grabbed his hand and wound her fingers through his.

He turned to Agent Jones. "Okay. What time do you want us?"

"Let me get it set up." Jones pulled out her phone. She patted the top of the two hands in front of her, still holding on to each other. "Thank you!"

She stepped out of the room to call Vicente and make the arrangements. She wanted to make sure the best sketch artist was available to be there as well, the moment Señora Herrera-Malave's memory could provide a description.

By 1:30, she was at the precinct, Grandmother and Grandson in tow. She wasn't about to let them out of her sight and give them downtime to rethink their decision.

Agent Jones' phone rang. Her partner was on the other end of the line.

"Miranda! Are you sitting down? Judy Ward is James Ward. She has your Y-chromosome! I'm on my way back to the church!"

"Whoa…slow down there, partner. Start from the beginning."

Whelan filled her in on his morning, ending with, "Judy Ward's your killer! You were right all along. She's been out-playing us this whole time!"

It devastated Agent Jones that she couldn't be in Kansas City to help make the bust. But if Whelan missed her and Judy caught her flight, she was supposed to be headed back to Miami. Either Judy was coming to get the last of her things from Ferretti, or she was coming to kill him. She wondered for a moment if he was born in August.

Chapter 37

Agent Whelan raced into St. Vincent's. It was largely empty, save a few people cleaning up and removing floral arrangements to be delivered either to the cemetery or back to Evelyn Ward's home. He left Cannon at the hospital to watch over Mulligan and hopefully attain more helpful information.

Whelan yelled out, "Judy Ward?"

Everyone froze in place, save one man who approached him. "She left over forty minutes ago."

"Where's the cemetery? Was she headed there?"

"I don't believe so. There's no graveside service planned. This was it." He went back to his flower collecting.

Whelan called in for someone to alert the airlines. Her flight was scheduled for 2:20. He gave strict orders to hold her and not to let her board. Looking at his watch, he wondered if it would be too late. It was 1:58. He was at least forty-five minutes from the airport. It was pointless for him to try and catch her personally.

His own flight was scheduled to leave in two hours, but he was going to have to disappoint his mother and son. His sole focus right now was to find Judy Ward. He aimed his car in the direction of Evelyn's home. What had they missed before in their search? *Is there a secret room hidden in that basement? Maybe a cellar in the backyard?* Various deductions entered then fled his mind every few seconds as he worked through his acceptance that Judy Ward was the 12 Pills Killer.

No one was at Evelyn's when he arrived. The surveillance team had been dismissed. Whelan wasn't sure if the search warrant was canceled or still valid, but under the circumstances, he felt confident the judge would see it his way. He picked the front door lock and stepped inside.

Flower arrangements crammed Evelyn's living room. Whelan tip-toed around some and made his way to the back of the home. More vases were covering the kitchen table, and three more easels displayed the largest floral sprays Whelan could recall seeing.

He took a seat at the table and admired some lilies in front of him. The tag was readable: *Love and Prayers, The Carsons.* He looked at another vase and flipped the card around so he could read it. *Heaven's Blessings Upon You and Your Family—Call if we can do anything, The Peters' Family.* For almost three minutes, Whelan went tag reading throughout the home. Perhaps a specific name would trigger a memory or take him in a new direction. Any connection that would lead to unraveling Judy Ward would help.

There were flowers sent on behalf of the church and some from Father Cassidy personally. The bulk of them were churchgoers or neighbors. None indicated anything to Thomas. He slid into a recliner in the front living room.

About to doze off, he heard the lock on the front door being turned. He stood and cocked his firearm, aiming it toward the door.

As it opened, he yelled out, "Don't move! FBI." He could see nothing but yellow roses, and then the vase they were in fell to the floor.

The woman behind them was frozen in terror.

He lowered his gun. "I'm sorry. I thought you were someone else. Please come in."

The woman didn't move. He approached her and kneeled, picking up roses. "I'm so sorry. It's been a crazy day. Let's see if we can find another vase for these."

"You're the officer who was chasing Joe at the church!" the woman managed to spit out.

"Yes. I'm Special Agent Thomas Whelan with the FBI. And you are?"

"Helen Gentry. I live down the street. I knew Evelyn for over forty years. I even have my own key." She began to cry. Her fear broke, and grief resumed. She fell into a chair in the front living room.

Whelan reached out and patted her arm. He retrieved the last of the flowers and went to the kitchen. Another vase was quickly emptied into the sink, and he stuffed the woman's roses inside. He returned them, placing them on the coffee table before Helen, after removing another vase so they would fit. "There, all better," he said.

Helen looked up and smiled thinly. "Thank you. What was all that about? At the church?"

Whelan hunted down a broom and dustpan and set about cleaning up the broken vase in the doorway. "Well, Joe Mulligan is a drug dealer, and I—" He cut himself off. "You knew that, didn't you?"

"I'm aware Evelyn needed some pain management in these past few months, yes."

Whelan wasn't sure what he should reveal. *But if she knows anything helpful...*

He had little to lose. "We believe that Judy Ward is caught up in some illicit activities. What can you tell me about her? You knew her as a child?"

"Yes," she said. Her demeanor was cautious.

"Look, I know about James," Whelan cut to the chase. "I'm trying to understand what trauma James might have gone through as a child. Something which would have affected him deeply enough to want to hurt others now. Were you close enough to know?"

"Trauma? No. He was loved by Evelyn very much. She doted on him constantly."

Whelan tread carefully. "Did someone hurt him? Where was his father? Laurence, was it?"

"Laurence was Evelyn's third husband. He passed two years ago. Before that was Wilfred, they divorced. He was a drunk, and after you get rid of the first one, the second one's easier."

"So…who was the first one? James' father?"

"I think his name was Charles. Evelyn did speak about him once. Otherwise, she always steered clear of that subject. They were divorced before she bought this home. He had a bit of money and kept up a generous child support until James graduated high school. Evelyn worked as an interior designer until about five years ago. Mostly window dressings."

"Did she? I didn't know that." Whelan realized he knew nothing about Evelyn Ward. "You never met Charles then? Was he Charles *Ward?* She kept his name when she got remarried?"

Helen pursed her lips. "No, yes and yes. I never met him. Evelyn kept his last name, for James' sake. She wanted him not to feel like he was being abandoned by her—by taking a new name. I think Charles had been out of the picture for about two or three years when Evelyn and I met. We met at church! And once we learned we lived eight houses from each other, why we became quite close. I've been in this home at least once a week since 1978."

"James graduated in '85?"

"Sounds right."

"So you knew him pretty well from…thirteen to eighteen? Then he went to college, graduated, and then became Judy, before setting out on a path as a teacher…."

"What are you asking me, agent?"

"Nothing…trying to get a timeline. You talk to Judy recently? This week?"

"I spoke to her briefly when I checked on Evelyn two days before she died."

"She happen to mention the name of this woman she's seeing now? The one she's leaving her husband for?"

"She's leaving Ferretti? For a woman?" Helen began to chuckle. "I had no idea."

"Why is that funny?"

"Well, I mean, she went through so much to *become* a woman. To wind up dating one now—well, that's not for my generation to understand. Any of it."

"Can you imagine the confusion she went through as a child? It had to have been hell."

"Well, God bless her now," said Helen.

Whelan studied her briefly. *God save her. Cause I'm taking her down.* "Did you ever observe anything when James was a teenager, which might have led you to believe he could commit harm against someone else? Outbursts? Fights? Surely Evelyn shared a story or two about a fight with her son. Every mother has fought with their children." *I sure had my share…*

"No, sorry. She loved that child to death. Not strict *enough,* in my opinion. I think she was making up for the father's absence."

"Maybe she was making up for the father's…mistreatment?" suggested Whelan.

"If she was, she never told me that directly. As I said, I think she mentioned him once in forty years."

"In what context? Do you recall?"

Helen leaned back and closed her eyes a moment. "I was over for dinner one Sunday. James wasn't here. He was at a friend's. We were watching *60 Minutes* on the television. They were showing a story, and out of nowhere, Evelyn said, 'I should have killed Charles when I had the chance.' I didn't think much about it. A lot of women would like to kill their husbands from time to time. I didn't believe she was serious. It was just a comment."

"You didn't ask her what she meant?" asked Whelan.

"I did. She said 'nothing.' She was venting, and then she apologized for having said anything. I told her I understood. There were times I felt like wringing John's neck—my husband. He's helping take flowers to the gravesite."

She looked around the room. "My goodness. She was popular. Look at all these. Judy's supposed to return the day after tomorrow. I hope they stay fresh. I'm going to turn the air down to help keep them up."

Helen stood and began working her way through the jungle toward the thermostat on the wall.

Whelan excused himself and headed down to the basement. He poked around for ten minutes, finding nothing new since the last time, a few short days ago. He surfaced and interrupted Helen in the kitchen, adding water to a new vase.

"Honestly, agent, you dumped out these beautiful lilies? Evelyn had extra vases under that cabinet. You could have asked." She shook her head and mumbled under her breath.

Whelan displaced his guilt with a flash of his teeth. "Helen, I'm headed out. It was nice to meet you."

"You too, agent."

"Oh, you didn't finish your account a minute ago. The *60 Minutes* story… do you remember what it was about?"

Helen shut her eyes again. When they popped open, she looked pleased with recovering her memory. "Domestic abuse."

❀ ❀ ❀

Chapter 38

Special Agent Miranda Jones was pacing up and down the hall in the Miami precinct. Señora Maria "Frecita" Herrera-Malave was under the care of the hypnotherapist for over an hour. When the door opened, Yosvani raced in and fell to his grandmother's knees. She was sitting on a sofa.

Looking pretty well-rested if you ask me, Miranda thought. *Maybe I should try that.* "Frecita, how did it go?"

"Fine agent. Thank you. I feel wonderful."

"Uh-huh, and?"

"And? Oh! No, I'm sorry. I didn't remember his face. It's all still a dark blur."

The therapist was putting an old-fashioned tape recorder into a duffle bag. "I think another session or two, and she might be able to recall some details. She did pretty well up until that moment. She's agreed to come back next week."

"Next week!" Agent Jones wheeled back to Señora Herrera-Malave. "Frecita, we're on the clock! I need a description today— yesterday! Can't you try again *now*? Maybe in an hour?"

"We got all we're going to get today," said the therapist. "We could try tomorrow, but she has plans."

"Cancel them!" Jones was beside herself. "I can't express the urgency of this matter any stronger. Frecita, please! You must try. Another life is on the line!"

"Well, I can do it before my hair appointment. 8:00 a.m.?"

"Yes! Thank you. I'll make sure you get here on time. And I've arranged for that twenty-four-hour protection I mentioned. They can drive you home now."

"I need to go to the store," said Frecita.

"Anywhere you need to go. You let them know. Yosvani can follow you the whole way."

When they were gone, Miranda fell onto the sofa. She looked up at the therapist. "Got an hour for me?"

He cackled and walked out the door.

I wasn't kidding…

Agent Jones glanced at her watch. It was after 3:00. Judy Ward's plane wasn't set to come in until 10:00 p.m. If she was even on it. She dialed her partner. "Where are we at?"

"They don't believe Judy Ward boarded the plane," he told her. "We can't verify the flight manifest yet. They're trying to reach the pilots now, but her ticket wasn't scanned. There's a layover in Atlanta. I've got local agents heading there to inspect the plane in person the moment it lands."

"Okay. The witness is a bust so far. We're trying again at 8:00 in the morning. I'm going to go secure a room for me again tonight, and then I'm having dinner with Vicente Mansilla."

"All right," said Whelan. "Call me the moment you have anything new."

"Yep. Ditto." Jones hung up the phone. Killing time waiting on your next planned step was one of the hardest things for her to handle.

She checked into her hotel again and decided to take a swim in the pool before dinner. A few laps helped her unwind some frustration, and by the time Vicente picked her up, she was showered and refreshed.

Mansilla listened to her update on the drive to the restaurant.

"So she's still in Kansas City?" he concluded.

"Looks that way. She's set to land any minute now in Atlanta if she did get on. I'm expecting a call the moment it's cleared. I don't suppose your team has come up with anything new? Nice that you guys let that last video surface, by the way."

"Yes. Not our grandest moment. That kid disappeared and, while we're pursuing it, our lawyers say it will be impossible to convict him of anything or retrieve any money. It would be nice if he would make a gesture and donate it to the families of the victims."

"I'd wager he's holding that out as a plea bargain in case they do come up with charges strong enough to stick. I'm glad he finally put it out, though. It led me to Maria Herrera-Malave, and I know she saw the killer's face. If she winds up identifying Judy Ward, our case is solved. Judy can't run forever."

"What if she saw someone else?"

"One step at a time."

The restaurant was at the top of a hotel, with a view of Key Biscayne in the distance. Everyone around them wore smiles, mostly couples out for a romantic evening. Quiet laughter escaped colored lips as cocktails flew. Jones and Mansilla were the odd pair, growing more tense as time passed. They ordered drinks and tried their best to small talk on the restaurant's rooftop patio until the call came in.

"Agent Jones," Miranda answered.

She was on the line for less than sixty seconds. "Judy wasn't on the plane in Atlanta." She dialed Agent Whelan and shared the confirmation.

"I figured," said Whelan. "We tracked down a rental car in her name. She paid cash, so it wasn't easy. We've got a BOLO issued, the airlines have been notified, including all the private ones, and I've got any credit card in her name flagged to alert us the moment she swipes it. We've stopped wasting resources chasing hotels. I'm sure she's staying at this woman's home she's having an affair with, but damned if we have a clue who that is."

"I wondered why she refused to tell us the other night," said Jones. "If she was innocent, she'd have told us."

"Maybe. Or, maybe," Thomas said, always the devil's advocate, "it was because she knew she was off the hook, and why bother mixing up someone else in this crazy mess? Especially someone you love?"

He was quick to reject his own theory. "But I don't think she's innocent. I think it's her. And we *had* her. Twice! She's manipulated every move we've made since."

Agent Jones' neurons started firing. She looked at Mansilla, who was listening in, of course. "Whelan, what if there *is* no other woman?"

"Huh?"

"If she knew we were getting close to catching her as the 12 Pills Killer, she might have played us there too. I mean, who would have made up *that*? Right? We bought everything she sold us."

Whelan pondered the possibility. "I don't know. She sounded pretty convincing. I believed what she was telling us. Or, at least, I believe *she* believed it."

"If she *is* a sociopath, a part of her *might* believe it. Or she's a skilled liar. Or hell, maybe she's telling the truth. I'm saying we can't trust anything she told us to be real."

"Agreed. I spoke with a neighbor of Evelyn Ward today. I think Judy's father abused her as a child—when she was still James. She's falling into profile the more we learn."

"Yes, that fits."

"Now, how the hell do I find her?"

"Keep doing what you're doing. The one thing you haven't done is set up roadblocks on the highway, and I don't think we'll ever get clearance for that. Besides, if she did hit the road, she's had hours on us, so it's a moot point. I'll be back tomorrow afternoon. This witness had better get her clicker working."

"Good luck."

"You too," Agent Jones hung up from her partner.

Mansilla was staring intently at her.

"What?" she asked.

His gaze shifted to the open sky. "I'm feeling helpless. I don't like it. I'm vested emotionally on this one and can't do a damned thing to help."

"I understand completely. I've walked in those shoes." Jones looked down at her own feet. "But never wrapped in duct tape."

Chapter 39

Saturday morning, 12 Pills began the ritualistic cook. It brought joy and comfort, reliving memories of helping mom in the kitchen. *Make enough on Saturday so Sunday you can rest and appreciate leftovers.*

The schedule had already been bumped up out of boredom earlier in the week. 8 of 12 would be delivered today.

I'll prepare the next two batches as well.

The happiness of watching a malevolent bastard get their recompense was too intoxicating to wait a week between any longer. The thrill didn't continue another six days as it did in the beginning. Now it was lucky to last three.

A triple batch had never been mixed. A miscalculation in the volume of liquid per expandable air in a hot burner caused an overflow.

Stupid! Stupid! Stupid! We mustn't waste!

Releasing a sigh, 12 Pills scrapped the entire batch and started the cook over. By noon, there were a dozen little blue pills divided into three baggies. 8, 9 and 10 of 12 were ready to go.

That should get me through the week. Let's see how it unfolds.

Clean-up brought nearly as much satisfaction and pleasure as the cook.

Clean that mess! Do you think God's house is dirty?

8 of 12 was extracted out of its cardboard home. The executioner stood over the remaining bottles pondering, then grabbed 9 of 12 as well.

Just in case.

12 Pills closed the door at the top of the basement, casting darkness on the staircase and the names adjacent to the empty holes on the board. Alongside 8 of 12 was *Mark Whitfield.*

❦ ❦ ❦

"What do you mean, you released him!" Agent Whelan was yelling at Special Agent in Charge Kendrick. Mark Whitfield had been sent home.

"He hasn't broken any laws. He's been dismissed from the bureau. He wasn't on house arrest when he left home unreported earlier this week. Frankly, the agents who were surveilling him are in more trouble than he is."

"But…" Whelan stopped himself. He plopped in a chair across from Kendrick.

"But?"

"Given his closeness to Kavanaugh, I suppose I was hoping he might have insight still to share with us. Hell, I don't know what I'm thinking."

"I do," said Kendrick. "You want him punished for being an asshole. Well, he has been. He went against direct orders to stay put and in touch, and he's lost a career he's been developing for the past fifteen years because of his actions. His best friend is dead. His marriage is over. He's been punished."

Whelan looked at Kendrick and accepted the truth of it. He nodded in agreement.

"He said he would stay in town for a while," said Kendrick. "If you think he might have insight on a specific lead, call him. He's agreed to be as cooperative as he can. He can't impede our investigation any longer."

Whelan kept nodding.

Kendrick stood and came around and put his hand on the shoulder of the young agent. "Let it go, Whelan. You've got a killer to catch."

"Yes sir." He stood to leave, shaking Kendrick's hand.

Before Whelan made it to the door, Kendrick said, "Oh and Whelan—catch her soon, would you? I'm getting tired of Channel-44, calling me every day for an update." He winked at Agent Whelan.

"Yes sir!" Whelan was happy to leave the weight of Mark Whitfield behind.

❀ ❀ ❀

"Jane!" yelled Mark. "I can't find my clubs!" He was buried three feet deep in his hall closet.

"Sold them yesterday on Craigslist. They went fast!"

Mark poked his head out and stared at his wife. She was idly flipping through the pages of her latest magazine subscription. "Tell me your joking."

"Relax, I got an incredible price. Two hundred dollars!"

"I paid twenty-six hundred!"

"Oh…" Jane pointed her head back toward her lap. "Well, he seemed like a nice man. It must have been his lucky day. Good for him."

Mark stomped toward his wife then stood over her. "If you really want a divorce, and we have to wind up selling off everything in this house, I'd think you'd want top dollar. You could have had fifty percent of at least a thousand dollars. Now you get a hundred. Tell me, does that make you happy?"

She paused and looked up. "Yes. For those clubs? Absolutely." She stood up to answer the doorbell. "But, I promise to be more sensible moving forward."

She'd ordered pizza delivery for lunch. The delivery man dropped off four pizza boxes, then made two more trips to the car to retrieve salad, rolls, wings and bottles of soda. After giving the driver a generous tip, she yelled for the kids to come down and eat. They had friends over for the Fourth of July. The afternoon would be full of video games, the evening full of fireworks. Six boys came storming down the staircase.

"Please tell me we're not eating my golf clubs on one meal from Rosanni's Pizzeria," Mark commented.

"Only your drivers and putters. The irons are buying burgers for dinner."

When the boys' paper plates were full of food, they dispersed back to their respective areas of the house.

"How much do you think I should ask for that golf cart you *had* to have? You've used it twice; because we don't live close enough to a course for you to drive it there! What did you pay for that? Seven thousand?"

Mark sat down in an overstuffed lounger. Luckily, his pizza was keeping his mouth full, or it would be relaying comments he'd regret later. He finished his two slices and went back to start on another pizza. He yelled at Jane from the kitchen. "This two-liter come with the pizza? Did you order lemon-lime? What happened to our usual?"

"I ordered the usual!" she screamed back. "They brought what they brought. Drink it, don't drink it, I don't give a rat fuck!" She marched into the kitchen to pour herself some and get another slice.

After filling a glass over ice, she held it up to the kitchen window and looked at it. "Strange. This looks like Sweet-Light. Remember that diet powder I tried a few years back? They came in those little individual tubes. Supposed to be full of acai or some crap."

She raised the glass to her lips. Before she could take a sip, Mark slapped it out of her hand. It crashed to the floor, shattering. Light blue soda went racing along the grout lines in the tile.

"Mark! What the hell?" Jane was livid. She knew he was pissed because she sold his clubs, but her hand was in pain from being hit.

"Don't drink that!" he yelled. "Don't drink any of it! It may be poisoned!"

Jane was in disbelief. "Poisoned? Really?"

"Yes! Really! I may be on the 12 Pills Killer's hit list!"

"What?" She was having trouble digesting his words. "I thought they thought *you* were the 12 Pills Killer! They cleared you of that, and now you think you might be a *target*? Really Mark…that's not even a topic you should be joking about now."

Mark took both of Jane's shoulders in his hands. He looked deep into her eyes. "Jane, I love you. And I give you my word right now that I'm not joking. I'm as serious as I've ever been."

Jane tilted her head. She looked at the soda bottle on the counter. You couldn't see the color of the liquid through the green plastic. Her eyes wandered over to the half-eaten boxes of pizza and other items strung along the counter. Then they drifted up to the ceiling. "Oh my God."

She sped to the staircase, Mark fast on her heels. "Boys! Boys, stop eating! No one eat anything! Don't drink anything!"

Jane threw open her oldest son's door. He and three boys were playing video games. "Stop eating! The food may be poisoned! Did any of you drink anything? Any soda!"

They all looked at her like she was crazy. She was at the moment.

"No," they grumbled.

Her son asked, "What's this all about? What do you mean, poisoned?"

"I mean poisoned like the rotten apple in *Snow White!* I mean dead in an hour poisoned like you'd better say your fucking prayers dead!" She was hysterical.

Mark had shared the same, more downplayed conversation with their younger son and his friend in the other bedroom. He came back in and put his arms around Jane from behind. She turned around and began sobbing into his shirt.

"Boys," he said, as calm as he could be. "Don't eat or drink anything else that came from the pizza place today. Did any of you have any soda?"

The group sobered up quickly. "No!" they all cried out.

"I think we're all fine. To be safe, I want everyone to get to the car. We're all going to the hospital to get a quick check-up, then you can come back and play games."

No one moved. Even to ten-year-olds, the conversation was surreal.

"Everyone to the car, now!" Mark raised his voice.

The boys all ran downstairs.

Mark pushed Jane's face off his chest far enough to look at her. "I think we're all okay. Let's go make sure."

He took her hand and led her downstairs. They all piled in her SUV and headed off to the hospital. On the way, Mark called Agent Thomas Whelan and filled him in. "I didn't lock the door," he concluded. "Please go in and take care of it."

He hung up and looked at the group of scared little boys in the rearview. Tears fell from his eyes at the realization they were about to put six young children and his wife through the horrible pain of having their stomachs pumped. It was going to be one shitty holiday.

❀ ❀ ❀

Chapter 40

Agent Whelan stared at the soda on the floor of Mark Whitfield's kitchen. He was on the phone with his partner. "Cusack's taking samples of everything to be sent to the lab. We suspect the soda's been tampered with. Pizza place swears they put regular cola in the car. The delivery guy says he just grabbed what they loaded. All we can come up with is that Judy swapped it out of the guy's hatch right here in front of Whitfield's."

Jones considered how that was achieved. "She's still got a listening device on his home."

"Yes," Whelan agreed. "Only way. She must have been ready and given a forty-five-minute notice for an opportunity, which she acted upon. I've got agents knocking on neighbors' homes right now to see if anyone saw her make the soda swap."

"Double check with the pizza employees. If she swapped it at the restaurant somehow, maybe someone saw her."

"Agreed. Miranda...?"

"Yes?"

"Today was sloppy...and desperate. This upped the game. She was prepared to take out an entire family to get Mark. That breaks the M.O."

"She already did that earlier this week by having only four days between murders."

"We're running out of time. We can no longer rely on what we thought were the established rules of the game. She's cheating."

Agent Jones sighed. "I know."

"How's it going in Miami?"

"Ugh."

"That promising?"

"Our time this morning was a bust. The witness is coming back on Monday to try. The shrink thinks she should have a breakthrough soon. *He* says she's doing great. But the one thing I need her to remember isn't happening. I don't know what *great* means to him. Today the old woman remembered a recipe for mango salsa over baked snapper. Great… I mean, really, out-fucking-*standing*."

Whelan had to laugh.

"So, I'm scheduled to land around four."

"Need a lift?"

"No, my car's there. I hope. I didn't plan on two nights originally. Hey, catch Ward before I get home, would you?"

"You sound like Kendrick. He said the same thing."

"Yes, well, he *is* training me for advancement." It was Jones' turn to laugh. "It's called 'delegating.'"

"Uh-huh," said Whelan. "I'll make sure to have the whole case wrapped up for both of you by 5:00 p.m."

"Awesome. See you soon." Jones hung up the phone.

Whelan looked back down at the grout in Whitfield's kitchen. The forensics unit had cleared all the food and soda. For the first time in three weeks, Whelan felt sorry for Mark Whitfield. He was a crappy agent and husband, but did he deserve this? *Was he that bad as a child?*

He was trying to figure out why Judy Ward would want to take revenge on twelve former students. Had twelve—or more—kids done something traumatic to her? What could it have been?

Picking up a broom from the hall closet, Whelan swept up the broken glass on the floor, then proceeded to mop up the spill. He poured a bit of bleach on the tile. When cleaned, he continued to do the same with the countertop.

This small gesture helped with any guilt he might have felt at having put Whitfield through total hell this week. He'd orchestrated the end to his marriage and his career. He tried to reassure himself that it was Mark's own doing, which led to this and that he was a bystander in an otherwise self-destructing life.

Whelan's phone rang. He looked at the call: Mark Whitfield. *Speak of the devil.*

"Whelan."

"Tommy, it's Mark. How's it going over there?"

"We're wrapped up. I'll lock the door behind me. How's your family?"

"Rough, but we'll survive. I wanted to make sure if there's anything you need from me, just ask. I need to see this killer caught. More than ever. He's gunning for me."

"She," corrected Whelan. "Our top suspect right now is Judy Ward."

"I thought it was a man's DNA they found under Susan's nails?"

Whelan filled him in on Judy's past. "What I need to know, Mark, is if you can recall ever doing anything to Judy when she subbed for your teachers. Anything that might set off a psychotic episode years later."

"I don't think I ever had Judy Ward as a substitute. If I did, I don't remember."

"*Any* substitutes? *Any* teachers? Any other students? Anything at all that would cause someone to want this kind of retribution?"

"No. I've been thinking about that for weeks. I got nothing. Tommy, this shit scared me today like I've never been."

"I'm sure. It would anybody. The watchdogs show up yet? I called in for two agents to escort you home and then watch the house. I doubt she'll try to strike again so soon, but we can't be sure."

"If she does, I'll be ready for her."

"Mark, she has to have ears on your house still. I think we need to do another sweep. We missed something."

"Do it. Do whatever you need." Mark was looking at his boys. They were recovering from their stomach pumping. The prospect of losing them caused him to tear up again. He was also choked a bit. "Tommy, do whatever you need to do to find and bring this bitch down. Or so help me, God, I will."

"Don't do anything stupid, Mark. You don't need to go from law enforcer to lawbreaker in the same week. We'll find her. We'll prosecute her. The right way. So it sticks, and she gets the chair. But let us do our job."

"Okay, Tommy. Make sure you do." Mark hung up the phone.

Whelan looked around Whitfield's house a last time before shutting the front door.

Uh-huh. I'll get right on that. Where oh where are you, Judy Ward?

❄ ❄ ❄

Judy Ward was returning to the home of her new love, Lisa Harmon. They'd met at one of Evelyn's chemotherapy sessions about fourteen months ago when Judy was in town visiting. Lisa was younger by eight years and had never been in a serious relationship. She was a nurse at the hospital, and the attraction was immediate. Neither one was looking for love, but there it was.

They fell as fast as they did hard, and within a month, Judy was making visits to Kansas City every two to three weeks. It worked out particularly well, as Lisa's home was a seven-minute drive from Evelyn's. Judy could see two birds with one plane ticket.

Lisa talked Judy into staying the weekend after the service on Friday instead of returning to Miami. "Didn't you say you had business to attend to here anyway?" she had questioned her.

"There is some I could attend to tomorrow," Judy had agreed. She didn't need much coaxing.

When Judy walked back into Lisa's home Saturday afternoon, she headed straight for the kitchen. "What smells so wonderful?"

Lisa was coming up out of the basement. "Cornbread and green beans. I wanted to make fried chicken for dinner, and I was in the mood for a big pot of homemade beans to go with it. I let them cook for about three hours like my grandmother used to do."

"They look amazing," said Judy, stirring the pot. "Ham, onions, mushrooms—they're a full meal by themselves! And do I smell bacon?"

"It's in the cornbread, with jalapeno and cheddar. I use honey instead of sugar. I think you'll love it."

"Sounds like you're trying to fatten me up," said Judy.

"Well…" Lisa reached in and tickled Judy's ribs. "You have lost a few pounds this year. I think you could do with a bit more padding on these."

Judy kissed her. "What were you doing in the basement?"

"Laundry," said Lisa.

"Well, I'm going to run back out for twenty minutes, and when I return, I'll help you fry some chicken. I haven't done that in ages."

"Sure."

After Judy left the room, Lisa noticed the door to the basement hadn't shut all the way. She secured it and turned back to the stove. *Cooking's best with someone you love.* Her grandmother always told her that when she was young. She began humming as she filled the cast iron with oil.

Chapter 41

Whelan found himself back at Evelyn Ward's home for the second day in a row. He was surely missing a clue. *What am I not seeing?*

The house was pretty much as he had seen it the previous day, except the flowers were scattered about a bit more, opening up the room to walk around easier. He assumed it was Helen Gentry, the neighbor, making herself useful. He went down to the basement. Every foot of wall space was inspected and tapped to make sure there were no hidden compartments. He analyzed the floor plan and square footage in his head to see if it matched the main floor of the house. *There has to be a hidden room.*

He relaxed for a moment on the sofa, gazing into the blackness of the television mounted on the wall. It mirrored his reflection. Standing up and moving closer, Whelan started looking at himself. He was thin—gaunt—his mother would call it. *I need to look after myself better. I've got to find Ward and put this one behind me. I need to prove to the bureau I can still do this. I need to show Miranda I can do this. Did I get back on the horse too soon? Damn you, Eddie Morrison, I'll not let you break me.*

A door slammed upstairs.

Whelan marched up the steps and opened the door to the kitchen. He expected to find Mrs. Gentry playing with the flowers again.

The woman sorting through the arrangements on the table was picking individual flowers out to put together into a new bouquet—

a cheerier one by the looks of it. She jerked up in shock when Whelan threw the door open, stifling a startled scream.

Whelan was equally shocked. He drew his weapon and aimed it. "Judy Ward, take a seat. I need to ask some questions, and I may place you under arrest."

Judy's face took on an expression of amusement. "Honestly, agent, you're determined to be in my life some way, aren't you? Arrested? For what?"

"For the murders of at least nine people and the attempted murder of Mark Whitfield."

"Who?"

"Don't play dumb with me any longer. You sold that act last week. I'm not buying it now."

"Agent, I haven't killed anyone. If this is your way of making a joke, I'm not sure I get it."

"Take a seat, Judy."

She did as instructed. Whelan called in for a car to pick her up and then rang Agent Cannon. Both were on their way. Still leveling his gun, he dragged a chair out from the kitchen table and took a seat.

"Do you have to point that at me?" she asked. "I'm not running away. I don't like guns. What if that thing accidentally went off?"

"Guns don't *accidentally* go off. People do."

"Exactly."

He looked at her. She was beginning to get a look of concern on her face. It was sinking into her head Agent Whelan legitimately believed she was guilty.

"Why did you do it, Judy? What set you off?"

She sighed. "I haven't done anything. You've got the wrong person. I know you think I'm this 12 Pills Killer. Why don't you lower your weapon, and we can laugh at that together?"

"You're the only one who fits. You've already admitted you knew some of the victims."

"Some, yes. Not all. Not *most*. Agent Whelan, I imagine *lots* of people knew some of them. What makes you think it's me?"

"I think you're lying about not knowing the rest. What did they do to you? Did they know you used to be a man and make fun of you? Snicker behind your back when you walked away?"

"Ahhh…" Judy teared up. "You think that I must be so fragile as to let children goad me into such a rage I'd seek out revenge on them for some *comments*? That *would* make me a monster, wouldn't it? Agent Whelan, the hell I've faced in my life, the lengths I've gone through to find myself—be comfortable in my own skin…." She cut herself off and wiped at her cheeks.

Continuing, she sank back into her chair, a bit more relaxed. "I assure you, agent, it would take a lot more than some ten-year-olds making fun of me to break me. And for the record, they didn't. My students never knew about my former life. Most of them loved me. And I loved many of them. I loved Jackson Kenny. He was adorable, the sweetest child. I would never harm him or any other child, then or now, for any reason. It breaks my heart that you think I could have killed that child. Yes, I know he's a man now…was—but he'll always be that sweet little boy in my head." The waterworks continued to stream down the sides of her face.

Whelan lowered his gun but kept it in his grip on his knee. "That's a beautiful sentiment, Judy. All of it. One that a psychopath would have."

He stared through slits below his squinched brow. "By the way, what's your girlfriend's name? I'm going to need her address too."

Confusion took over Judy for a moment, then anger. She crossed her arms. "It's been a long week. Fuck you, Agent Whelan.

Do you think I'm going to let you drag *her* into this nightmare? *You're* the psychopath here. When we get to the bureau, I'd better have an attorney waiting. I'm sitting here, giving you full cooperation. But you don't want it. You want to chase ghosts. We're done here."

"If you want to give full cooperation," said Whelan, "you'll allow us to draw some blood and run your DNA."

"And when it doesn't match some sample you have, I'll be free to go? You'll leave me alone forever?"

"You'll be free to go…for now. I can't promise forever."

"No. I suppose no one can."

The pair sat in silence for three minutes until Agent Cannon arrived. More agents swarmed in and hauled away Judy Ward. They escorted her to a car and drove off.

Whelan looked at the bouquet Judy started building before he interrupted her. *Who were you going to give those to?*

※ ※ ※

Judy's blood was drawn and sent to the forensics lab at the bureau immediately.

Agent Jones landed at Kansas City International and headed straight for the office after being filled in by her partner. Two hours later, she was pacing back and forth in front of the lab door. It opened. Agent Joe Cusack almost ran into her, racing out to give results.

"Not her," he said.

"It has to be," said Jones. "Run it again."

Cusack reached out and touched Agent Jones' shoulder. He looked her in the eyes until he knew she could hear him. "My team made no mistakes, Miranda. It's not her."

Agent Jones resumed her pacing, her eyes to the ground. After a few seconds, she wheeled on him. "How sure are we that the dried blood under Susan's nails is our killer's? What if it was someone else's?"

"We ran a Raman spectroscopy test on it. We identified that blood as having been the same age and decay as Jacob's body. To within a day. Now, of course, we can't say that Susan Jacobs didn't scratch some other man the day she died to have collected such a sample, but what are the odds?"

"Slim," sighed Agent Jones, "to none." She walked away silently. At the end of the hall, she remembered to turn around and thank Agent Cusack for his quick work and diligence—and for coming in late on a holiday.

"You're welcome, Agent Jones. I'm sorry this didn't wrap your case up for you." He returned to the lab to thank and praise his team and help with cleaning up before leaving.

Jones returned to the holding room where Agent Whelan was perched opposite Judy Ward in a staring contest. Both looked up anxiously as she entered the room.

"It's not her," she said.

"It has to be," said Whelan. "Did they run it twice?"

Agent Jones grimaced. He'd parroted her exact thoughts from three minutes ago. She looked at Judy Ward. "You're free to leave, Mrs. Ward. I'm sorry we've put you through all this. Truly. We won't be bothering you any longer."

Judy stopped in the doorway and turned back to the agents. "I hope you find your killer soon. Good luck to both of you." Then she was gone.

Agent Whelan stood open-mouthed, looking at his partner for answers.

"What? You said it yourself a week ago. We're looking for connections. We made one. A *wrong* one. A horribly wrong one. Time to move on."

Whelan didn't move, aside from his head shaking back and forth uncontrollably.

Miranda moved to him and put her arm around his shoulder, nudging him out the door. "Come on. I'll buy you a beer."

In the parking lot, Whelan looked at his partner as the sun began to set. "I'm not fit company at the moment. Can I have a rain check? I don't want to be in a crowd tonight."

"Why don't you come by the house? I'll order a pizza, and we can watch the Royals game. There's supposed to be a big fireworks show at the stadium tonight afterward. They're going to broadcast it. Should be fun."

"I don't want to intrude on you and Derrick. The two of you should make an evening of it. We can start fresh in the morning."

"Derrick needs to get used to you being in my life. He won't mind." She said it innocently.

Less innocent thoughts ran through Whelan's head. "Actually…I'm wiped, really, another time. Oh, and I'd like to fly out to D.C. tomorrow. I think I need a day to re-process everything— formulate new suspects. I've been wanting to question my mom about this case too. She knew Whitfield and other friends of David's and mine. It's a long shot, but you never know. I'll be back in the office Monday."

"Of course. If any new leads turn up between now and then, I'll give you a call."

"Thanks. Oh, and keep a close eye on Whitfield. After this morning, I think he might try to play detective—off the clock and without any rules."

"Do I sound terrible if I say maybe I'll let him?" she asked.

"Yes. Oh, and I might have fucked up. I told him Judy Ward was our prime suspect. I'm going to call him on my way home and update him so he won't go after the wrong person."

"Yes, that wouldn't be very helpful at this point. Oh, speaking of not very helpful, I forgot to tell you the new sweep of his home discovered two bugs. I'm going to have to hold a training. Those should have been caught the first go-'round."

"Probably done by some of his buddies we let go. They weren't doing their jobs. What the hell were they thinking? Where were the bugs?"

"One was under the cap that goes over the refrigerator door hinge at the top. The other was wedged under a heavy metal suit hanger in the master closet. No prints were picked up from either. He scrubbed the serial numbers, so they're going to be practically impossible to trace. Tech is taking a look anyway."

"Okay."

She sensed his despair. "Whelan, cheer up. Think of today as having ruled out a suspect. That's progress!"

"Yeah…" he conceded.

"You know, most serial killers take years to be caught. We've been forced to go at break-neck speed under the circumstances. We need to give ourselves some credit."

"I'll credit myself when it's due. I'm concerned 12 Pills' failure to get Whitfield today will press him to move faster on number nine."

"Yes. I didn't want to voice it, but I've been thinking the same thing."

"Hell, maybe I should stay in town tomorrow."

"And do what? There's no fresh lead at the moment," said Jones. "Go see your son. Talk to your mother. Clear all the bats from your belfry for a day so it can accept new possibilities. I'll hold the fort." She didn't intend to reach in and hug him, but she found herself holding him a moment. She let go and hopped in her car.

As she sped out of the lot, Whelan sniffed the air once more where she'd stood. He smiled and headed for his car.

Chapter 42

"Come on, Tommy, throw the ball!"

Whelan was out cold on the flight to Washington, D.C. His nightmare returned, amplified.

Tommy was trying to read the arranged signals from the catcher behind the plate. None of the finger combinations were making sense. Tommy paused a moment. He'd been here before.

He looked into the stands. The crowd was roaring. Eight of them were standing. He could see their faces. They were children between seven and fourteen years of age. Each held a giant post-it in front of their chest:

JACKSON KENNY – 1 of 12

PAUL DUKE – 2 of 12

TRACY STAMFORD – 3 of 12

SONJA CUEVAS – 4 of 12

TONY BALZANO – 5 of 12

PATRICK KAVANAUGH – 6 of 12

FRANCES MOFFETT – 7 of 12

MARK WHITFIELD – 8 of 12

Whelan looked back to their faces after reading each sign. They were now adults—their frozen expressions filled with fear—orange pill bottles protruding from their mouths. Their eyes all stared vacantly in Tommy's direction. A ninth person was standing. The face was blurry. It was impossible to tell if they were a man or a woman. The one clear thing was their pill bottle, with a cap marked in Sharpie—9 of 12.

12 PILLS

Behind Tommy, the sound of dried grass crackling as it burned grew louder. Tommy turned to see blue patches of wolfsbane in the outfield rise quickly. They grew tall, with huge blossoms, which then exploded into cerulean flames. The scoreboard above the fence was melting at the bottom, but the digital score was still visible.

It read: Home – 1, Visitors – 7.

He looked beyond the fence, to the street behind it, where cars were lined up with angry parents. A lone kid sat in an old Subaru, looking through the door window to try and watch the game. His eyes locked on Tommy's before filling with blue fire. Teardrops fell from his eyes and singed the car door like acid.

Tommy believed he knew the boy. He looked at his face again. It was engulfed in flames. The boy opened the car door and began a slow, deliberate march toward him as the fire consumed his body. A giant blaze of sapphire moved across the field as Tommy stood petrified on the pitcher's mound. It stopped two feet short of him, and a lone arm extended out toward him, holding a pill bottle. The arm was chewy caramel—melting—dripping flesh onto the ground. There were eyes in the flame. Irises Tommy felt he recognized. *Who do they belong to?*

As always, the moment the plane touched the runway, Agent Whelan woke.

The woman seated next to him was staring at him. "You okay?"

"Did I say anything? A name!" Thomas snapped at her.

"No. Nothing." The woman leaned back toward the window to put any amount of distance between her and him she could.

"I'm sorry. It… it's important that I remember." He sounded cuckoo.

The woman avoided further eye contact by staring out at the passing trees.

Whelan struggled to retain any new details, but it all soon vanished.

He couldn't help but dwell on the notion he only had days left to save the lives of four more people. *I shouldn't have left. Why did I come here?*

❧ ❧ ❧

Whelan's mother, Kathryn, insisted on picking Thomas up at Dulles International. His son Connor was the first person he saw when he exited the plane. They held a long hug.

"Dude, I swear you've grown an inch," said Thomas.

"You say that every time you see me," howled Connor. "Maybe a half-inch this time, though!"

"My turn!" said Kathryn and squeezed her way in.

Thomas' ex-wife, Georgia, graciously offered to let Thomas stay the night at their home in D.C. Her ex-mother-in-law had been there several days already and planned to fly back to Kansas City with Thomas in the morning.

It was a beautiful cottage home on a street where old maple trees canopied the cars and sidewalks. The two-bedroom house was small, but the school system was A-rated, and she felt safe in the neighborhood. Thomas' name was still on the deed. They agreed to keep it in both names until Connor went off to college. All of their arrangements had been amicable.

Georgia was rocking in a chair on the front porch when Kathryn pulled the car to the curb. Connor raced inside to fire up the latest video game to show his dad. Kathryn made an excuse to get inside, and the exes were alone.

"Hi, Georgi, you look well," said Thomas.

"You…don't," was all she could manage. "I'm sorry, I meant… You don't look healthy, Tom. You look tired." She stood up and hugged him. He felt thin. "Well, I'm making one of your favorites tonight. Maybe you can put on a pound while you're here."

The hug felt impersonal on both sides. There was little emotion left. Thomas hoped that could be salvaged into a friendship for Connor's sake but knew Georgia was still working through some of her anger over the downturn in their marriage. It was unfair to fault her husband for placing priority on catching a dangerous criminal over being present for his family, but she blamed him regardless.

He instinctively went for the refrigerator like he'd done a thousand times. A brand new six-pack of his favorite beer was in the door. He looked up and smiled. "You *do* still love me!"

"Yeah-yeah. Go play with your son." She goaded him.

Two hours later, they sat down for a formal meal. Kathryn insisted on holding hands and saying grace. "God bless this food we are about to receive. Bless this family. Thank you for this beautiful day and these moments. Amen."

She opened her eyes in time to see her son and his ex-wife holding hands for an "extra" moment. The look they shared was one of understanding. She decided she'd take it. It was better than hostility. They'd work on compassion another day.

"Meatloaf!" said Connor. "Mom…seriously? You said you were making something good."

"Are you kidding," said Thomas. "Your mom makes the best meatloaf I've ever had."

"She puts too many onions and peppers in it."

"That's what makes it so good. Pick'em out. Put'em on my plate. I'll eat them. And I know how much you hate mashed potatoes and gravy! And peas with butter and cream…yuck!"

"No way, man. I'll take your peas, and you can have my peppers," laughed Connor.

Georgia interrupted, "I think I made plenty of everything. And remember to save room for blackberry cobbler."

"You made blackberry cobbler?" asked Thomas.

"*I* made blackberry cobbler," said Kathryn, "and your son turned the crank on the ice cream machine for over an hour this morning, so you've got homemade vanilla to go on it."

"Gee everybody…" Thomas teared up out of the blue. "Thank you. All of you. I love you all more than you know."

Kathryn's eyes moistened with heartfelt emotion. "Well, don't wait so long to come visit in the future. You've forgotten you have a family. Who loves you too."

"Never," said Thomas quickly. He looked directly at Connor. "I never forget any of you—not for a second."

The rest of dinner and dessert continued with lighter conversation as everyone caught up on each other's lives. Afterward, they all watched fountains and twirled sparklers in the backyard. It was a day late, but no one was checking the calendar.

Chapter 43

Agent Miranda Jones was finding herself bored Sunday afternoon.

Derrick flew to New York that morning for a meeting with a cable channel. There was an offer on the table to star in his own television fitness program. They loved what he was doing online and wanted to bring that to a new audience of TV viewers.

She spent the day trying to rest and unwind. Every hour would bring a new hypothesis which she would cross-reference against existing data on the case. She kept tabs with the agents out in the field today and followed up with Mansilla in Miami to see if there were any new developments. By 3:30 p.m. Agent Jones was more restless than rested. She cleaned up, put on one of her favorite blouses, and navigated her way toward the plaza for some shopping. At 6:00, she realized she hadn't eaten all day, and out of the twenty-plus restaurants to choose from, she made her way to Slap-Happy's Bar and Grill. Their happy hour lasted until 7:00, and she decided she needed a little "happy."

Perhaps her sub-conscience coaxed her into feeling closer to her partner in his absence. Maybe she secretly longed for more flirting from Reggie Johnson, who clearly had a severe crush on her. She smiled as she walked in, but it faded when there was no one at the bar she recognized.

Maybe I should call Agent Cannon and see if he's up for a drink?

She stopped herself. *Why am I looking for company right now?*

Normally, she enjoyed her alone-time. She seldom had any, so it was treasured when she did. The pressure of the case was getting to her. Every lead they had fizzled out. It could be merely days—even hours—before the next person on the killer's list was discovered. *Hell, they could be dead already, and we simply don't know it yet.*

She threw back two tequila shots before ordering a beer and some potstickers, then tried to lose herself in the television above the liquor bottles. It worked. On her third beer, she didn't notice the man taking a seat beside her.

"You're eating my usual 'go-to,'" he said.

She turned her head. "Reggie! I was just thinking about you." *Shit. Why did I tell him that?*

"Lucky me!" he said. "I'm pretty much *always* thinking about you." He flagged the bartender and ordered two shots of Patron and another round of beer for each of them, then added another order of 'go-to' and some fried pickles.

"Where's your partner tonight?" Reggie asked Agent Jones.

"Visiting his son in D.C. Do you have any kids?"

"Not yet," he smiled wide. "You?"

"No. Hasn't been in the cards. And I'm sure not getting any younger."

"A beautiful, vibrant girl like you—you've got plenty of time left. What are you, twenty-six—seven?"

Miranda giggled. "Sure. Let's go with that. We'll knock off the past eleven or twelve years like they never happened."

"Amen!" cheered Reggie. "That would save me a mistaken marriage and a nasty divorce. Might still be driving my Beamer instead of a Toyota."

"Nothing wrong with a Toyota," said Miranda. She raised her delivered shot glass. "Here's to hard-working middle-class grunts like ourselves."

Reggie clinked along. His eyes darted back and forth across hers until they grabbed and held them. "Grunt is the last description I'd ever give to you. I can't imagine you described as anything less than exquisite perfection."

She radiated. Her sub-conscience won out. She was receiving the validation she'd been seeking. She was clutching to anything that made her feel better about herself in the face of her failure to solve her case and prevent more people from being killed.

"How's it going with your hunt? Catch your killer yet?" he asked.

So much for feeling better. "No, I'm afraid we hit a dead-end yesterday. I thought we had her...but...."

"The killer's a woman?" asked Reggie.

"It *was*, but the DNA didn't bear out. Well, it was a *man's* DNA, but...oh, forget it, it's complicated. And I shouldn't be talking about it anyway. I'm rattled. I was sure we had it in the bag, but apparently, we didn't. And I'm so tired of flying!"

"Flying?"

"Yes!" snapped Miranda. "I have to fly back down to Miami tomorrow. There's a woman down there who saw the killer's face, but she can't remember it. Can you believe that? She wouldn't even have come forward had I not gone down there and put up a fuss! She's received two hypnotherapy sessions now, and the shrink says she's getting real close. We're hoping the third time's the charm. With any luck, by this time tomorrow, I'll have a real witness and the killer behind bars."

"That's great. Congratulations!" Reggie raised his beer mug in toast.

"Oh, Reggie, I'm sorry," said Miranda, finishing her glass. "I didn't mean to go on like that. I should know better than to talk about an active case. Forgive me for venting. I've got too much alcohol flowing through these veins, and I needed to unwind on someone a moment. Let's talk about you. How was your weekend?"

"It's all good, Miranda. I love hearing any and everything about you." Reggie's smile was broad before his face shifted to a more serious, flirtatious tone.

He lifted her arm and turned it palm up, putting two fingers on her wrist, then proceeded to stroke gently up to her elbow and back to her hand. "Your veins look fine to me. Just like the rest of you. *Very* fine. Do you have time for more than an appetizer?" he asked. "I've been trying to buy you dinner since the first night we met. And there's a respectable bottle of Cabernet on the menu I've been wanting to try."

"Reggie... You know I'm involved. Believe me, if I weren't...but that's not the case right now."

"Right now? Right at this moment? Where's this mystery man I'm supposed to be competing with?

Miranda grinned. "It's a competition now? Oh my... He's in New York."

"He left you all alone? Oh, uh-uh..."

"For *one* night."

"Mmmhmm..." Reggie's eyes twinkled. His head cocked to the side as his pupils chased Miranda's.

For a moment, she was spellbound. She was unsure if her intoxication was from the liquor or this suave charmer less than a foot away.

Reggie leaned in to kiss her.

❀ ❀ ❀

Thomas sat back in his chair after the last bite of cobbler and ice cream went down. "Best I've ever had. I think we have professional chefs in this family." He rubbed his overstuffed belly.

"It was all delicious," said Kathryn. She stood and began clearing the table.

"I've got it, Kathryn," said Georgia. "Why don't you go out on the front porch and visit with Tom? Get in some one-on-one time. It's beautiful out tonight. Connor promised me he'd help clean up."

Thomas looked at his son, who begrudgingly nodded.

"As soon as you're finished, come get me, and we'll squeeze in another level or two on that new game before bed," said Thomas.

Connor was happy again. "Deal!" He raced off to the kitchen while his father and grandmother made their way to comfortable rockers on the front porch.

Thomas lit two tiki-torches filled with citronella oil.

"You miss this house?" asked Kathryn.

"Of course. This neighborhood. This town. All of it. I thought I was making a life that would last forever here."

"And then the FBI got in the way. And your conscience got in yours."

"I blew it. I don't know if it was worth it."

"You've said before that you made your choice. I would argue you had no choice. It's part of who you are. It's in your nature. And for what it's worth, no one in this house thinks any less of you for having taken the road you did. It may have cost you a wife, but it gained your son a hero. He looks up to you like you wouldn't believe.

Brags to all his friends about how his dad is out there putting away bad guys."

"Really? I don't know if that's much of a trade."

"Take it, Tommy. Take it where you can get it and put the rest behind you."

"Thanks mom. I try."

"So tell me about your current case. I love to hear the details. It makes me feel like Miss Marple."

"Well, don't freak out on me, but it's the 12 Pills Killer."

"I knew it! Georgia owes me a dollar. Go on!"

Thomas squinted his eyes in disapproval. "And…after a month since being brought on board, we've still no idea who it is."

"None? Surely you've tracked *something*."

Agent Whelan laughed at his mother. "Your confidence is reassuring. Thank you. Actually, yes. There's a house right outside Traverse City, Michigan, that I believe the killer rented around February of last year. Lived in it for three months. No one knows his name or remembers his face."

"No one? Bullshit. Where did he grocery shop? Where did he buy his gas? Where did he order pizza from once in a while? *Someone* in that town saw him. I'd bet a few."

"You're right. I think I'll head back up there and see if I can get in front of the local news. Make an announcement, and hopefully, someone will come forward."

"See there, I've practically solved it for you," Kathryn teased him.

"I wish. We're on the clock. We think he's going to strike again any day now. Any hour…"

"Oh honey, I'm sorry. I know that's maddening for you." She paused and looked at the screen door to make sure no one was eavesdropping. "*We*? How *is* this new partner? A woman, you said? How's that going?"

Thomas pounced, "Oh, there she is! I wondered when Miss Gossip 2020 would surface."

"I'm looking out for your best interest."

"Fine, whatever. But please, don't ask me when the last time I got laid was."

Kathryn feigned shock. "I wouldn't dream of it! And besides, I don't have to *ask*. I can see it's been a while…it's written all over you."

Whelan's jaw fell open.

"So," said Kathryn, "tell me the rest. I want to know everything."

"I knew you would. I'm hoping to jog your memory and see if you can think of anything I'm missing. There's a connection here I've been unable to put my finger on, and you know a couple of names on this list. Maybe you'll have a thought that's evaded me."

Thomas spent the next twenty-five minutes filling in his mother on Agent Miranda Jones, the case details, the shake-up at the office, discovering Susan Jacobs, and the victims' names. He held his phone out with the list so she could read them for herself.

The names hit her harder than she'd expected.

"Not Jackson Kenny! He was so sweet. A considerate and kind boy, that one."

"Yeah, that's what I've been hearing. I knew him as a buddy, but to hear it from the perspectives of adults, talking about a child, it's been an eye-opener."

"Well, of course it would be. And Paul Duke? Patrick Kavanaugh and Mark Whitfield!"

"Mark was an *attempt*," Whelan interrupted. "12 Pills tried to put it in his delivery order, possibly take out his whole family. Mark caught it in time."

"It seems like just a few years ago, he was at our house all the time. Oh Tommy, have you talked to your brother?"

"Yeah… not much help, other than to connect Susan Jacobs to Mark. We connected them ourselves right before that, so, not too revealing."

"Well, go ask him about Kavanaugh again. I think they hung around quite a bit too."

She looked through the names again. "Balzano was a bag of hot air. I hate those awful commercials. And Frances Moffett? Was that Franny from school?"

Whelan nodded.

"Oh, she was so talented that one. I loved her in that musical. What a voice. And Sonja Cuevas… Oh! She was such a sweet little thing—what a shame. I don't know how you do it. So sad." She handed the phone back to her son.

His jaw fell open again. "Mom. You *knew* Sonja Cuevas? How? Where? *How?*" He grabbed his mother's arm in excitement.

❀ ❀ ❀

Agent Jones put up her first two fingers like a cub scout and pressed them against Reggie's lips as he leaned in to her. "That can't happen, Reggie. I'm incredibly flattered, but I love Derrick."

Saying it out loud to another admirer felt real—felt right. She stood up, nearly wobbling off her bar chair along the way. "I shouldn't have come in here tonight. I don't know what I was thinking."

"Whoa! Take it easy," said Reggie. "I'm sorry. I felt a spark, and I thought you were feeling it too. It's fine. Sit. Drink your beer. Let's pretend that didn't happen and go back to being friendly like we were sixty seconds ago." He pushed her pint glass toward her.

Miranda paused. She *had* felt a spark. That's what was bothering her. "I don't think I should stay Reggie, I'm sorry."

"Miranda, it's okay. I get it. Please, don't let this ruin our budding friendship. Let me at least walk you to your car and be the gentleman I set out to be this evening. Don't take away my last shred of dignity."

Agent Jones sighed. Now she felt terrible. She looked into Reggie's eyes. He was sweet and sincere. *And handsome, damn it.* "Okay. Eat that last dumpling while I run to the restroom, and then you can walk me to my car."

Chapter 44

"*Mom*, how did you know Sonja Cuevas?" Whelan repeated himself.

"Well, there were several of us single mothers that needed help with you kids back then. You remember 'Old Mabel'?"

"Yeah..." Whelan reflected.

Mabel was one of his main babysitters when he was in elementary school. She was the strictest out of all of them and wasn't easy to forget. She often wore a head wrap with colorful African tribal patterns. Sometimes she'd trade up to an official Zulu hat. Thomas was never sure how much hair she had—or didn't have— tucked away under all that material. She weighed over 250 pounds and always made quite an entrance, throwing her oversized crocheted bag in a chair on her way in and pointing her finger. "You'll be in bed by 8:30, young man. Now, where's your homework?"

Whelan smiled with the memory. "She wasn't our favorite babysitter."

"Well," continued Kathryn, "she was *ours*. She was the main person most of us in my circle used when we all had other plans, and none of the regular mothers were available. Jackson's mother worked a lot of nights, and I worked some. Patrick's mother was on a bowling league—I think Mark's might have been on that—plus her husband dragged her away for date nights when he decided he wanted a little from the missis instead of one of his side whores."

For the third time in the past half-hour, Whelan's mouth fell open. "I didn't know any of that."

"Of course not. Why would you? You were a child. You were all growing up fast enough as it was. You weren't supposed to know the sins of the parents."

Whelan wondered for a moment if his mother wanted to open up about some of her own past sins, but that would have to wait. They were getting off-topic. "So, Sonja Cuevas?"

"Yes, I'm getting there. Well, Mabel—Old Mabel, as you kids called her—she was a blessing. I know you considered her too tough and not a lot of fun. Well, us mothers were all spread pretty thin. If anything came up on short notice, Mabel was usually available at the last minute and didn't have a problem with having an extra child— or three or four—dropped off at her place or whatever home she was at for the evening. I'm sure she preferred it, actually. She'd make two or three times the money for the same time on the clock! Smart woman."

Whelan bobbed his head up and down rapidly. His eyes were wide.

"Well, you boys didn't need a babysitter by the time you reached junior high. You were more than capable of looking out for yourselves. But some of the women I hung with had children younger than you. One was Yolanda Presley. Her daughter Charlotte was about five years behind you. She still needed a sitter. She had a friend—from Raytown, I think—Sonja Cuevas. I wouldn't normally remember some little girl I met but a few times while dropping off or picking up some kids at Mabel's, but she made an impression. Prettiest little face, that one. So sad…"

Kathryn hung her head. "It's an ugly world." She looked at her son as tears filled her eyes. "Are you sure you wouldn't rather sell cars?" She tried to make a joke and cheer herself up.

"I'm sure." Whelan put his hand on top of his mother's. *Holy shit! My mom met Sonja* and *Charlie!*

She interlocked her fingers in his and smiled.

Whelan returned the kindness. He was a bit more appreciative of how marvelous his mother had been—still was. "I didn't know you ran kids around to help your friends out. I didn't realize you even had many friends. I feel like I didn't know anything about you."

"No. A child's focus is pretty much solely on themselves. They are the whole world until they grow old enough to understand it's bigger than them. And that's okay. That's the way it should be. You weren't supposed to look upon 'mommy' as an individual, with dreams and challenges of her own, her own friends and relationships and personal interests. 'Mommy' is just 'mommy,' caregiver, home provider, food provider… toy provider…."

Kathryn locked her eyes on Thomas. "And at least I got one of you right," she kidded.

Whelan smiled, but he couldn't afford to digress any longer.

"Mom," he continued. "This is important. Did Mabel have any babysitting clients in other towns? Maybe Lee's Summit or Kansas City? Any kids from Saint Vincent's?"

"Oh yes. For certain. She was popular. Word spread around the area. Trustworthy, dependable babysitters were hard to come by. I heard she was making a bundle working around Sunset Hill. That Saint Vincent's crowd has money. She got so it became a full-time job. Probably made more money than I did!"

Whelan's mind was in overdrive. His mother might have solved his case. Old Mabel could be the 12 Pills Killer! *Babysitter! We never had "babysitter" on the list! Fuck substitute teachers and Santa Claus. It's Old Mabel!*

Agent Jones' rolling corkboard flashed into Whelan's head, with the list of victims. All of a sudden, his mind linked the missing information he'd been struggling with every time he studied the complete list. *I was babysat alongside all those names—all those kids—at one point or another in my early childhood!*

"Mom, do you have any idea where Old Mabel—Mabel—is now? Where she lives? I don't want to jump the gun, but I think she might be our killer!"

"Oh sweetie, I'm sorry," said Kathryn. "but that's not possible. Mabel's dead."

Reggie's dumpling took forever to eat, and he'd taken the liberty of ordering another round of beer while Miranda was in the ladies' room. They small-talked about baseball and the stock market for a bit before Miranda insisted on leaving.

"Fine, we'll go, but *I* insist on picking up your tab."

"All right, but don't think it's going to get you any favors," she said.

"Nope." He threw his hands in the air. "Hey, I'm on best behavior, I swear."

"Uh-huh." She smiled and shook her head.

The bartender returned the credit card receipt for Reggie's signature. The bill came to $70.88. Reggie tipped $12.12 and totaled the bill to $83.00. "Okay, let me get you to your car." He looked up at Miranda.

She was staring at the tab on the bar. She slowly raised her eyes to meet Reggie's.

He glanced back to the receipt. "That was a mistake, wasn't it?" He laughed, more to himself than to her. "I knew you were going to throw my game off."

❀ ❀ ❀

"What do you mean she's dead?" asked Whelan.

"She passed away about four months ago after a year-long battle with ALS. One of my friends saw her obit in the paper and brought it to my attention," said Kathryn.

Thomas typed on his phone, Googling Kansas City obituaries. "What was her full name?"

"Mabelline Johnson. I never knew her middle name."

He typed it in. After a moment, he found it on an obituary site and read aloud: "Mabelline Johnson of Independence Missouri – Born July 27, 1951 – Died March 3, 2020. She was preceded in death by her brother Marvin Johnson of Independence, Missouri and her parents, Wilfred and Bessie Johnson of Kansas City, Missouri. Ms. Johnson is survived by her sister Caroline Johnson and her son Reginald Johnson, both of Kansas City, Missouri. "Mabel," as her friends and family called her, is scheduled to be buried at Truman Memorial Cemetery on March 6 at 10:00 a.m. After a year-long battle with ALS, Mabel has rejoined our mighty Father in Heaven and will be remembered as a wonderful mother and friend to all. In lieu of flowers, the family has requested donations to the ALS Association or the American Diabetes Association."

Kathryn looked at her son. She didn't say a word. His brain was in processing mode. She called it his "think-tank" expression. She'd seen this expression on him many times growing up. She'd learned to let him work through all his thoughts, lest her interruption break them entirely.

Thomas replayed the events and conversations of the past few weeks in his head. He flashed back to the list of names Victoria Cuevas gave of those involved in her daughter Sonja's life. He saw Mabelline Johnson there, but it didn't click that she was "Old Mabel." Anyone on the list who was deceased was cleared of being the killer, and with no connections made, her name was dismissed as "useless" and dragged to the trash can. The hairs on his arm began to rise.

Whelan remembered the real estate agent in Traverse City, who was unable to recall the exact names of the possible tenants. *Trevor maybe or... Renaldo? Maybe... Mabel was survived by a son, Reginald... Renaldo—Reginald?* At Balzano's, Miranda said, *"He didn't even need to reach up to snip it...those hedge-cutters have at least a two-foot reach."* Gaia said he was brownish. *Caramel maybe... planted monkshood... Someone who has been planting dream lawns and gardens since 2001 would know his poisonous plants...*

Oh shit. The nightmare he'd been having raced into his consciousness. The screen that obstructed his view in his dreams the past few weeks fell away to brilliant clarity. He was on the pitcher's mound. He turned to see the outfield in blue flames, then lifted his eyes past the scoreboard and the fence to the street, to an old Subaru with a lone boy in it, staring at the world from behind locked glass. The face took shape. It was Reginald, Mabel Johnson's boy.

"Oh my God. Reggie Johnson is the 12 Pills Killer!"

❀ ❀ ❀

Chapter 45

Agent Jones' eyes darted back to the receipt. He'd scrawled in a tip of $12.12. Her mind overlaid that on the most recent bottle cap with 7 of 12 written in Sharpie. The '12s' were a match. She looked at the '3' on his total of $83.00. It had the same little curlicue in the tail as the 3 in the third victim's mouth. Her eyes shot back to Reggie's as her right hand instinctively reached for her firearm tucked into the rear of her waistband.

"Easy agent. Let's not make a scene. You've got less than an hour to live, and if you want me to save you, we need to leave *right* now. Calmly, and without drawing any attention to ourselves."

"What do you mean an hour—" Miranda began to hiss before cutting herself off. She looked at her beer on the counter, a half-filled pint glass. There was a greenish tint to it. She looked at Reggie's beside it. Yellow. *Son of a bitch...*

She froze in place, her sense of reason scrambled. Rationality competed with alcohol for working space in her head.

"I've got an antidote," said Reggie, "but if we don't get it in you before the poison is fully digested, nothing can save you."

He's going to kill me. It's his only choice. How do I warn Whelan?

Miranda's self-preservation mechanism kicked in. "Okay."

She stood and began ambling toward the door, Reginald locking a firm grasp on her upper arm.

He led her to his car. Before placing her in his passenger seat, he took her gun.

"Agent Jones, you look scared. Don't be. I'm five minutes away. We have time."

When they turned into the driveway of Mabelline Johnson's home in Westwood, Miranda looked shocked. "You're three blocks over from Evelyn Ward's."

"Who?" asked Reggie.

"Never mind. Someone I once knew."

He marched her into the basement and tied her hands behind a concrete support column for the home. He had the decency to put her in a folding chair first instead of the floor.

Agent Jones looked around her. "Very tidy, Reggie. You want to come over and clean *my* basement? Maybe we could wash some laundry together."

"I'm good, thanks." He placed her gun and cell phone on the work table. The phone rang as he let go of it, and it startled him a moment.

Jones watched him jump. *Not as cool under pressure as he thinks. That makes him more dangerous.*

Reggie showed Miranda the caller ID; it was Whelan.

❀ ❀ ❀

"Answer it," he instructed, swiping the call open. He placed it on speaker.

She tried and failed to make her voice steady. "Hello, Agent Whelan."

Reggie smiled. *She's trying to sound impartial.*

"Miranda!" Whelan was hysterical. "Miranda, 12 Pills is Reggie Johnson! I'll explain later how I know, but you've got to get him *now*. Maybe he's at Slappy's. If not, look up his mother's home,

Mabelline Johnson. He might be living there. I can't make it back tonight. My plane doesn't get in until 12:40 tomorrow afternoon."

"Oh, Whelan..." The sadness in Jones' voice was prevalent. "Partner, your timing was almost perfect, but fifteen minutes too late. Fifteen minutes is a lifetime right now. My lifetime."

The other end of the line was silent for a few seconds as Agent Whelan's wheels turned. He could tell he was on speakerphone. "Reggie?"

"Present," he answered like he was a child being called on at attendance.

Whelan wanted to yell and spit through the phone, but he took a breath and willed calm into his voice. "What is it you want, Regg? Let her go, and we can talk about it."

"I can't do that, I'm afraid. She's too important now. She's going to secure my safety. I'm assuming Agent Jones is the first call you made when you figured out it was me? No one else yet?"

"No."

"Excellent. You're smart, Tommy. I'll give you that. Stay smart. Tell no one, and I'll let her live."

"Hey, Reggie," said Miranda. "If you boys are going to talk a while, how about taking me upstairs and giving me the antidote first?"

Reggie looked at his watch. "We have time."

Whelan's stomach dropped. He wasn't certain she'd been dosed until that moment. He didn't know the full recipe for the magic formula but doubted anything could counteract the poison.

His gut spoke out, "Miranda, try to vomit! Reggie, you bastard! If she dies, so help me, God, you'll see the end of my gun instead of a courtroom. I swear to you!"

Agent Jones leaned over as best she could and started trying to get her gag reflex to kick in. It was challenging with her arms secured behind her back.

Reggie stood watching her, amused and curious to see if she could succeed.

She glanced up and caught his expression. "Whelan, I think it's too late. I've digested too much by now. Based on our lab calculations, I've got about fifteen to thirty minutes left, depending on the dosage he gave me."

"Smart woman," said Reggie. "Two smarties..." *Don't be smart with me! You'll get another ass-whoopin'!*

Thomas lowered his voice again. "Reggie, what do you want? What is your end game?"

"Isn't that an interesting question?" Reggie considered for a moment. "I'm not sure now. You've made this intriguing again for me, Tommy! I didn't give you enough credit. I thought for sure you'd be sidetracked with Whitfield a lot longer. I set him up so sweetly. What cleared him so fast?"

"DNA. Susan Jacobs."

"Ahhh..." he rubbed at the back of his neck like her scratch was three minutes ago instead of three months. "So it was my mistake, not your brilliance. Maybe not so smart."

Whelan was growing impatient. "What now, Reggie?"

"I have five more birdies to take down. It doesn't matter in what order any longer. Doing it by birth month was just to kick off the game and get it going. But the rest will get their prizes sooner than later now. You two have left me no choice."

"What's with the birthdays anyway, Reggie?" said Whelan. "What happened? Was it a birthday party that upset you?"

"It was *all* of them!" screamed Reggie.

Miranda jumped in her seat as the psychopath in front of her flew from levelheaded to enraged, his temples pulsing.

Reginald continued, "Do you know what it's like to be made to sit in a car on the curb, watching a birthday party through a roll-up window that you *weren't* invited to? Watching while your mother, the hired help, works the party like an employee? She couldn't leave me at home alone—there was no one left to babysit poor Reggie! They were all in *there*, having fun, playing games, getting presents, eating fucking cake and ice cream while I sat in hot cars, freezing cars, watching through windows! Over and over, every week. Someone's fucking birthday…for *years*…."

He became eerily calm before continuing, "So now, you all get to play *my* fucking birthday game. Winner takes all."

Whelan's face sunk as an image flashed through his head. It wasn't a nightmare this time. It was a genuine memory of looking through his dining room window and seeing eight-year-old Reggie Johnson sitting in the car, watching his party. He didn't know him then. Thomas wouldn't have him in class until two years later. And by then, he'd forgotten all about it.

Like every child, at every party, who noticed Reggie, not one had ever invited him to come in and join the fun. Most never even realized he was Old Mabel's son. And it wasn't her place to ask the people paying her if he would be allowed.

At least, that was her belief. She'd never tried. She'd decided it was an important lesson to let her son see that you have to work your way in this world. There were no free rides.

"Reggie…" Whelan stumbled for words, "I… I'm so sorry. We were *kids,* Reggie. Little children. I saw you for a few seconds, and then it was out of my head. Just *children*…"

"It wasn't out of *my* head. It was burned there. I spent much of the '90s eating cold meals and doing homework from the backseat of an '87 Subaru hatchback. All those years watching, and never even a single piece of cake!"

"Reggie," said Miranda. She put as much sincerity in her voice as she could manage. "I'm so sorry. That was horrible for you. But please don't do this. You can have a better life now. You *do* have a better life. You're successful. You're handsome. I imagine everyone wants to be in your life now."

She closed her eyes and wished she could take back that last sentence.

"Right… you made that abundantly clear earlier. Tommy, get on your plane tomorrow and get here. You know where I'm at. I'm going to save her, for now. But if anyone else shows up before you or with you, I'll kill her. Tell no one, Tommy. I've got ears everywhere. I'll know. One misstep and your partner will be meeting Jesus like a sinner at a revival. We'll be waiting."

He hung up the phone.

Miranda was at a loss for words as she fought back against panic.

"Reggie…" she tried to speak. She cleared her throat. "Reggie, the antidote? The clock's ticking."

Reginald Johnson stared blankly into Agent Jones' eyes a moment.

For the first time since she met him, they appeared soulless.

"Agent Jones," he said, "I lied. There is no antidote."

❁ ❁ ❁

Chapter 46

Miranda wasn't the only one whose phone was on speaker, so was Whelan's.

Kathryn looked at her son with shock and disbelief. Playing detective vicariously through her son's conversations over the years was fun and entertaining, but for the first time since he'd joined the FBI, she realized the truth of his job—its dangers and horrors. She was speechless.

Thomas ran inside and found Connor playing a video game where he was flying through space in a dogfight. "Son, I'm so sorry, but I have to go. I know who the bad guy is, and my partner's in danger." He gave Connor a bear hug.

"It's okay, dad. Go get him!"

Whelan smiled at him. "You're amazing. So much smarter and wiser than I was. I love you." He gave him another quick hug.

"Love you too, dad." When Thomas walked out of the room, Connor changed the game on the screen to one where he could shoot criminals in the city.

Georgia looked at her ex-husband. "Kathryn filled me in. What can we do?"

"I'm going to have to hire me a charter. Mom, I need your rental."

She handed him the keys. "Don't worry about me. I can take a taxi. Leave your bag unless you need it. I'll bring it with me tomorrow."

"I'll take her to the airport in the morning. We'll be fine," said Georgia.

12 PILLS

Whelan gave both women a quick hug with a "love you" attached to them, and flew out the door.

After Georgia locked it, she turned around and mumbled to herself, "And be careful."

Pointing his car toward Ronald Reagan Washington National Airport, Whelan put in a call to Agent Cannon. He instructed him to have a charter plane ready, at whatever cost. This airport was twenty minutes away. It would have taken over an hour to get to Dulles.

"And tell no one. I'll deal with any fallout later." Whelan finished his instructions to the younger agent.

The Cessna flight was the first one he could remember where he didn't fall asleep immediately after take-off. There would be no scary dreams this time. The nightmare facing him was real, and he had under two hours at maximum speed to formulate a game plan.

❀ ❀ ❀

Forty minutes ticked off the clock on Reginald's lab wall. Miranda watched every time the minute hand passed the twelve. She kept waiting for some sort of stomach pain, or perhaps for her eyes to grow blurry or her head to become dizzy.

Reginald was checking on her every five minutes now. His look was one of bafflement. He'd glance back and forth nervously from the clock to Agent Jones' face, then turn abruptly and march upstairs.

As ninety minutes came and went, Miranda's thoughts grew more and more erratic: *I didn't get to say goodbye to Derrick...or to Whelan... I'm never going to get that promotion now... Did I eat breakfast? What was it? I know I had something besides coffee... My dad's going to die old and alone... I hope the cleaners don't keep* *that new suit I turned in. That cost me $280... Whelan's last mental image of me will have a pill bottle sticking out of my mouth...*

A few minutes before 1:00 a.m., Reginald came bouncing down the stairs. He didn't look confused this time. He took a seat opposite her, holding a glass of light blue liquid. He held it up to the lightbulb, turning it, side to side, his neck matching the angles and the rhythm, like some poor confused puppy. Then to her shock, he upended it into his mouth and drank it all.

Oh, shit...he's killing himself! What about the other killings he has planned?

Her face processed every emotion it could over the past two hours. It was now drooped—given up trying to comprehend.

He chortled at her, willing her to understand.

She did not.

"That was diluted Gatorade."

She shook her head, lost.

"You can relax now. You weren't really dosed. You're going to be all right."

He'd put her through mental torture. Her face was still blank when tears started streaming down it.

While she recovered, he pulled out his laboratory equipment and went about making up a batch of the genuine article right in front of her.

Neither spoke for forty minutes as Miranda nursed herself back to sanity—and sobriety.

"So," she cautiously said, "all that—just to fuck with me?"

"Well, you wouldn't let me fuck you the way *I* wanted to."

She wasn't sure how to respond. *He's dangerous—intelligent. He's planned this game for a year—played it over and over in his head—practicing.*

Jones spoke up, her curiosity getting the better of her. "If you didn't poison me in the bar, what was it you put in my beer?"

"While you were in the restroom, I reached over the bar and grabbed a bottle of blue curacao. One little splash. Not enough to taste.

Agent Jones watched the flask of liquid cooking, turning bluer before her eyes as he added the extracted flower pigment. "And that?" she nodded toward his batch in progress.

"The real McCoy. And it's not orange-flavored."

Miranda was replaying her actions in the bar from earlier. Her eyes revealed her thoughts.

"Thank you for sharing your case update with me," Reginald goaded her. "I had no idea that old woman in Miami saw my face or that you were pushing her to remember. I figured if she'd described me three weeks ago, you'd have arrested me by now. And I knew you might have my DNA when I saw the police tape around Susan Jacobs' house. That was two strikes against me. Anyone who follows the game knows that on the third one, you're out. I was going to charm you here tonight—or force you. Either way, you were coming with me. Can't have you or your partner messing up the end of my game now, can I?"

Miranda was regaining her wits. She put on her softest voice. "Reggie, please don't do this. We can work this out. I can get you a deal in turn for saving the last five people you plan to kill."

He chuckled. "Right. You don't have that kind of pull."

Reggie walked over to her and cupped her cheeks in his hands.

Miranda didn't fight it. She wanted him to feel her, to know she was a warm, living being. She looked into his eyes with as much compassion as she could muster at the moment. "Let me go, Regg. I can save you from a death sentence."

"This game wasn't designed to have the loser saved. It was always them or me." He stroked her skin. "It's a shame you had to be so fucking beautiful. I didn't see you coming. But I always allowed for adjustments—for the unknowns. Like you. You're part of 'them' now."

Reggie mumbled as he went back to work. "Was always them or me."

She knew he'd have to kill her once he dealt with Whelan. She was only alive now to keep Whelan in line until Reginald could subdue him. Would Whelan call the cavalry or come alone, as asked? One way, she was dead. The other way, they were both dead.

❁ ❁ ❁

Whelan arrived at Kansas City's downtown airport, twelve hours earlier than Reggie was expecting him. Perhaps the surprise factor would give him a chance. He'd looked up Mabelline's address. *Westwood!*

Half an hour later, he parked alongside the curb, a block down from the house. He stuck to the shadows as he made his way toward the home. Slipping into the side yard, he peered through windows, looking for signs of Reggie. The house was dark. His partner had hinted on the phone earlier that she was downstairs. And this wasn't a two-story home. That left the basement.

On the other side of the house, he could see a light coming from a ground-level window. He didn't want to give himself away, but he could see nothing from his current vantage, so he moved alongside the brick wall. Turning his phone brightness as far down as it would go, he fired up the camera in selfie mode. He inched it along the grass until he got a view of the basement, angled back in his direction.

318

Agent Jones was tied to a chair. *She's alive!* His heart started pounding double time.

There was no sign of Reggie. He watched for a couple of minutes. There were empty beakers on a table and other lab equipment scattered about. The window was locked. Slipping through the darkness, he made his way to the back door. He picked it in twenty seconds. A little click invited him in. It was the kitchen. His gun led each corner he went around. He opened the basement door. It gave silently.

One step after another was taken until he could see Miranda's feet. Another pair of shoes stood next to them. Each step down was one foot up on his partner's legs—and the vile creature beside her. When he got to the bottom, Whelan froze, disheartened. Standing beside a still bound Agent Jones was Reginald Johnson, with twisted, maniacal lips.

"Hello, Thomas. We've been expecting you." Reginald was holding a large syringe filled with blue liquid. The needle was already implanted in Miranda's jugular, and his palm was on the plunger.

"You can put your gun down now, Agent Whelan. Unless you think you're faster than me…? It takes but a few drops entering her system at this concentrated level, flowing directly to her heart."

"Miranda?" asked Whelan.

"I'm fine. I'm betting he's not faster than your bullet."

"Yes!" shouted Reginald. "Let's all bet, shall we?"

Whelan's brain flew through scenarios—one, two, three—all ending with his partner dead. He would never be able to work another crime if he let a second partner die in front of him while he stood helpless.

He flashed back to his old partner, Agent Jay Pierson, making him wait in the SUV instead of going into the forest with him as his backup. The intel said the shack Morrison used in those woods to store arms and supplies was vacant. It had been dreadfully mistaken. What was supposed to be a quick surveil exposed ten men walking around with assault rifles and sidearms. And Eddie Morrison himself.

I should never have let him go in alone.

Whelan's eyes fixed on Reginald's a moment. He willed the evil monster to explode into blue, fiery flames and go straight to hell. Of course, this didn't happen.

As if reading Whelan's mind, Reginald tilted his head and smiled.

Whelan gave in and moved to the table, placing his gun down.

Agent Jones' heart sank. "You've just killed us both, Tom."

"He's being smart, Miranda," said Reginald. "I told you he was smart. Good boy. Now come sit in that empty chair." He pointed to one at the other end of the table.

Whelan obliged.

Reginald threw him a pair of handcuffs, police issue. "Cuff your hands to the right table leg."

Agent Whelan complied once more. He nudged the table's top upward with his shoulder in an attempt to gauge its weight. It was solid and heavy.

"Tighter!"

Thomas tightened them as much as they would go. He gave them a forceful yank to show he was secured. He noted a light flashing on the stairwell post.

"My silent alarm," said Reginald. "You triggered it when you came in. Thank you for the warning. I knew you wouldn't be able to hold out until your other flight came in. We've been waiting up for you. I have to say, I didn't expect you for another hour at least. You're remarkable in your diligence. Kudos."

"What now, Regg? You hold all the cards."

"You've made the game fun, Tommy. You and Miranda. Though the credit mostly goes to you. She played against my weakness for her, but you...you solved the puzzle. Too bad you won't win the game."

Whelan focused on the lunatic before him. He pondered his conversation with his mother a few hours ago. *We aren't supposed to know the sins of our parents.* "What was it, Reggie? What set you off? Old Mabel dying? Your mom used to beat you or something, Regg? Everyone loses their parents at some point. What was it about *her* death that prompted you to go out and start killing people?"

Reginald Johnson glared at Thomas Whelan for a moment. He reflected on his mother, comments she'd made when he was growing up, actions she'd taken to ensure he turned into a first-rate, upstanding man. She was strict, yes. She took a belt to him on occasion, yes. When he was delinquent, he needed punishing. When he was righteous, he deserved rewarding. Didn't every mother teach their children to worship God, keep a clean house, do chores and work hard in school?

The lessons his mother imparted to him were never shared with another. No stories were swapped. Had there been, he might know that most mothers don't nurse their children until they're four. Most don't whip their child's bare asses with a belt until they bleed so severely they can't sit for two days. Most don't lock them in cars for hours at a time because they don't trust them home alone or with a neighbor while they're out working. Most celebrate at least one of their own child's birthdays before the age of eighteen. And most don't share a bed with their teenage son, especially when their home has two bedrooms.

All of those things were justified in Reggie's head. He never blamed her for any of it. You don't blame a mother for taking on all that her role encompassed. You praise her. His mother was a saint in Reggie's eyes. She kept him fed and clothed. He had a roof overhead every night. She kept the monsters in the world away, both real and imagined. She doctored him when he was sick and always made sure he took his medicine.

"Time for your medicine," he mumbled.

Reginald knew Whelan was trying to bait him—throw him off guard with careless questions. He cleared his throat. "Clever-clever, Tommy… but this is *my* game."

He was gleeful as he pulled the needle out of Miranda's neck. He walked over to Whelan and inserted it into his.

"Reggie!" screamed Agent Jones. "Damn you, Reggie, don't do this! There has to be another way."

He ignored her, leaning close to Whelan's ear and whispering, "I've put her through hell tonight, Tommy, and now the final straw is knowing she couldn't save you. I may leave her here to watch over your body for a couple of days. She's been a bad girl, and she needs punishing. Oh, I'll have to kill her eventually, but not until I'm certain she's learned her lesson."

Whelan did his best to look him in the eyes, through the corners of his own. With utmost sincerity, he said, "Reggie, I'm sorry I didn't invite you in for cake."

The remark threw Reginald off a moment, but he recovered. "I'll bet you are. It's time, Tommy. Any final words?"

"Only three. Take. The. Shot."

A deafening gunshot filled the basement, echoing off the concrete walls. Agent Whelan's face was sprayed wet with blood and a bit of gray matter from Reginald Johnson as his forehead ripped open in front from the rear-penetrating bullet. The forward momentum carried Reggie to the floor behind and to the left of Whelan. His hand was wrapped around the plunger, and the syringe ripped free of Whelan's neck on his way down.

Miranda looked toward the stairwell. Standing behind the bottom post was Agent Phil Cannon. He lowered his weapon and came on into the room. He untied her first, then moved to uncuff Agent Whelan.

"Cannon!" she exclaimed with delight. She hugged him, then followed suit with Whelan when he was freed. Grabbing a towel off the table, she wiped some of the insides of Reginald's head off Whelan's face.

Agent Cannon bent down and rolled Reggie over. His eyes were open, forever filled with a look of surprise mixed with terror.

Whelan looked at the body. "Fitting."

Agent Jones knelt and retrieved the syringe. She held it to the light. "I don't think you got any. It looks full."

"If it was what he said it was, I think I'd be feeling it already."

Cannon got on the phone and called in to the office. He looked back at his lead agents. "This place will be swarming with everyone soon."

Whelan looked at him. His eyes moistened, but he refused to let any tears fall. He grabbed Cannon and pulled him into him tightly. "Thank you."

Cannon allowed himself a broad smile. "Well, we should wait upstairs." He turned to head up.

"We'll be up in a minute," said Jones.

"You got it."

When he left, Whelan looked at her curiously.

"Whelan…Thomas…I …We…" she was lost, trying to spit out her thoughts. She'd never been more emotionally spent and was trying to express too much at once.

"I know Miranda. It's okay, partner." It was her turn to be gathered into him. They held each other for a long moment before releasing their arms.

Jones was the first to speak. "I need to call Derrick. He needs to hear how much I love him. He needs to hear it right now."

Whelan nodded. "I know. After the medic checks you out, go home. It's over. I'll cover for you with Kendrick. Don't come in today. You can give your full report tomorrow. I'll stay and get them started. I'll come by around ten to check on you."

He moved deliberately away from her toward Reginald's body.

Miranda walked to the stairs and looked back at him. He was still staring down at the floor. She moved on up and out, in the direction of certainty.

Whelan turned back, ready to leave this nightmare behind. It had been quite an evening. When he first came down the steps, he didn't notice the table set up to the side, with the remaining pill bottles lined up. He read through all the names. Number ten was another girl he knew from elementary school, and number twelve, December, read *Thomas Whelan*. He pondered that for a moment. He was supposed to be feeling euphoria right now. They had caught and killed 12 Pills. It was over. But the only sentiment in his heart as he marched up the stairs, was guilt.

Chapter 47

Gerrard was cooking fish tacos for everyone at the Tiki-Taco on Grand Cayman. It had been a week since the case wrapped. The agents were given time off to rest and renew themselves before their next assignment. This time, Whelan brought his son and his mother, and Miranda brought Derrick. Agent Cannon joined them but with no other family.

"Phil," said Thomas, "we're your family now." He raised his beer bottle. "Here's to family—blood *and* water—bonded forever."

"Here-here," everyone toasted.

Agent Cannon grabbed Connor for a little Frisbee action on the beach.

Derrick gave Miranda a kiss and then ran over to join them.

"So, you two back on track?" asked Whelan.

"Definitely." She looked at her new friend with an understanding and a connection few in this world would ever share. Events had permanently bonded them. Turning her head to watch the guys on the beach, she said, "He asked me to marry him three times in the past two years."

"Why not beat him to the punch?"

"I did. On the plane down."

"*And?*" asked Kathryn Whelan, no longer hiding her eavesdropping from the bar.

"Well, what do you think?" Miranda beamed.

She turned back to Thomas. "It finally felt right."

"Congratulations," he said.

"Thanks. I'll tell you what *didn't* feel right. I got an '*un*-invitation' from Judy Ward and her fiancé, Lisa Harmon, for their impending wedding ceremony. Talk about moving fast! Have you ever been *officially un*-invited to an event?"

Thomas retrieved a card from the bottom pocket of his cargo shorts. "I got mine on the way out of the office. I was going to show you, but I forgot all about it."

"You think she was trying to be funny?"

"She *did* tell me we seemed fated to be in each other's lives," said Whelan. "Maybe this was her insurance against it."

"Well, *I* didn't think it was that funny. I've been served with restraining orders that offended me less."

A burst of laughter escaped Whelan. He gave her a hug and a kiss on the forehead, then ran out to join in the Frisbee action.

Miranda pursed her lips a moment, but the more she thought about it, the more she saw the humor. She decided to let it go. She turned around to Gerrard behind the counter with a grill full of fish. "That smells amazing."

"Yah, m'lady, caught fresh dis mornin'." Gerrard's Cayman accent flowed freely like the ocean breeze.

"You're lovely and kind to Whelan. What did he ever do to deserve such a special friend like you?" It was an innocent enough question.

"He never told you? He saved the lives of my family and me eight years ago. He was a rookie, but he listened to his gut. He got a good gut dat one. I owe him every'ting. No 'ting will ever be enough to repay dat mon. Dat toast you all took? You don't know yet, how much to heart he takes it. We made da same toast. Now, we are forever brothers."

"From different mothers," Kathryn quickly added.

Gerrard reached over and grabbed Kathryn's hand, kissing it gently. It was ebony and ivory coming together in the sweetest of ways. "You da bestest ma-ma."

"You too, Gerrard." She leaned over and kissed him on the cheek. "Now, let's not get all mushy and let that fish overcook. I'm hungry!"

An hour later, seven full bellies were sitting under the giant thatched roof, sharing whopper fishing tales, and discussing whether or not to fish again tomorrow or go snorkeling. Thomas looked around at his family and felt the love.

His phone's obnoxious ring jolted him from his contemplation. "Sorry," he said to the table. "I thought I turned it off."

He answered, "Whelan."

He was on the phone for a minute, his face strained and contorted. "Yes. Yes, I understand," he said more than once.

Everyone's eyes were on him when he hung up.

Kathryn spoke first, "What is it, honey?"

Whelan didn't know whether or not to say anything in front of Connor, but he'd hear it on the news if not from him. "Eddie Morrison broke out of jail."

Faces were stoically silent.

Connor was the first to speak. "So...don't just sit there. Go catch his punk ass again. That's what you two do—catch bad guys...."

Whelan and Jones looked at one another and began to smile.

THE END

Thank you for reading **12 PILLS**. I hope you had as much fun reading it as I did writing it for you. Did you figure out the killer before the reveal?

If you enjoyed this novel, please tell a friend, and please leave a review on the site where you purchased it. Reviews go a long way to help independent authors like myself grow and establish an audience, so I may continue to write more stories for you.

A follow-up to **12 PILLS** is now available.

MURDER AT PARKMOOR has been released and picks up shortly after the events you've just read.

I've also started writing the third Agent Whelan Mystery!

Stay tuned to my website for more information and purchase links. www.kirkburris.com.

Have a blessed day!

Kirk Burris

Made in the USA
Coppell, TX
19 September 2022